DREAM THIEVES

DREAM THIEVES

STEVEN LEE CLIMER

ISBN: 979-8-88785-012-2 (Paperback)
ISBN: 979-8-88785-013-9 (Hardcover)

Library of Congress Control Number: 2022951904

Any references to historical events, real people, or real places are used fictitiously. Names, characters, and places are products of the author's imagination.

Book design by Allison Chernutan.

Printed in the United States of America.

First printing edition 2022.

emily@fracturedmirrorpublishing.com
Fractured Mirror Publishing
Knoxville, Tennessee

www.fracturedmirrorpublishing.com

DREAM THIEVES – 25th Anniversary Edition
by Steven Lee Climer (Original Publication)

Finalist — Best First Novel of 1997, International Horror Guild Awards
Winner — Best Fantasy 1997, Under the Covers Book Reviews Reader's Awards
Winner — Best Horror Novel 2000, EPIC (paperback edition)

REVIEWS OF THE ORIGINAL PUBLICATION

"*Dream Thieves* is a fast-paced book with urks and turns you don't see coming. Delightful and refreshing, it's something new to chalk up in the list of must-reads."

- Frightnet

"...*Dream Thieves* is a fine first novel...The book's fantastic premise becomes utterly believable, mainly because Grimm himself—with all his anger, his ambition, his petty jealousies, and grand hopes—is so convincingly drawn. This one's quite imaginative..."

- William Hughes, Editor and Publisher
Dread: A Magazine of the Uncanny and Grotesque

"I used to believe that Dark Fantasy was just another name for horror, set in strange and blurry worlds. Steven Lee Climer redefined my perception of the genre with his debut novel *Dream Thieves*. *Dream Thieves* earned Climer a nomination for best first novel from the International Horror Guild, and it's a shame he missed out. If he can continue to produce material this inventively satisfying, though, then I'm sure he hasn't long to wait before some serious recognition falls his way. I cannot recommend it highly enough."

- Richard Wright, *Masters of Terror*

"A dark fantasy, *Dream Thieves* is a chilling tale of mythic proportions, one that lingers in your mind, but not, I hope, in your dreams. Set in Germany, it portrays, in stark and chilling word-pictures, a man's descent into blackness. Edward Grimm is a woodcarver of note, hired by royalty to carve carousel horses, but he is also a man who is unable to dream, or to create from the wonders he feels lies in the dreams of his young nephew. Dreams he conspires to steal with the aid of a magic potion he has procured from a Gypsy. But, magic potions have to be paid for in full, and how Grimm pays has to be read, savored, and enjoyed. This is a haunting work, not only for the beauty of Mr. Climer's incredible prose, but for the unusual concept, the deftly drawn characters, and the mood that draws the reader deeper and deeper into the soul of Grimm. I wish I could tell you more without giving away a plot that is intricate in design, as finely carved as Grimm's Zoltan, and imbued with an extraordinary vision. I loved it."

- Under the Covers Book Reviews

"Not much gives me the creeps. In my spare time, I research serial crime—murders, rapes, that kind of thing. It takes quite a bit to get to me. *Dream Thieves* did it. Distinctly uncomfortable. Slightly nauseated. Definitely appalled. That would just about cover it. In every sense of the word, horror.

Perhaps, it is the choice of victim that produces such a visceral response. Cruelty to a child, especially by a family member, is chilling.

Edward Grimm is a man of enormous talent, a woodcarver extraordinaire. He is also a sociopath, without a hint of empathy or compassion. One goal drives him brutally forward: Grimm is unable to dream, and he will do anything to steal the dreams of others. Tragically, the dreams he covets the most belong to his young nephew, Gustav. With the magic of a gypsy woman, he will find a way to capture those dreams. And the cost to everyone he involves will be beyond belief.

Dream Thieves is presented in a relatively new format, available on diskette or by download. And, yes, even though I had a hard copy of the text, I read the entire book on computer. No problem. Current wisdom insists consumers will set a limit on how much they are willing to read online, maintaining that documents cannot exceed X numbers of pages. If so, we need to get beyond that mental block. It reads fast, it's portable, and, when on your computer screen, looks just like that report you're supposed to be working on. And you can always print it out if staring at the monitor begins to bother you.

The only distraction came in the form of numerous typographical errors. Hard Shell is still a fairly new company and, no doubt, every project will be an improvement on the process, but such mistakes are among the easiest kinks to smooth out. A first read should have picked up on these stumbles.

Dream Thieves reads (probably not coincidentally) like the original Grimm's fairy tales, those stories you skimmed through as an adult and then hid from your children. Blood-curdling stuff that would keep the kids sleeping in your bed until their 18th birthday. The origin of the phrase "fairy tales" would be an interesting one to trace, since most fairy tales contain more murder, torture, and abandonment than prime time television can stuff into a few hours.

Climer's novel is genuine horror, told in an almost baroque style that occasionally lulls the reader into a false sense of security as the charming Bavarian landscape flows by. And yanks you back with a claw to the throat. At times, the events are so disturbing, pulling away seems the only decent action.

Dream Thieves is that gruesome accident you want to look away from, but can't. It amounts to literary rubbernecking. The only consolation being that the victims in this case never existed and, so, cannot suffer."

- Lisa DuMond

FOREWORD

I've *never* written an introduction for a novel before. I've probably never even read more than one or two introductions in my entire lifetime. But I've agreed to write this one. And as I sit here, bleary eyes focused on a flickering computer screen, half empty cup of coffee on the table beside me, I can't help but wonder why I was so willing to write these few words of introduction for a writer I've never even met.

Steven Lee Climer and I have never crossed paths, so I don't owe him anything. He's never lent me money, or baby-sat my kids, or walked my dog in the pouring rain. We're not old high school chums, or drinking buddies, or second cousins once removed on our mothers' side. As a matter of fact, I never even knew who Steven Climer was until last year and have only read a few of his works of fiction.

I would have probably continued not knowing who Steven Climer was, not even caring who he was, were it not for a small press anthology called DEAD PROMISES. You see Steve and I both have stories in that anthology: mine is a reprint of an earlier work; Steve's is a disturbing little ditty called "High Lonesome Road."

I almost hate to admit this, but "High Lonesome Road" spoke to me like few stories ever have, bringing back all but forgotten visions of a childhood spent in rural America. Steve's story called to me with memories of lonely country roads, clapboard houses, and catching fireflies in a mayonnaise jar on a hot August night. His story also spoke to me of ghostly things, of lost and lonely spirits wandering aimlessly through forests of tall trees.

I finished Steve's story with great enthusiasm, amazed that I had found a true gem of a story in such a tiny little anthology. Better yet, I had found a writer with the potential for greatness. A new writer that had not been corrupted by the system, had not sold his soul, or tarnished his vision, for the almighty dollar. A writer who believes that the telling of a good story is all that's important.

I was so impressed with "High Lonesome Road" that I immediately recommended it for a Bram Stoker Award. I also opened up a line of communication with the author, praising him for his talent, and begging him to please send more stories my way. Steve was more than happy to respond to my request, and I became his much-devoted fan.

So I sit here now, having just read DREAM THIEVES, wanting to write an introduction what will do the book justice. I want to heap words of praise upon Steven Lee Climer for his wonderful novel, but words escape me. I am a writer left speechless by one of the finest stories I have read in a long, long time.

Like the main character in his novel, Steven Lee Climer is also a master carver. Words are the medium he works with: words, sentences, paragraphs, and pages. He takes a scene, a plot element, a block of dialogue, and then, with sharpened tool in hand, he begins to chip and whittle away, refining the moment, making it perfect. He glues and he polishes, layering on the suspense in fine, even coats, creating visual elements that dazzle the eyes and chill the bones. He lures us in, and then charms us, with the subtle texture of his words, and the smoothness of his dialogue.

I could go on and on about Steve's talents as a writer, but I won't. From the moment you start to read DREAM THIEVES, you will know that you are in the presence of a master storyteller, a carver of haunting visions and nightmares. Enjoy the book, but beware of the sharpened chisel in the author's hand.

OWL GOINGBACK

Bram-Stoker Award-Winning Author of
CROTA AND COYOTE RAGE

I am a man in misery, my bones long replaced by this hard oak. I am a man imprisoned within this tree, within this sarcophagus, painted and carved.

I can see her. I can almost touch her from here. She is before me, my tangled web of English Ivy curling about her feet. It was not always this way. In the years that have passed, I've almost forgotten what truly brought me to this point in time. I have no regrets, even though I am without the two things I longed for most.

Edward Grimm squatted by the fireplace in his lonely dwelling, far away from the well-traveled paths leading northward to Frankfurt. He stared into the flames, his coal black eyes void of any reflections. Grimm was a tall man, when he stood, and wore a shaggy, but small, beard and mustache tipped with white. He was not an elderly man, but he was old in his heart.

Grimm replaced the poker by the hearth and stood. He went to the window and looked out into the gray winter afternoon. He was expecting his brother to come by with his son, Gustav. Grimm loved when Gustav came by, not because he loved his nephew, but because he loved what he could see in Gustav's face, the dreams in the boy's eyes. It was something quite unknown to Grimm.

For as long as he could remember, he had never had a dream. He had heard others talk about what they had seen in their sleep, but Grimm's mind offered only desolation. Although he longed to dream, he knew desire and dreams were two entirely different things. Desire was not inspirational, and often self-motivated. He had desire, but he wanted a dream.

He did not desire money, he was comfortable. Grimm earned plenty of money with his gift for carving tools. Others had expressed jealousy because they dreamed of having a skill such as his. He hated those people. They had a dream.

"They are here." Grimm said as he saw his brother, Alexander, and Gustav coming off the main trail. He pulled the door open in anticipation of Alexander's knock.

"Good afternoon, brother. It's good to see you," Grimm bent to the blonde seven-year-old. "And how is Gustav today?"

Gustav was always a little intimidated by his uncle, even though he was told it was silly. "Hello, Uncle."

Alexander unwound the scarf from his neck. "Such a blustery day. Thank you, Edward, for watching Gustav while I go to town. It has been difficult, since his mother passed away."

"I know," Grimm replied. Although brothers, they looked very different from each other. Alexander's eyes were large and brown, his mouth, pleasant. He was a good looking man, a loyal husband and father. His children were beautiful and healthy; Grimm had no children. Alexander's wife, when she was alive, was warm and caring; Grimm had never experienced a woman's love. He had always envied his brother's life.

"I shouldn't be too long," Alexander said. "Please make sure he stays out of trouble, he's a mischievous one, my Gustav."

"Don't worry about him, he is in good hands." Grimm looked down at Gustav and pulled the boy close. They watched as Alexander bundled up, once again. He left the cottage, and soon disappeared around the first bend in the dirt road.

Grimm leaned toward Gustav. "Well, what have we to do today?" He paused and looked into the boy's innocent eyes, as if to steal his soul. He tried hard to love Gustav. Perhaps he did, in some way, but his jealousy overpowered his compassion. "Ah, yes, I remember. You were going to tell me a story, something you had dreamed."

Gustav smiled at his uncle. "Can I see the workshop, please? I want to see the carousel horses again!"

Grimm paused; he knew if he went along with the boy's wishes he could get him to speak. "Certainly. I started a fire in the stove just in case you wanted to go out there."

Grimm took Gustav by the hand, and they walked through the tiny house, which consisted of only three rooms: a kitchen/dining area, and two bedrooms. Between the two-bedroom doors was a third door which led to the workshop out back.

Gustav could hardly contain himself when Grimm opened the workshop door. "Have you made any new ones?"

"Yes, for King Leopold in Scandinavia." Grimm said.

Gustav tugged at Grimm's shirttail. "Can I see it? Can I play on it?"

"Of course, of course."

Gustav gaped. He stood before one of the carousel horses for which his uncle was famous "It's the best one yet, Uncle!" he exclaimed, stroking the shiny black leg of the stallion.

"Thank you." Grimm lifted little Gustav onto the steed. "How does he feel?"

"Like the finest show horse ever! Better than any of the circus horses!" Gustav took the reins in his hands.

Grimm watched the boy's smiling face. Ideas and fantasies were swirling upon it. "Would you like to see the drawing he came from?"

"Yes!"

Grimm walked over to a small workbench that contained all his carving tools and bits. There, he located a pencil drawing made by one of the king's artists. Grimm envied the artist who could see this beast in his mind.

"Here it is." Grimm took it to Gustav. "This is the king's favorite horse. He asked me to carve a carousel horse from this picture."

"He's a fine horse, Uncle, but not as good as this one!" Gustav shouted and pretended to dig in with his heels.

Grimm studied Gustav. He could see that expression on his face again, the look that drove Grimm to the point of insane jealousy. "What would you do if you had this horse in real life?"

Gustav's brain raced with fantasy. "I would go to the *Schwartz-wald* and find the green dragon that Father told me about. Father tells me the story at night about the green dragon of the Black Forest."

"I don't think I've ever heard the tale. Why don't you tell it to me?"

"In the Black Forest, there's a castle belonging to an ancient queen. The king went out one day to kill the dragon, because it was killing all the animals and burning the trees, but the dragon killed the king before he could kill the dragon."

Grimm was fascinated. "Yes, yes, go on."

"Then, a bad king came to the castle and kidnapped the queen, who was the most beautiful woman in the land. He took her to the dragon, and said the dragon could have her, if the king could have the castle and land, and if the dragon would never kill any more animals." Gustav paused for a long breath. "The dragon answered that if he could keep the castle and the queen, the bad king could have the land. The bad king agreed, and the dragon now sleeps in the dungeon of the queen's castle and guards her so she can never escape."

"And you would go kill this dragon?" Grimm asked.

"Yes, because whoever kills the dragon will set the queen free, and win all the land for himself, and be king."

"Would you like to be king?"

Gustav touched the hard black points of the horse's mane. "I would love to be the king."

Grimm smiled and lifted the boy from the horse. "Would you like to name him, Gustav?"

"Can I?" His eyes were as bright as points of sunlight.

"Yes." They stood together and look at the steed's face.

"I don't know." Gustav studied the tall head and face. The mouth was ferocious and lined with red paint. The eyes were angry and dark. For a moment, they almost seemed real.

"What kind of name would a king's horse have?"

"He would be called…Zoltan." Gustav smiled, "Yes, his name would be Zoltan, my grandfather's name."

"Your grandfather's name. "Grimm retreated into memory, calling up the image of his father. Zoltan, before Grimm, was a woodworker. He carved religious figures. In fact, one of Zoltan's pieta carvings still rested in one of the great cathedrals in Hamburg. Father created those pieces out of love for Christ and God, the very spirits that had left Edward Grimm with emptiness in his soul.

"Zoltan is a good name for this horse." Grimm told Gustav.

Gustav played for nearly two hours in the workshop before falling asleep on the wool rug by the fire. Grimm watched the boy as he slept, replaying every word, every image the child had expressed. In his mind, Grimm could see the queen and the green dragon, but only because it was told to him by another.

"Little boy," he whispered, "Why is it you were given such a wondrous gift, and I have nothing?"

Hating Gustav, Grimm looked into the fire, and spoke to the flames as if they were a direct line to the Devil, or God, himself. "I must possess what he has. How do I get this gift for myself? How?"

Someone knocked on the door. As he rose to answer it, he looked through the window; it was Alexander. He knocked again.

"Wait, wait, I'm coming," Grimm called, pulled the door open, and wintry winds slapped his face. "It has gotten cold outside."

Alexander stepped in quickly. "Yes indeed, the storm just whipped up. I was coming up the road, by the bend that turns to your place, and the winds came, and the temperature dropped in a matter of moments" Alexander looked past his brother's thin shoulders and saw Gustav sleeping by the fire.

"Just look at him."

Grimm saw love in Alexander's eyes, the love for his son. "He's been asleep for nearly an hour. He played so much, I guess he tired himself out."

"Yes," Alexander was removing his coat, "but I wish that were it."

"Oh?" Grimm's eyes narrowed as he greedily prompted his brother for information. "Would you like some tea? The water is already hot."

"I could use a warmer. I'm so cold, I think my soul is frozen on a stick." Alexander laughed a little then sat at the kitchen table.

Grimm wanted to hear none of this babble, he wanted Alexander to talk more about Gustav. "He seems to be sleeping peacefully, would you like me to wake him so he can get ready to go?"

"Oh, no," Alexander declined. "He hasn't been sleeping well at night. He has been waking with bad dreams, you see. Since his mother died, it's been getting worse."

Grimm was like a sponge. "Really, what are his dreams about? Does he tell you?"

"His mother, mostly." Alexander watched as his brother dipped his fingers into the dried tea on the table, pinched some, and mashed it inside two metal tea balls. "That, and a host of unpleasant things. I was away, teaching at the university, as you remember, when Gretchen died. I think much of his trouble stems from the fact that I wasn't home to take care of him, but you were here, thank God."

Grimm sat a cup of steaming water before Alexander. "I did my best."

"And I thank you so much." Alexander dipped the tea ball in the cup, and it sank to the bottom. "I thank you for the tea, also."

Grimm smiled. "What else has he been dreaming about?"

"A strange combination: Werewolves and the Virgin Mary. He says her image appears to him."

"Most unusual."

"I don't know what to make of it, I am a scientist not a priest." Alexander withdrew the tea ball and sipped the hot, murky liquid.

"Well, at least he is sleeping now." Grimm cast his eyes at the slumbering child. "I wonder if he is dreaming now."

Alexander set the cup on the table. "It is getting dark, we must be getting on if we plan to make it home before nightfall. The gypsies are about again, and I don't feel like running into their begging hides—if I can help it. In the spring we may move to the city."

"Spring is a long way off, brother." Grimm rose out of the chair and carefully walked over to the sleeping child. "You may change your mind. You never know what could happen between now and then."

He critically observed the boy's face as he approached. Gustav's brow moved in sporadic jerks, indicating a sense of tension and fear. His little lip quivered momentarily. Grimm touched him. "Gustav, wake up. Your father is here. It's time to go home."

"Oh!"

Grimm knelt, "I didn't mean to startle you. What's wrong?"

"I was having a bad dream." Gustav saw his father approaching behind Grimm. "Papa, I was having one of those dreams, again."

Alexander looked at his brother. "Why don't you tell us about it? Sometimes talking about it helps, I heard one of my colleagues at the university say."

Grimm felt near to salivation, like a dog presented with a steak. "Yes, yes, Gustav. What was it about? I will listen."

"It was about Zoltan, Uncle."

"Zoltan?" Alexander gave Grimm a puzzled look.

Grimm explained, "I carved a new carousel horse, and Gustav named him after his grandfather."

"Zoltan was running, and I was on his back. I couldn't get off him. I grabbed his mane, but it made him crazy. Mother came and tried to help, but Zoltan hurt her. He reared up on his back legs and kicked her. She was dead, I am sure of it." Tears welled in Gustav's eyes.

Alexander knelt and drew the boy close. "It's all right. Zoltan didn't hurt mother. He's just a dream. Don't worry, it was just a dream. She died of a disease, Gustav."

Grimm stood. His mouth suddenly swam with a foul taste. He wanted to kill his brother with a poker for crushing the boy's dreams. "Alexander, I still have a few finishing touches to put on the horse before the king's men come for it tomorrow."

"I understand, we'll let ourselves out." Alexander held Gustav in his arms a moment longer and then asked him to get his coat.

"Uncle, can I come and see your horses again, soon?" Gustav asked while buttoning up.

"Yes, of course." Grimm touched the child's blond hair. "The next time you come to see me, I will have a surprise for you."

"A surprise?" Gustav's eyes grew big.

"Yes, a surprise. A wonderful surprise."

I always considered myself a child of God. He had given me a gift. But, when I turned to God, He turned from me. A father unwilling to help his children is not worthy of a child's love.

I had heard it said many times that the gypsies were witches in league with the Devil. If they were, they may be my salvation, I was prepared to become the Devil's personal artisan. I really knew nothing of them, directly. Except for the times I took money to the camps and paid to watch the women dance.

Alexander was truthful about the biting winter winds. After nightfall, it became even worse. Grimm had been on the trails for more than two hours. He was taking a great risk being out in the forest past dark. Many things live in the woods through the region, things far worse than any nightmare.

Grimm hoped the gypsies were in the area. They usually brought their caravans through the countryside this time of year, but they had so many campsites, it was difficult to pinpoint which one they would be occupying. Grimm knew of four such locations. He had already been to three, and now he was on the trail to the last, deep in the woods.

Grimm had no gloves, and his hands were wrapped in strips of linen. He knew he could not stay out in the cold much longer. He could not let his hands be damaged by frostbite, they were his livelihood. He brought thirty gold pieces, and prayed they would be enough for the services he sought.

Grimm saw the flicker of lanterns in the distance. The trail opened up into a clearing, nestled within were several large wagons and tents in a circle. The gypsies were proud, they preferred to be called *Rom* for the area of Romani, which they called home. Grimm recalled the proper nomenclature for the clan known within gypsy society as the *Vitsa*. These were their tribal trails.

The camp seemed warm and inviting, as the light from the oil lamps stretched into the night. The light called to Grimm, promising him warmth, and possibly, an answer.

Grimm could see a few Rom males tending to chores about the camp and moving silhouettes on the window shades of the wagons. Grimm knew who he was looking for. She was known as *Phuri Dai*, or the senior woman of the clan. Many said she was just as powerful as the chieftain, and she commanded powers and knowledge not accessible to *Gadje*, or non-gypsies. She was whom Grimm sought. He approached the second wagon, unchallenged, and climbed the short set of stairs. This was the wagon traditionally inhabited by the *Phuri Dai*. He gently knocked on the door and then waited for a response.

As the door slowly opened inward, a shaft of heavenly light sliced through the night. Grimm wasn't sure if the light came from an artificial source or from the young woman who stood in the doorway. Her hair was as black as the wing of a rook, so black that the light lent it a bluish cast. Grimm's confidence dissolved as he looked into her eyes, an intense, other-worldly green. He could not look away, nor could his mind recall anything but the simplest words.

"Hello. I do not mean to disturb you. That is, I know it is late."

"What do you need?"

Her voice captivated Grimm, and he struggled to regain his composure. "I have come to see *Phuri Dai*. I think she is the only one who can help me."

"One moment." The green-eyed woman left, and the light severed.

Grimm stared at the door now shut before him, the young woman's face imprinted on his memory. The effect was much like looking at the sun, then closing his eyes. As the image of the sun would still burn behind his lids, so the image of her face remained imprinted, perhaps, forever.

The door creaked open once more. The girl was there, but she did not speak as she led Grimm into the sacred realm of the *Phuri Dai.*

Grimm drank in everything his eyes could see, both direct and peripheral. The wagon was strewn with copper and metal objects. Drying herbs and plants hung in the windows, anticipating the warmth of the sun in the morning, their heady scents filled the chamber. Grimm walked across creaking, old floorboards, patched in spots with pieces of packing crates. The wagon was warm, he felt welcome. Then he saw the *Phuri Dai,* sitting at a small circular table aglow with candles and lamps.

She was older than the trees, and the abstract light enhanced the deep crevasses etched in her face. She was a small, shrunken woman. It was as if she were made of cotton, then boiled until the fabric contorted to form thick, heavy skin. Her head, as round as a melon, was topped with sparse, wire-like, gray strands of hair.

"Who has come to see me?"

When she looked up, Grimm was again confronted by intensely green eyes. "My name is Edward Grimm. I am an artist—a carver."

"Grimm. I have heard of you." Her voice quavered, whether from her great age, or infirmity, Grimm was unsure. His heart thundered. He thought, *she is a witch, and she knows my core is bad.* Or she might be just a crazy old woman. "Thank you, I am honored that you have heard of my carvings of carousel horses."

"I've never seen your horses, sir." She non-verbally prompted him to sit, glancing at the chair across from her. "I am sure they are beautiful."

Grimm's heart sank. She knew his soul, he was certain of it, but how? She was only a woman. No, she was *Phuri Dai.*

"Grimm," she said, "this is my granddaughter, Elena. She is

part of *Vitsa Manush, Manouches,* and *Sinti.* Her father is *Shondor Manush,* Chieftain of the Vitsa."

Elena's piercing gaze further unnerved Grimm.

"Elena is a talented dancer, the old one continued, "but, of course, you know already that Rom women are all great dancers. Elena, fetch your brother and his fiddle."

Wordlessly, Elena followed the elder woman's instructions. She was well trained. The word of the *Phuri Dai* was the word of God, Himself. It was unthinkable to deny anything they asked for or demanded. Elena went into the cold night.

"Forgive my ignorance, but how shall I address you?" Grimm asked the old woman.

"I am known by many names, and I have many faces, man." She was not afraid to look into his eyes and never glanced away. "You, sir, may call me Ilis."

Grimm could not lie as he looked into those ancient, eyes. "Madame Ilis, I fear my request may insult you." Ilis held up her hand to silence him. "No more, not yet. First, I want to look at you."

Grimm was puzzled, "Look at me?"

"Not at you, inside you." She leaned her wrinkled face close to him. "I want to see for myself what you want."

Grimm sank slightly in his chair. For the first time since he was a child, he was frightened. Perhaps his grandfather's words were true. Beware of the gypsies, they claim to be animal doctors, nomads. It is all a ruse, they are nothing but heathen witches, and will steal your soul.

Grimm's desire for Gustav's dreams was greater, and he would overcome any fear in his heart and mind. He was determined to have them by any means. If he had to trade his soul, he would.

"You are so quiet, Grimm," Ilis said, pouring oil from an urn onto a glossy, black ceramic tile.

"I have nothing to say."

"Untrue, man." She laughed at him. "You have much to say, but you are afraid." She held the tile coated with oil in front of him. "Spit on this, but not too much."

Grimm thought her request silly, yet he swirled his tongue slightly, gathering saliva. Then, gently, he spat into the thin oil.

"Good," Ilis said as she tipped the tile from end to end. The oil and spit combined, creating peculiar shapes on the tile. "Do you know what a black mirror is, Grimm?"

He had heard it mentioned before, but really had no idea what it was. "No, Madame Ilis, I don't."

"With the use of a candle flame, the black mirror can see into the soul. It does not lie. You have added your essence to the mirror, and now I will see for myself what you desire."

Ilis held the tile close to the candle flame and tipped it from side to side. The oil moved in waves and ripples, reflecting strangely on the black surface. She frowned, studying the images she found there.

"The desire of your black heart is a great one, Grimm. You are one who hates. Jealousy will destroy you. Ah…"

Her prediction terrified him. He knew it was true. He forced his tongue to move. "What is it, what else do you see?"

"I see, Elena." The *Phuri Dai* placed the mirror on the table as her granddaughter returned with a handsome young man. "My dear, Elena."

"This is my brother, sir," Elena said, and the young man bowed. "He shall play the fiddle while I dance for you."

Grimm looked at Ilis, then back at the brother and sister. The dark-haired boy couldn't have been more than sixteen, yet he was sturdy like all Rom men. He wedged the instrument beneath his chin and began to play.

Elena flowed with the music, becoming part of the melody. Every fluid move drove Grimm's lust into a frenzy. She swirled, twirled; he lusted greedily. Elena was a drug to his eyes, a narcotic for his glands. She swept Grimm into her web. Upon conclusion of the dance, Elena left the wagon.

Grimm was numb. Never before had he seen such a woman. Never before had he felt such lust. He must have her. He was finally getting everything he deserved. First, he would have dreams and now a woman. He would take these things that God stripped from Alexander and claim them as his own.

"She is a wonderful dancer, sir." Ilis' comment broke Grimm's trance. "We have much to talk about." She paused, looked deep into his eyes. "What would you pay for a dream?"

Grimm couldn't contain his thoughts; his passion had been released. "Anything, anything I have. I would pay with all the gold and silver I possess."

"Gold and silver pay for the material, for that is what it is. What you desire costs, sir, it costs."

"What is the cost?"

"It is living forever, for as long as you possess what you want."

Grimm was solemn and honest, "That is not a payment, that is what I want."

"You may think so, now."

"You haven't told me anything useful," Grimm said, impatient and growing more agitated. "You talk in riddles. What is it you offer me?"

Ilis' face soured. She swiftly snuffed all of the candles and lamps, save one. Grimm watched as she put things away and placed other things on the table.

Grimm felt the urge to apologize. "I'm sorry, Madam Ilis."

"There is no need for atonement, sir. I am prepared, and able, to grant your wish which is nothing new. Many before you, and many to come, all share your passion. You, in turn, will give yourself to the spirits. They will give you the ability to capture the child. His dreams will come to find him. When they do, that is when you can capture them."

Grimm had not mentioned the child, had not spoken his name, as far as he could remember. The *Phuri Dai* had seen the boy in Grimm's eyes; they had revealed to her the blackness of Grimm's soul, his foul intentions. Once again, cold fear gripped him.

"I still don't quite understand." Grimm watched her in the dim light.

She was grinding things with a mortar and pestle and adding a foul colored liquid to it. She murmured words Grimm couldn't follow. He could do nothing but watch her prepare the concoction. Finally, she completed her mixing and mumbling and poured the potion into a small vial.

"What should I do, once I capture the boy?"

Ilis took a small wooden stick and lit the end of it from the flame inside the lantern. She then relit all the candles and lamps. "You are an impatient man." Ilis placed the vial in front of him.

"How much do I owe you?" Grimm asked.

"You, sir, owe me nothing, but you owe everything to the spirit world."

"What should I do with this?" He held the potion up and inspected it.

"The spirit and the dream are one, together locked in harmony. To capture the spirit means to capture the dream." She could see her words confused Grimm. "Use your talent and fashion an elegant carousel. Do not put figures upon it, create a base and canopy only. Once you have the boy, place him on the carousel. Beware from this point on, for you know not what he is dreaming or what will come."

"What shall I do when they come?"

"Just as with the boy, sprinkle the potion upon them and whisper the words, *ator malcuth theraputae*. His dreams will then be yours, and you shall live for as long as you possess them. I fear for your soul, sir."

"Don't waste that energy for me, Madam. I am prepared. I have waited a lifetime for just this." Grimm felt triumphant.

"Once you go forth, there is no turning back."

"Why would I want to do that?" Grimm stood and turned to leave. Just then, Elena reentered the wagon.

"Here." Grimm pulled out the gold and placed it in her hand. "This is for your dance."

Elena courteously accepted the money. "Thank you, sir."

"No, it is I who thank you. You are a beautiful woman, perhaps one day you and I may become close, close friends."

Elena allowed Grimm to raise her hand to his lips. They were dry upon her soft flesh, but warm. She felt as if they were feeding leeches, sucking the life force from her.

She retracted her hand. "You must be a rich man."

"I am richer at this moment than in all my life." Grimm smiled and peered into her eyes. The greed and lust she perceived repulsed her, but she did not allow her own gaze to waver.

"I take my leave of you, now, but I assure you, Elena, I will return."

I had decided my own fate. I looked forward to it like a great meal in front of a starving man. The anticipation nearly drove me insane. I knew the carousel I would create would be a masterwork. I planned the position of every leaf of every vine, each little detail on cornices and columns, and each position in which a dream figure was to be fixed.

I decided to go one step further. If I were to put so much of myself into this ultimate work, I wanted it to be as beautiful as possible. I decided to build a carousel large enough to house a calliope. A means to provide music to dream by. The area in the center was carefully planned so the calliope could be grand, and the steam machinery would not take away any of the beauty.

Each time Gustav came to see me, he had such tales, such fears. He was still deeply troubled by his mother's death, but I loved it. Although I did feel some remorse, it was his inability to deal with her passing that allowed his mind to create the dreams I craved.

I hated him more every day.

Grimm gathered all of his resources to purchase the fine wood for the canopy and platform. He took every cent he'd saved from years of carving for royalty and bishops and went into town. All the way, he thought not of the carousel's beauty but of the ultimate prize—Gustav's dreams. He didn't care for the child. In fact, he'd had thoughts of what he could do to the little boy to make him conjure images. He sometimes fantasized about having power over the boy and making him do whatever he wanted. Like it or not, Gustav had all the control.

Often those fantasies were uncontrollable and entered forbidden realms. The realms Grimm's own father crossed when he stole into the boy Grimm's room at night and caused such pain and fear. Always after an encounter, he created the most fantastic pieta.

Christ rested in His Mother's arms, each new carving more real, more persecuted, and more inspired than the last. Grimm's father turned to his young son who had the gift of the craft; he praised him and called him the inspiration. Grimm hated the pietas. He hated Christ.

What did He know? God gave Grimm nothing. Grimm could only copy what another saw in his mind. His mind was vacant and void, often shrouded in hateful, shadowy memories. Others brought work to him. Surely, Grimm had enough talent to make a living. Many considered him an artist, a fine craftsman. Grimm knew better.

Grimm pushed into Schoenberg as the sun traveled through the afternoon sky. Blustery winds kept the clouds away and the heat of the sun's rays warmed his reddened cheeks. Schoenberg was the closest town with a ready supply of fine woods available. The town rested on a narrow neck of woods near a small river that eventually entered the Danube. Nearby, men harvested an unusual number of trees. Also, by route of the river, traders brought in exotic types of wood for the furniture craftsmen around Schoenberg.

Grimm trod the frozen streets until he reached the lumberyards, on the edge of Schoenberg. He'd been there many times before. Zoltan, the horse for King Leopold, began as a fir tree from this town. In particular, the lumber came from Resteller's lumbering mill, before which Grimm now stood.

Grimm pulled the bell by the front door to signal a customer was on the premises. After a few moments in the licking cold, the immense wooden door opened. Victor Resteller, a bald, middle-aged man with smiling eyes, led Grimm into the warm sanctuary.

"Greetings, Mr. Grimm. It's been a long time since you have come to Resteller's."

Grimm looked at Resteller; he liked this man well enough, but he always seemed too friendly, too eager to please. It made Grimm nervous.

"Hello, Victor. How have you been?" Grimm said with false courtesy. He said only what was expected, nothing more.

"Business is good." Victor said. "Tell me, how did the horse turn out?"

"Very fine, perhaps one of the best I've done." Grimm answered.

"Has the king seen it yet? What did he think?"

Grimm hated the questions Resteller always asked. He seemed to take great pride in anything made with wood from his store. Almost as if he should get some credit for providing the raw materials, but none of the talent.

"The king has not yet seen it, but he will be sending his people to get it today. I expect them late."

Resteller proudly grinned and adjusted his suspenders. "Well, what fabulous piece are you starting on today?"

Grimm was purposely vague. "I'm starting a big project, but I don't know yet what it will be when I'm finished."

"I've received shipments of mahogany and cherry, plus many others, since last you were here. Would you care to see them?"

Grimm wasn't very interested, but it paid to be cordial to Resteller. "I would love to see your newest lumber, I may be able to use it in some way."

"Wonderful, follow me." Resteller led Grimm into the bowels of the immense, barn-like structure.

They walked past the large cast iron stove, and Grimm thought how dangerous it was. Hot coals and fire so close to dry timber; it was an accident waiting to happen. Grimm thought of how unfortunate it would be if such a thing should happen.

Resteller led Grimm to a large bin full of rough lumber. The wood was rich and deep in color. The bark was still intact.

Grimm decided he could use that skin for shingling on the carousel. He didn't pay any attention to the babbling Resteller, whose only concern was to unload the expensive wood. Resteller didn't really care about the work, Grimm knew. He only wanted to make a profit on wood the furniture makers had passed up. Grimm stroked an exposed split in the lumber and admired the grain. There were very few knots and impurities.

"How much are you expecting for this wood?" Grimm said.

Resteller interrupted his endless stream of words to think. "I really haven't thought about it. I expect it to bring a good price…" His eyes analyzed Grimm's face. Grimm's features were cold, perhaps it was the winter, or just his nature. In any case, Resteller knew the wrong quote could offend the buyer and send him to a rival. "I hope to get 200 marks for the lot."

Grimm watched Resteller pick at his fingernails, as was his habit when he was nervous. Internally, he smiled. "That is acceptable." Grimm looked back at the wood stacked against the stone wall, "It is for all of it, correct?"

"Correct."

Grimm pulled his money out and counted the proper amount. "I also need pine delivered to my workshop."

Smiling, Resteller greedily accepted the payment. "Do you want to pay for the pine, today, too?"

"No, I wish that to be on my credit." Grimm said. "I will pay you later, after the king's men come for his carousel horse."

"Certainly, I'll have it all delivered tomorrow, before noon if that is acceptable."

"Very well."

Grimm returned to the wood and touched it again. He thought of Gustav. It wouldn't be long until everything came his way.

It was getting very late, the sun creeping toward the horizon as Grimm tidied the workshop before the king's representatives arrived. He had propped open the rear door of the workshop. Often, the space became musty, the air laden with tiny motes. The winter breezes kicked the piles of sawdust and wood shavings into shifting dunes. He swept at them, unable to control their blending waves. He was ready to give up, when he heard many footfalls breaking the frozen earth.

Grimm rested his broom against the wall and wiped his forehead with a rag. In the doorway stood one man. He cautiously looked in. Grimm admired his heavy, black winter coat of fine wool and high leather. The man had fair skin and hair, his cheeks stung red by the wind.

"Hello! Is this the residence of Edward Grimm?" The man smiled with perfect teeth.

"Yes, I'm Grimm. Please come in, I've been expecting you."

The man entered and was followed by three others. Grimm looked at the quartet, who could have been brothers. He'd often heard that Scandinavian men looked remarkably alike. Perhaps the king enjoyed being surrounded by fair haired, beautiful men.

"I am First Lieutenant Alvis Carr, and I represent King Leopold. I trust the horse is finished?" the first man said without much fanfare.

Grimm looked at him with false hospitality. Who dares come into a man's home with such arrogance and disrespect? "Of course, the stallion is right over here. I have him covered because I was cleaning."

The group collected around the protected and hidden carving. Grimm walked over proudly, pulled the canvas away from Zoltan. It was apparent from the gasps that the horse was acceptable.

"Herr Grimm, I think you have outdone yourself!" Alvis said.

"Thank you."

Alvis approached the horse. He leaned close to inspect the fine craftsmanship, and caressed the carving like it was a woman, his fingers slipping over the slick black surface, the hard points of the mane and across the slope of the saddle.

"You have done a tremendous job." Alvis slid a finger in Zoltan's mouth. "Even the tongue and teeth are perfectly detailed."

"You're too kind." Grimm smiled.

"And look at these." Alvis moved to within an inch of the horse's eyes and paused to admire them. Grimm was intrigued with the attention Alvis seem to show Zoltan's eyes. They were lifelike, deep brown, glassy, and surrounded by the narrowest band of white with stretches of meandering red vessels. It was as if they watched everyone in the room.

Grimm grew tired of the inspection, "Sir, now, about my payment."

The talk of money brought Alvis out of his staring match with the carving, "Certainly, I have the agreed upon amount with me."

Alvis fumbled through his coat. After a moment, Alvis found the cloth bag. With an embarrassed smile, he handed it to Grimm. Grimm opened the bag, poured the contents into his hand and counted quickly.

"Do you not trust a king, Herr Grimm?"

Grimm realized his act offended the messenger of King Leopold, "Forgive me, I always count. Especially, if my customers are from so far away. It would be too difficult to work through any discrepancy. It is not meant as an insult, it is good business. If you do not feel the horse will be adequate, I can always keep it."

Alvis backed down, "I didn't mean to imply any indiscretion, sir."

"It is all right." Grimm enjoyed seeing this man, who hid beneath the power of another, stripped of any power at all.

"Well, we should get this out of here before the sun totally sets." Alvis waved the other men to work.

"I have enjoyed doing business with the king. If he needs any more work done, please do not hesitate to ask me."

"Yes, I'm sure he will be pleased with this piece and send much more work your way. In fact, he is planning a new summer residence, and I know he will be looking for workers. He is building a wonderful new church with one of the largest pipe organs for hundreds of miles."

Grimm's ears perked up at this information. "Tell me, has the king secured a maker for this organ yet?"

Alvis tried to keep his attention on the men and Grimm at the same time. "Yes, he is using a young man named Julian Keefe, from Ireland. He presently is here, in Germany. In Hamburg to be exact, repairing an organ there."

"Do you know what church?" Grimm asked.

"St. Benedictine's, why?"

"I am thinking of adding some brass fixtures to some future work of mine. I am looking for someone qualified, and if this Julian Keefe is not yet working for the king, I would like to discuss things with him."

Alvis smiled, "Oh, from what I have seen and heard, he is the finest to come along in quite a while. The king has not yet sealed a commitment with Mr. Keefe. He doesn't expect to be ready for his services for a few months, by summer at the earliest."

"The work I have in mind for Mr. Keefe would only last for a month or so. Do you know how long he will be in Hamburg?"

"At least three more weeks," Alvis said.

Just then, one of the men with Alvis came to him. "Sir, we are ready to leave."

Alvis looked to the horse wrapped and bound in heavy canvas. "Excellent. Well, Herr Grimm, it has been a pleasure."

Alvis shook hands with Grimm. "I look forward to seeing you again."

"Yes, I hope so."

Alvis pulled his hand back and stepped through the door, behind the exiting form of the horse Gustav had named. "Goodbye."

Grimm walked behind them and shut the door. He dared not move, he dared not think until he was sure Leopold's men were well away. At last, it was safe to be alone with his thoughts.

"I have great plans for you, Gustav," Grimm muttered,

reaching for the broom. He began sweeping the floor where Zoltan had stood. "There is much, much work to do. I must keep this area clean if everything is to go my way."

I had been gathering inspiration for more than two weeks. I poured over books and drawings to use in the creation of the carousel's exoskeleton. The meat for the inside would have to wait.

I came across a beautiful, highly detailed etching of many ancient Greek buildings. I was particularly entranced with Doric-styled buildings and elected this vogue for my cage. As I gradually studied the style, I fell into fascination. The way the columns rose to support the entablature. The shaft's swelling at the entasis.

I began assembling what I wanted by cutting and pasting and copying. Soon, I had a plan to work from. I had eight columns. Each one was topped with an architrave, and a triglyph-framed metope waiting to house one of Gustav's captured dreams. At last, I was ready to begin my work. But first, I had to see Elena once more.

Elena had joined Gustav as one of Grimm's obsessions. He never recovered from the wounds of her slicing green eyes. At last, he felt as if God were ready to reward him. Grimm thought he was deserving of heavenly payment for the sacrifices he'd made.

Grimm scraped together the little money he had left. Gathering materials for the carousel platform and works housing had all but exhausted his resources. But the carousel was the most important thing, the most intense effort he'd ever put forth. He could not let go, not stop now. And through the boy he would live, and through Elena he would take love.

She would want to give herself to him, she was only a woman. Elena, a gypsy girl, at that. It would be her good fortune to marry an outstanding citizen and escape her vagabond lifestyle. They would marry and Grimm could have her for his collection of dreams. Perhaps they would have a child, and Grimm would have yet another outlet for his pain.

The forest was not as harrowing as the initial journey to find the Rom encampment. Grimm found himself doubting more and more the powers of the old hag. She had promised he would eventually have all that he needed to have a dream. But there was a price; everything came with a price. What would the cost entail, and when would he start paying? Perhaps when the payment started, everything else would, too.

The frozen ground crunched beneath the weight of his boots. It was late afternoon and the gypsy lights could be seen easily through the stiff web of hibernating wood. The camp hadn't shifted at all. Grimm thought they probably had decided to settle for the winter. The valley was protected on all sides by the sloping hills and forest. The winds could never penetrate this haven, and the snows never got more than six inches deep.

Grimm hesitated, almost stumbled, as he trekked through the camp to the trailer of the *Phuri Dai*. Perhaps it was the cold, freezing his feet into cumbersome blocks of ice that had to be dragged up the rickety stairs, or just fear that made it hard to approach the door. He remembered the night being sliced open with the eyes of green. Elena eyes were like razors when she laughed.

Grimm lifted his hand like a wooden mallet and cracked it softly upon the door three times. There wasn't an immediate answer, but he could hear the stirring of people inside. Finally, the door pulled open, and a rush of hot air met Grimm's cold face. His breath exhumed in spurts, like a geyser.

Elena cut him. She said nothing, a characteristic of an obedient Rom girl. He liked that about her. She didn't have to use her voice to say a word, however.

"Hello." He stumbled inside, shaking the ice blocks from his feet.

Suddenly, to Grimm's utter surprise, Elena addressed him. "I did not expect to see you again." Her hair was pulled forward, her brunette locks kept her neck warm.

"I had a few concerns, and I needed some answers to questions I did not ask before." He closed the door behind him.

"The *Phuri Dai* is not available right now. I cannot disturb them." Elena paused and looked at Grimm. "What is your name?"

Grimm's heartrate rose, he was taken quite off guard. "I… my name is Edward Grimm."

"Edward Grimm." Her green eyes seemed to slice a piece of his face away while she openly flirted with him. "What is it that you do? You seem to be well off. It is rare to see someone with money so far removed from the city."

"Yes, but I do not work in the city. I am a sculptor; I make all sorts of things for people."

"Rich people?" she asked.

"Very rich," he answered.

"Have you ever made anything for a king?"

"Yes, I have made many things for kings, queens, dukes, and American presidents." Grimm enjoyed her questions. He felt important, if only for a moment.

"How fascinating. Do you go to grand parties and balls? Are you celebrated?"

"I get invitations, but I do not go," he said. "I am not comfortable in those situations."

"Why?" she asked. "You create such masterpieces. Surely, there is a desire to meet the artist."

"I do not know about that…"

Suddenly, the door pulled open, and the *Phuri Dai* entered with the help of a striking young man. "Mr. Grimm," she said.

The young man fired a look of anger at Elena, then at Grimm. "Elena," he barked, "you know to never let *Gadje* into the *Phuri Dai*'s home."

Elena's gaze pored over the young man. He was lean, his face rugged. His eyes were just as piercing as Elena's, but of deep, bottomless brown.

"I am sorry, but I did not want Mr. Grimm to wait in the cold." Elena returned the young man's jealous glare, and it was obvious to Grimm they were lovers.

The old woman broke the tension, "It is all right, Sennett, I will allow it this time."

Grimm looked at the man named Sennett. He stood proud, like an arrow or tree. His body was strong, vibrant, his movements conveyed a predatory sexuality. He had known Elena's flesh, and he, also, had been cut with her eyes. Jealousy took root in Grimm's brain.

"Sennett, you can go now," Elena said. "I will talk to you later."

Sennett looked at the *Phuri Dai*. She touched him lovingly. "Everything is fine. Let him pass."

Sennett turned, without a second glance at any of them, and left. Grimm sighed deeply, hoping the women did not sense his fear of the young tiger.

"Sennett is a very loyal and caring man," the old woman said while moving to her familiar seat. "He is very protective of us."

"I understand. I imagine many men come to take advantage of the women here. I have respect for him."

"Many think he will be the next leader of the Vitsa," said Elena.

"That is many, many years down the road." The *Phuri Dai* looked at Elena. "Now is not the time to talk of this. Elena, please tend to Sennett."

Elena started to leave. Grimm watched as she passed within an inch of him. She brushed him like a swan's wing, and his heartbeat skipped. The door opened and closed. Elena was gone. Grimm fumed as he thought of Sennett. She was going to see him, and possibly be with him.

The *Phuri Dai* brought Grimm back from his obsession momentarily. "Mr. Grimm, I did not expect to see you this soon. What is it you need?"

She sat down, and he sat across from her. "I don't think this magic is working, I haven't felt anything."

"It is because you have not done anything yet. Things do not happen out of the sky. My friend, you must work hard to make it work. That is a part of the payment."

"Tell me, tell me how to do it."

"The boy, take the boy, soon. The potion gets stronger only if used. If it sits too long, it will sour and be very dangerous."

Grimm paused to contemplate the warning. "I have plans, the boy will be coming to my house tomorrow. Then, I shall make my move, but…" he hesitated. "How long until his dreams come for him?"

The *Phuri Dai* dragged a dense cackle from her throat. "Maybe the very minute you use the potion, maybe never. Some give up dreams, or they never had them to begin with. Herr Grimm, you know it is true."

"It is true." He lowered his head, but then brightened slightly, "I've heard about his dreams, he dreams often."

"A dream, or a nightmare?"

"What difference does it make?

The flames reflected in her eyes. They licked and danced. There was another eye looking through hers at him, like a window from somewhere else, somewhere sinister.

"Go now, Grimm. Time to harvest what you have sown."

Grimm wanted to say more, but it was clear he had been dismissed. The words spun around in his mind. They wanted to fall through the bottom of the funnel, go out his mouth, and get a reaction, but there was a blockage. Perhaps it was that seedling of jealousy. The old woman planted it, clearly. However, she didn't know that Grimm feasted on it. He could not wait for that fruit to ripen, to see Alexander broken and that he was the golden one now.

He rose, speechless. The *Phuri Dai* did not look at him. He turned, walked across the creaking dry floor. As he pulled the door open, fingers of cold clawed his face.

The gypsy camp was alive with activity. The men from the surrounding towns and villages were out tonight seeking thrills. All over the encampment, small circles of folk congregated around some of the young girls. They danced around fires, which gave them shadows and light. The gypsy men protected the women and collected the money the *Gadje* men paid.

Grimm's gaze darted around the camp. He paused momentarily at each of the bonfires, hoping to catch a glimpse of Elena. He knew she was dancing for someone else. He wanted her to dance only for him. And Sennett, he had made love to her on more than one occasion. Grimm knew it. Not just a dancer, friend, or confidante. He had made love with the girl, the girl who cut with her eyes. Grimm would take her, too.

Sennett stood by a smaller fire, and a young woman sat nearby, singing beautifully. It wasn't Elena, however. Grimm spotted the man who ran the feed store in the village, and fully expected to run into his lumber peddler in the small crowd.

The man from the feed store held up a bundle of cash. Sennett moved over to claim it and to ask his request. Blades of jealousy ripped across Grimm's face, body, and heart. He could feel the hot blood pulsing. If Elena could only see him bleed for her, surely she wouldn't pursue this young Sennett, who looked so wild.

Grimm wanted to run across the encampment and throw him in the fire. He wanted to destroy him, because he had Elena. What was it about him that made Elena's heart race? What powers had he possessed to make her surrender her virginity to him? Sennett was strong. Grimm could see the tightness of his clothes against his lean body. His sleeves were rolled to his elbows, even though the night was cold. His forearms were heavily muscled from hard work, and fine dark hair trailed to his wrists. Sennett's hands were beautiful, almost feminine, yet rugged. His palms were small and his fingers long. These were the hands that touched Elena.

Grimm's hands were not beautiful. They were blocky, his

fingers like small sausages, and he struggled to make his fingers do the work they must. He did not have the young body Sennett did. Perhaps Elena could only be pleased by a brash, unshaven boy's raw sexuality.

Elena might think of Sennett as the man she wanted to be with, but what about when she was ready to marry? She couldn't marry someone like Sennett. Grimm thought. He didn't have money, or the potential for earning enough of it to make a difference in Elena's life. He, Grimm, could make a difference. He could sweep Elena into a lush life; she would never want for anything.

Grimm quickly glanced back at Sennett. He still stood by the fire. He was enjoying the show as much as the other men. Grimm thought this to be in his favor. Elena would not want a man whose eyes strayed so easily.

"Herr Grimm."

He turned to see Elena standing in the shadows of one of the wagons.

"I see you cannot stay away from this place," she said quietly. "I also see you have found my wagon to hide behind. What are you looking for?"

Her breath flowed gently forth with every word she uttered. Fingers in the fog taunted Grimm, tempting him to step into forbidden streets.

"I wanted to see dancers." His foggy breath quivered.

"Did you want to see me dance?"

Any answer Grimm offered would be as clear as glass.

Elena would know the truth no matter what he said. "It was you I came to see."

"You don't have to be ashamed, Mr. Grimm. I will dance, if you pay. It is how I make my money. I make my money many ways."

He dangled in her web. A few more moments of intensity, and he'd trip the signal cord, then she'd come down like a black widow to wrap him in silk for a later meal. Grimm knew this was happening. Part of him wanted Elena to take him and twist him, another knew the danger and warned him.

Then, it was like another being erupted from Grimm's flesh. Perhaps Elena razored it out of him, the beast of passion reached out. Grimm wanted her now, the way Sennett had her, and he wasn't going to let her back away.

"Elena, you are the one I came to see." Grimm seized her wrist in a vise-like grip. "There's something…I have to have…"

Elena's expression turned from that of a coy tease to someone in fear for her life. "Let go of my arm, you are hurting me."

Grimm turned back to the bonfire. He wanted to see if Sennett was still there. He was. Grimm was about to look away when Sennett made eye contact with him. It was momentary, almost not enough to count in the space of a fractured second. Grimm dismissed Sennett. He was a beautiful man, and most likely too stupid to realize what Grimm was about.

Grimm returned his attention to Elena. "Please, don't be afraid of me. I can pay anything you want. If it is money, I can get plenty." Suddenly, a hot flash impacted against his face. Heat permeated his eye, he felt his hands being wrenched from Elena. Before he knew what was happening, Sennett threw him to the ground. He pushed Grimm's face into the frozen soil and punched furiously at the sides of his head.

"Stop! Sennett!" Elena yelled, pulling at the enraged young man.

Sennett backed off. Grimm struggled to his knees.

"You, *gadje*. Bastard, I'll kill you!"

"He did nothing to me, Sennett."

"Rapists are not tolerated here, *gadje*!"

Grimm couldn't believe what he was hearing. Sennett was accusing him of trying to rape Elena. Grimm struggled to stand, but tremors of pain ruptured through him. He coughed, and blood came out his mouth and nose.

"I didn't do anything."

"Sennett, get out of here!" Elena pushed the young man back. "I'll take care of this. You do not know what is going on."

The visitors to the camp paid no attention to what was

happening in the shadows of the wagons. Frequently, the gypsy women had made extra money in the dark, and the shadows were the best place to be discreet.

"Sennett, leave now, or I shall speak to my father and *Phuri Dai*. You know the rules."

He paused for a moment. His angry eyes highlighted by the distant flames. For all Grimm knew, Sennett's gaze was fire, itself. Then, without another word, Sennett wheeled and stalked off.

"Are you hurt?" Elena asked while helping Grimm to his feet.

Attempting to salvage some pride, Grimm lied, "I just need to get home and rest."

She moved closer to inspect the damage. "He did not hit your face. You will not be bruised."

Grimm was deeply shamed. He found it hard to look at her. He'd never needed a woman to help him. Men should be strong, women submissive. His father had drilled that into Grimm's head since his childhood. His father, like Sennett, hit him in the head, too.

"I shall be all right." Grimm felt nothing but overwhelming anger and humiliation. "Leave me alone, woman." He pulled away from her, bundled his cloak about himself swiftly, and sped off through the night.

Humiliation, no matter the age, hurts deeply. He would never forget Sennett. He would have revenge against him, and Elena would see it. He would prove his love was superior to that of a boy. Sennett would never be anything to her, but a mere boy. He would wait until the time was right to have his revenge. His head throbbed, felt as if it would burst in a fountain of blood. He scraped up the hard snow and held it to his head.

Grimm forgot about Sennett at the sight of his carousel platform. He had been such a fool. Gustav would arrive the next day, and Grimm was not prepared for him. Tomorrow would be the most important day of Grimm's life. Tomorrow he would become the host of Gustav's dreams—forever.

I remember a dream I once had. If, in fact, that is what it was.
Now, it is just a memory buried beneath a lifetime of lame
refuse I call existence. I never received the love or gifts that
other children did. I was teased with the temporary gift of a
mother and love only to have it ripped away. Alexander was
the prince. He was smart and handsome. The university gladly
took him in while I toiled in an art class at lesser institutions.
I learned, and I am grateful for learning technique. However, I
am only technique. I lack vision and imagination to create my
own dreams.

My own father had supplanted love and joy in my life with
pain, bitterness, and betrayal. I hated him. He had to hate me.
Perhaps it was mutual loathing that kept me alive. I lived only
to rejoice in his death. And the day he died the angels sang to
me in choruses. The angels, however, were lofty, pretentious
creatures that loitered in heaven. I begged and offered my very
soul to them. I asked for salvation. I received silence. Perhaps,
begging offended them.

Then, the day I prayed for the devil to take my father, he died.
His death was hideous and painful, and the most delicious part
was the chance I had to see it all.

He was helping his brother, who owned and operated an iron
smelting plant. I saw the chains that held the huge kettle of
molten iron, they were eaten with rust. My uncle was very
frugal, and he wouldn't replace the chains until they broke.
There had been many horrible accidents before; one man's
arm was burned off when he was splashed with melted iron.

My father was hoisting the kettle from the furnace, and he
carefully piloted the glowing, viscous iron toward a series
of dyes ready to cast. I was there, sitting out of the way,
occupying myself with drawings in the sand. I had drawn a

picture of the devil, my father, and the fires of Hell surrounding them. I was in a daze. I put forth all my mental energy into the image in the oily sand. I wanted him to feel the heat, the blinding pain of burning to death.

As I drew the pitchfork in the devil's hand, I heard the highest pitched noise I'd ever known. The sound was like the scream of a rabbit, high and resonant. I knew what it was the moment I looked up. The rust had finished its long meal.

My father wasn't standing directly beneath the kettle. If he had been, he might have died quickly. I was sixteen then, and I was close enough to push him clear. The kettle came crashing down, my father fell back, but the hot liquid gushed from the giant smelting pot, hitting him in the chest and abdomen. It stuck like honey to his clothes, making a second skin. I remembered falling into the millpond with my clothes on, and they clung heavily. It looked like that was the way it felt. I finished drawing the pitchfork.

He was still alive, screaming, his body wrenching in pain. The molten iron was melting his body. It burned a hole into his chest, and the incredible pressure created by the heat forced his innards to spill onto the floor. I remember him attempting to crawl for my help. His entrails snaking along behind, their trails looked like worm marks after a hard rain. I stood and watched him, and I think I smiled as he reached for my hand. I backed up one step. He saw my smile. The iron had begun to cool somewhat. It blackened. Then, my father's eyes rolled violently. He collapsed into a soupy mixture of floor dirt, semi-liquid metal, and his own insides.

That was, perhaps, the last happy day I recall. Except for the winter day when Gustav came to my door.

Grimm swept the floors in the workshop. He wanted to make certain nothing, not even common floor dirt, would interfere with his plans. The crackling fire in the stove was his companion as he worked. He thought about Gustav, about using the potion, and waiting for the first dream to come to its missing master.

His brother said he would be gone for two weeks at the

most. Grimm would have the boy to himself forever, not just two weeks. He swept a little faster. The cuckoo clock, which he made, whistled three o'clock.

Grimm leaned the corn broom against the work bench and wiped off a few stray grains of saw dust. He returned to the main part of the house, filled the copper kettle with water from a nearby bucket. He put it on top of the wood burning stove in the kitchen. Soon, ghostly mists of steam started climbing from the spout.

Then, Grimm heard his brother's familiar rapping on his door. Grimm turned as Alexander pushed the door open, knocked the crusty snow from his boots, and pulled little Gustav inside after him.

"I tell you Edward, I'd swear it is colder around your house than any house in all of Deutschland." Alexander knelt and un-wrapped the child as if he were a precious, stored porcelain doll.

"You look chilled to the bone, boy." Grimm smiled. "Come and give your uncle a great bear hug."

Gustav walked cautiously to Grimm but slid easily into his arms. Although this was his uncle, Gustav felt chilly in his embrace. It shouldn't be like that, the little boy thought. But then, the adults might not love him as much if he refused.

Gustav's uncle was strong and wiry. His uncle's hands were long like a spider's legs and could easily encircle him. Even if he wanted to pull away, the man, who reminded him of a great black spider, could keep him, forever if he wanted to.

Grimm touched the boy's fair hair. He thought of how soft and fine it was, like an angel's locks. "I've missed you, Gustav." Grimm smiled and patted the boy's head.

Gustav cast a glance of apprehension at Alexander, but then a smile forced its way across his lips.

"He has done nothing but talk of staying with you while I'm away." Alexander started to unload some of his bundle he brought in. "I've brought a few of his favorite things, in case he becomes homesick."

"I wish you weren't going to be away so long, father." Gustav pulled from Grimm and went to hug Alexander.

Alexander draped his arm around his son. "I hate it, too, but I want you to know it won't last much longer. In the spring we will consider moving to the city."

Gustav looked into his father's deep eyes. He could see his face reflected, and also the image of his uncle coming up behind them.

"If you are to move so far away from me, I must spend as much time as I can with you, now, dear boy." Grimm laid a cool hand on Gustav's shoulder. He knew how it would be: Gustav would be full of apprehension, but soon he would forget to be afraid. He would play, as any child would, and his trust would grow.

Grimm always wondered why Gustav feared him. Gustav wasn't a mind reader. He could have no idea of his uncle's intentions. Perhaps the beings in Gustav's dreams have warned him, Grimm thought. They call to him, singing like birds when wolves or men enter the forest.

"You are trembling from the cold, Gustav." Grimm held the boy's chin in his hands and looked into his eyes, searching them for a sign. How did he know? Who was telling him, and how could Grimm silence them so he could harvest Gustav's dreams? The boy's blue eyes were fearful and wet. In the glaze, Grimm saw his own obscene reflection. His own eyes were there, ugly, bottomless. Without a soul. Gustav's soul was a big, juicy, polished apple to Grimm. He felt the flesh of the fruit, yearned to take a bite.

Grimm broke his connection with Gustav for fear his eyes betrayed him. He turned to his brother. "Would you like some tea before you go, Alexander?"

"I wish I had the time. I want to be on the main road before night catches me. I do not want to be in these woods tonight. The gypsies are about. They bring nothing but anguish to the Christian heart."

Grimm listened to his brother's prejudiced talk, but kept silent about his dealings with the Rom. "I do not think they will come around here."

"I hope not, they bring werewolves with them, you know." Alexander summoned Gustav and embraced him. "I would not want one of them to get my baby boy."

Stone-faced, Grimm watched the father and son share love. He hated both of them. Father had always loved Alexander the most. It served Alexander right to lose the dearest fixture in his life. Grimm smiled, not in reaction to their love, but from the thought of denying Gustav to Alexander, forever.

"Gustav," Grimm said, "I have started some wonderful new carvings. I'm sure you will love them."

Gustav turned from Alexander; he could see Grimm's form outlined in the flickering firelight.

Alexander stroked Gustav's fair hair, "There, my son! New things to see! Uncle Ed may let you name them, or even play with them."

"If you want to, I can even teach you how to make things of your own. Maybe someday, you'll be able to make a horse like Zoltan." Grimm looked at the apple.

Gustav's eyes were swelling with tears. Perhaps it was the promise of toys, or the naming of beasts. Grimm was glad the child did not start crying.

"Zoltan?" Gustav whispered.

"Yes, Zoltan!" Grimm then realized it was the king's horse that lit the child's eyes.

"I like Zoltan. I dreamed of Zoltan. Father gave me books with drawings of the Friesian stallions. I think that is what Zoltan is." Gustav relaxed a bit and slid away from his father.

"You did?" Grimm replied, although that was not what he wanted to say. He looked at the plump apple, and thought, *You did? How dare you! I have nothing, and now you take what little I could steal from someone else. It is mine, but soon…*

The clock struck the hour.

"My goodness, it is getting late. I must leave now, if I'm going to get out of the forest before it gets pitch black." Alexander tightened his gloves, boots and scarf.

"One more hug, please, father." Gustav hugged Alexander hard.

"My, such a big hug." He returned the embrace.

Grimm simmered. Grimm seethed. Their love; the last slap in the face he could take. He decided then and there, it was time to pick the apple, and if necessary, make apple sauce.

Alexander broke the clasp, "I must go now. It is getting late, late, late. You don't want the werewolves to get me, now do you, son?"

"Oh, no! What would I do if you were gone, too?" Gustav replied, truly frightened.

Grimm interrupted the loving moment, "Gustav, it is time to let you father go. Come, I will fix some wonderful pancakes for supper, just the way you like them."

Alexander got free of Gustav and made it to the door. He opened it, and the winter winds licked like dogs to get at the hot meat inside.

"Good-bye, son. Good-bye Edward. I'll be back soon, I hope, and wish you a good time."

Grimm and Gustav watched as the door shut. He touched the boy's shoulders and looked down upon the top of his head. He could smell apples.

Then, he spoke to Gustav. "Why don't you take your things to your room? I'll start making the cakes."

Gustav gathered his possessions swiftly and hastened to his usual room. He could feel his uncle's eyes upon him—every movement under scrutiny. Gustav felt he was being cored like an apple. His uncle's stare burned holes into his back as he went to his room.

Grimm was watching him. He was planning, looking for loose threads in the boy's mind—seams with which to unravel the boy's soul. He sought an entrance, that hanging thread to pull.

Grimm wanted to see the boy, unwind all his dreams; and the carver would be there with needles to knit all the threads into his own make-believe world. A delicious blanket to enshroud himself, to experience all that he had missed. He would weave a truth for himself, even though Grimm knew all along that his truth was damnation.

Gustav stayed in his room, thinking. His thoughts ran rampant through gloomy woods. He thought of the dragon and the queen story. Then he envisioned Zoltan. The horse filled his memory. He remembered the hard points of Zoltan's black mane. The steed was so strong, Gustav knew he could just jump on his back and ride like the wind. Zoltan would know the way, Zoltan could find his mother.

But then he looked around the small, stale room. The floorboards were dusty and cracked. The window rattled with the harsh north wind's breath. Zoltan was not here, and Gustav wondered if the magnificent horse could find him. He had to believe it, like he had to believe in St. Nicholas. If you didn't believe in him, he wouldn't come on Christmas. There would be no chocolates in the Advent calendar. It is the same with the horse, Gustav thought. *I must believe Zoltan will come for me.*

"Gustav!" his uncle called from the kitchen. "Dinner is almost ready, come on!"

Gustav sighed and turned to the door. The floorboards creaked as he walked across the room. He then reached for the iron door handle. It was cold like ice and bit his palm. Gustav could barely grip it.

"Coming, Uncle!"

Grimm watched as Gustav rushed from the room. He noticed a troubled look on the boy's face.

"What's the matter?"

"The door handle was cold."

Grimm looked down his nose at the boy. So innocent, he thought. How easy it would be to overpower this child, violate that innocence, break and beat his spirit into submission. Why should he not suffer as Grimm had suffered at the hands of his father? *But that was when I stopped dreaming,* Grimm realized. At least, he could not remember having any dreams since that time.

Grimm considered, then dismissed harming the child sexually; that would erase Gustav's chances of ever having wonderful, fantastic, pleasant dreams, again. Nightmares would plague his mind. No, Grimm believed, instead, he could dominate by intimidation, and not risk losing the dreams.

Grimm lowered himself to the boy's level. "Gustav, do you remember Zoltan?" Grimm could see in the boy's face that he did. "Well, I'm making something so much better than the horse that…"

Gustav interrupted, awe and eagerness clear in his voice, "I don't think anything could be as good as Zoltan! Can I see it now?"

Grimm knew only too well how important the horse was to Gustav. Gustav had grown to love the horse, and Grimm intended to wring every ounce of advantage from that love.

"Yes, I suppose we have time before we eat." Grimm held out his hand, and Gustav's little paw was totally engulfed as Grimm's fingers, curled like talons, clenched the prey. Together, the uncle and nephew went into the workshop.

The place was immaculate. Nothing remained in the work area, except for the impressive carousel base. An expanse of fine, finished wood was pieced perfectly over a rough, wooden frame. The entire structure was wheeled and moved around a hollow, still unfinished center.

The canopy rested upon pillars reminiscent of ancient Greece or Atlantis. Grimm had truly put his entire talent into this piece. Each detail was perfect in proportion and context.

But something was missing. There were no figures upon the carousel. It was empty, void of shapes; naked, a skeleton with no flesh.

"Where is the horse?" Gustav looked up at Grimm.

Grimm was deeply entrenched in anticipation. It dripped

like saliva from the corner of his mouth. The boy was so close to the carousel. Just a few more steps, a few more moments, and the boy would give up his treasure trove of dreams. And Grimm would feast on them forever, as the images sought out their maker.

"I don't see any horses. Do you have them somewhere else?" Gustav pulled at his uncle's hand like a puppy pulls a shirtsleeve. Grimm looked down. Gustav was like sugar. Grimm could taste the sweetness. Surely the child's blood was strawberry jelly. Around him, a hazy aura formed. It clouded Grimm's vision.

"Sweet boy, use your imagination! The horse is there, there are a hundred horses if you wish. You have to wish very, very hard. Imagine the great Friesian stallions." Grimm reached out for the boy, "Here, step up onto the carousel." He helped Gustav scramble onto the base.

The movement rocked the carousel floor slightly. The new wheels squeaked on their track. Gustav smiled and giggled.

"Close your eyes. What do you see?" Grimm peered across the narrow space separating them. "Go ahead, it is safe to close your eyes. It's safe to dream whatever you want in here."

Gustav slowly let his eyes fall shut. "I can see Zoltan."

"My, what a nice dream." Grimm wanted to lash out, he could hardly stand the sight of Gustav. "Is there more?"

Grimm's mouth eased open; his tongue filled the space. The lights from the stove and kerosene lanterns glimmered on the saliva on his lips. He intently listened to Gustav as the boy's imagination cracked open.

"I see trees, a big oak tree. And there's a tree fort built into it. I built it, and I can fly up with the special wings I made from the leaves." Gustav was smiling, momentarily free from his nightmares.

Grimm could only listen with passion. It was so dreadfully unfair, so horribly wrong that he could not see these things for himself. His mind was a machine, long rusted shut from abuse. Perhaps it was his past tears, like those that now drenched his eyes, that had rusted his mind closed.

The boy's mind was soaring. Infinitely diving on streams of unfathomable images. Grimm's heart began to swell, threatening to split his chest right down the middle. He had to stop the child now, before his heart exploded.

Adults routinely dismissed a child's thoughts with false pleasantries. It took every ounce of strength Grimm had to pretend he was unconcerned. "That is wonderful," he said, noting the breathy sound he couldn't control. "Delightful, I am sure."

"Flying is my favorite thing to do in dreams."

"Sweet Gustav, it is time to eat dinner." Grimm pulled his nephew down from the carousel.

"Can we play more after dinner? Can we, please?" Gustav had forgotten his fear, and he hugged his arms around Uncle Grimm's neck.

I stood over the hot stove, preparing our dinner. All the while, I listened to Gustav. He was so energized, as if lightning had struck him. He glowed. He chattered like an agitated squirrel.

As he talked, I watched the pancake batter dribble onto the hot griddle. It poured freely, but never was able to spread very far. The heat congealed the mixture until it couldn't move. Slowly, the mix stiffened until it was nothing more than doughy disks that browned above the heat of the iron. I turned the pancakes as I listened to Gustav's amazing stories. Rage swelled like bile in my throat. I was persecuted in my own home, attacked by a child. But he bore a knife made of such metal that would cut jagged rips in my soul.

I looked down at the pancakes. To me, they looked as if they could be wooden. They certainly had the color and grain. Funny, I thought, how some things masquerade so easily as others. Insects masquerade as flowers and leaves, fish portrayed rocks, and little boys pretended to be innocent.

As I listened to my nephew's tales, I gazed at the cakes. I then thought of the potion and the Phuri Dai. Her words haunted me, drowning out Gustav's babblings. I found the boy's words were what I wanted to listen to, but her words became louder until I could no longer shut them out.

I remembered her instructions, how to use the potion, the magical words that lit the fuse; I craved trying it. I could no longer fight it. I wanted to own the images in Gustav's mind more than anything in the world.

As I removed the pancakes from the griddle, I thought it peculiar that I would think of Elena at such a time. After a few minutes, I understood why I had recalled my enchantress. I thought of Gustav's dreams as acquisitions. I would add his *wealth to my own. Elena was much the same. She needed wealth, prestige. These were important things to her. This was the reason she stayed with Sennett. He was nothing, nothing except the heir to the Vitsa.*

That meant power. Elena, as I was slowly realizing, had to have power, too. She had an adequate amount, now, as the daughter of the chieftain. But soon, like a drinker, it wouldn't be enough. Elena lived for the stupor money and belongings gave her.

Elena was this way, and I cared not for material possessions. I thought having her would add a new dimension to my life, the way owning Gustav's dreams would do so. I might even, I dared to think, start dreaming, again, if I were in love. I knew she would love me in return. I had everything she wanted. I had money, or ways to get it, and I had a good reputation. Kings came to me for art. Surely, she would take this into consideration.

Or would she be stupid and think that life in the Vitsa would be enough for her? Could she prefer power over few to influence over many? Maybe power over one was greater than influence with hundreds. I would know soon, for I decided that I had to have Elena. I would then have a family of my own, I would command them. She would be the wife, and Gustav would be my child.

I turned to see Gustav sitting at the table. His eyes were bright and innocent. Deep inside, something pulled at me. It was an instant of tension, perhaps natural love that I had for the boy. I saw his face and recognized my desire again. I reminded myself that dreams and desire are two entirely different beasts. Equally, they are dangerous.

We sat and ate. He could barely keep his mouth closed enough to swallow. Gustav was so happy, he was free, right now, of any coat of burden. He hadn't mentioned his mother or the Virgin once. Now in his dreams, he saw Zoltan, and the beast dragon from a story he had been told.

I smiled as I watched him slurp down some water. It was a true smile, a smile of love, a smile from the monkey playing on my innards. That monkey had to be slain. I sought him out as I listened to Gustav. He filled me with vision, and that drove me on, made me intense enough to find a weapon inside myself.

I grabbed a dagger of hate and jealousy from my heart, and I sought out that little monkey that loved Gustav. As I took hold of the screaming simian, Gustav yawned. I bore the blade high above the monkey's exposed neck, and I impaled it on my knife. As the monkey's slaughtered form fell to the base of my brain, Gustav finished his dinner.

I smiled at the boy. He must have thought I was smiling at him, but I was smiling as I kicked the body of the monkey aside. Gustav was getting tired, I could see his eyes drooping. But he tried to wake up.

I asked him if he wanted to go out and play a little more before going to bed. At first, he said he was tired. But I insisted. I was ready to make my move, and I knew if he wouldn't go, I'd certainly force him. I wondered silently if it might not be better if I did it by force. Then, maybe I could deal with it better I wouldn't think about anything, the monkey wouldn't be resurrected. Gustav would fight me, and then it would be easier.

If he didn't fight, if I tricked him, I did not know how I would feel about it. It was a decision that I was allowed to back away from, for Gustav remembered Zoltan. It turned into his idea to go out into the workshop and play, again. I guess the temptation of seeing Zoltan in his mind once more was greater than his need for sleep. I don't think he understood that he always had the power to see the horse, but children often lack such universal vision. The end of the world can come quickly, or seem to come quickly, in the minds of children. Perhaps, because Elena was so young, she thought the end of the world would be leaving the Vitsa.

I told Gustav to go on ahead without me. I had to clean up a little before I could join him. He grinned like the silly boy he was and traipsed off into the work area. I could hear him making galloping noises with his hands against his thighs. He neighed and spat like a stallion, also.

I lied to him. I had no plans to clear away anything, except the dreams in his head. I, now more than ever, had to taste the apple. The noises he made drove me to the brink of insanity. The galloping; the horse ran in his head, and he could see it! How could he see it when it wasn't there? How could he know what the mane would feel like? I hated this boy. I'm glad the monkey was dead. I only regret how I killed the monkey. I would have much rather bitten its throat out, and swallowed the meat and bloody fur whole.

On an eddy of rage, I traveled to my room. I tossed the door aside. I heard the wind scratching at the thin glass. The darkness held such secrets.

I pulled out the vial, a small token of those strange secrets. I remembered what the Phuri Dai said to me. I, in all truthfulness, only remember the parts that suited me best. I couldn't recall any warnings or consequences. She claimed that I would be damned to forever living, because of my mad desire to own the boy's dreamscapes. It wasn't a curse, or any form of damnation. I welcomed the chance to live forever just to see the dreams. I had been without dreams my whole life, it would be no burden to exist eternally if I could dream.

I rifled through my stale top drawer, dumping all my clothes onto the floor. I had not many valuables, but I kept what I had safe. It's true, I had relations with the gypsies, but that doesn't mean I trusted them. They were no strangers to burglary.

I pulled out the drawer and put it on the floor. I then reached inside the space where the drawer had been, and I retrieved a small jewelry box. I opened it. Inside, I kept the two most valuable belongings I owned. One was a button from my father's army coat, from a time when I thought he loved me. The other, was the vial of liquid given to me by the medicine woman. I struggled to remember her instructions, the magic words, and all that I could expect. The words were in my mouth instantly.

Ator malcuth theraputae.

I repeated them in my head. I inspected the potion in the small glass jar. I had to believe in it, I had to trust that it would work. I never thought, however, getting your heart's desire was as easy as this.

The door to the workshop was near to my room, and in a heartbeat, I was through the portal. I saw Gustav, running around the base of the carousel, pretending to gallop.

'I'm Zoltan! I'm Zoltan' Gustav cried. 'Uncle Edward, look at me!'

I looked at him, kicked the monkey, and walked toward the child. I smiled, telling him to slow down, that he might break it. He listened to me and came to a halt near me.

What I did then would amaze God himself. I told the boy I had a wonderful game to play. I called it statues. I told him to close his eyes and stand very still. He couldn't stop asking how to play, but I assured him that it was fun. I got up on the carousel with him. In my head, the words churned and burned.

Ator malcuth theraputae.
Ator malcuth theraputae.

I silently unscrewed the lid off the potion, and carefully poured a few drops into it. Gustav started to ask questions, but I assured him that this was the way to play the game. The same argument came back to me. Would it be easier to force the boy to submit, would it make completing this task any smoother? How would I feel if he just stood here, unaware of what was going on?

Either way, this was Gustav's ending on the planet. How would I tell his father, what would I tell his father? I was about to commit this child to an eternity of limbo. Not dead, but unable to live. Was it worth it? He's just a boy, my own flesh and blood. Then I remembered, I was once just a boy, my father's flesh and blood.

I gingerly tossed the few drops of potion from the lid. Gustav never even felt them hit the back of his neck. Once that was accomplished, it was easy to say the words. I never wanted anything more at this moment, than to have my own dreams and the love of my nephew, but I had made my decision, and no sacrifice was too great.

Ator malcuth theraputae.

I needed to say the words only once. They were like fire to a vat of kerosene. I stood aghast at what I saw and stood back so it didn't spread to me. From the tiny droplets of potion on Gustav's neck, I could see his skin turning brown. I knew what it was, from my years of experience working with it—it was *wood. Gustav was swiftly being encased in wood. could see the child trying to move as the grain spread over his shoulders, up his neck and down his torso.*

It was like he was freezing solid before me, only instead of ice, he was turning to timber. The petrifaction process engulfed Gustav's head, his features becoming the finest specimen of wood carving I'd ever seen. I was witnessing the spirits carving a child in wood, clothes, shoes, everything was frozen in time.

Then, as soon as it had started, it was over. Standing before me was a statue, better than anything I could have ever done. I was afraid to approach the thing, the carving that was once my nephew. I was afraid at first, but I reached out and touched a wave in his hair. It felt like virgin wood. The texture was sanded smooth, and the grain was clean. I still had difficulty believing what had happened. My nephew was gone, petrified before me in a form-fitted coffin.

That made my mind hatch another thought. Was he dead? I couldn't remember if the Phuri Dai said he would still be alive or not. I got closer, so close our faces almost touched. Kneeling beside Gustav, my fingers explored the face frozen in wood. His long eyelashes were perfectly preserved, as was his lips and his nose. My finger journeyed over his open eye, pausing to see if the ball was moist. It wasn't, just a seamless image in the wood.

I ran my hand down the side of his shirt, and down his pant leg. This was once the little boy who called me uncle. This little shock of wood used to play and tell me what he dreamed. No more would this little boy sit in my lap.

But what happened now? The very thought scared me witless. I didn't think I had the nerve to bring it this far. I had to be sure the child was alive. I pressed my ear against the wooden chest. The texture was cold and smooth, no heartbeat could be heard.

I was starting to panic. I was losing my head. Without another rational thought, I impulsively ran to my work bench. I selected a large spike nail -- the type I had been using to secure flooring to the base. I had to know; I was possessed with needing this knowledge.

I hastened back to the wooden image of Gustav. I retrieved my hammer from nearby and knelt by Gustav's feet. His shoe were flawless works of craftsmanship. There were even spaces for the loops in his laces.

I asked Gustav's forgiveness for what I was about to do. I don't know why I asked. Why would he forgive me this trespass after I had sealed him forever in wood? Perhaps, it was the act of violence I was about to perform that led me to plead for forgiveness. I knew, at that point, I would have probably fumbled the entire process if I had to force Gustav to succumb to the potion. For hesitation now pounded in my skull. I took a long, labored breath.

I wiped the perspiration from my eyebrows and positioned the nail. The shaft of metal perched on the top of Gustav's shoe. The tip fit snugly in one of the lace eyelets. Then, just like I killed the monkey, I raised the hammer high above my head. The first blow was met with extreme resistance. I thought the nail was going to bend over on itself, but the remaining blows drove the brad deep until the head was flush with the surface.

I stopped pounding, but my heart didn't. I realized I hadn't taken a breath during the whole process. I let air rush into my lungs, filling the sacks with life-giving oxygen. My eyes fell to the nail head in Gustav's foot. After a moment of hesitation, I noticed a dark drop of liquid swelling from the wound. I reached to the drop and smeared it around with my finger until a bright red splotch stained the surface.

Gustav's blood pooled over the nail in his foot. He must be alive, he must be. I had done it, finally. No longer would I be the one left out. I would now know the pleasures of dreaming. I hoped, though, that Gustav didn't die while inside the wood. I had a suspicion that the magic spell put upon him was somehow suspending all body functions, that except for dreaming.

I was so excited I didn't know what to do next. So, I sat, and I waited. I waited for the first dream to come find its master. The first figure of my greatest work was in place, now it was my turn to dream.

It had been two days since I used the potion on Gustav. Nothing had happened, no strange visitors came to my door. The only visitor I was expecting to come by was Alexander. I knew he wouldn't be coming around for, perhaps, a week or more. But when he did, how would I explain the disappearance of his child. How would I say I had stolen his son's dreams, life, lifeforce, and I did not intend to return him to the world?

I knew I would have to come up with a seamless story, a tale of Gustav's disappearance. If everyone thought he ran away, or was kidnapped, maybe they wouldn't suspect that I was, in any way, involved. I felt secure with the fact that no one would think to tear apart the wooden figure of Gustav in my workshop. What would they find if they pulled it apart? Would Gustav's spent body pour out onto the floor, or would he be alive?

The thought of what was going on inside the statue fascinated me. I watched the nail hole with renewed interest every morning. Each day I wiped fresh blood from the nail head. This, I took as a sure sign that somehow the boy lived on in his limbo.

I started to worry about the blood hole. Would the nail give Gustav an infection, would he bleed to death? I fetched some of my wood working bits from my bench and worked the wood around the nail head. I dug out the wood until I could securely fit the claw of my hammer around the nail top. I then wrenched the piece of metal from Gustav's foot.

In my mind, I heard him scream. It was horrific and loud, full of agonizing pain. I tossed the bloody nail aside and started to patch the hole with sealer. I hoped to stop the blood flow and give the child's wound time to clot and heal.

He was still alive, that's all I wanted to know. I really didn't care if he was in pain, I only cared that my prisoner was living still.

Grimm sat with his cup of tea and swirled in fresh cream. As the cool cream hit the hot liquid, it exploded into swirling, creamy brown clouds that reminded Grimm of river mud. All day long, he racked his gray matter, attempting to create a foolproof plan to explain the disappearance of the child.

He had tossed around the idea of blaming the gypsies, but that could turn out to be more devastating than if they found Gustav in the workshop. There was no way of telling what the *Phuri Dai* would tell people, or what she would do to him for involving them at all.

No, Grimm decided, it was unwise to accuse the gypsies. Although, he would love to frame Sennett for Gustav's disappearance, what sweet revenge that would be, no one would dare believe it. Many didn't believe in gypsy curses, but Grimm knew the extent of their abilities. Gustav and the potion were proof enough of that power.

Another story must be concocted. Grimm stared down into the swirls of cream. He made the connection again with the muddy river. The child wouldn't be discovered if he fell into the river. Grimm explored the possibility further. Deep in the woods, not far from here, the river snaked toward town. Here, the current was swift. If any little boy fell in here, his body would be swept away. It would be all but impossible to recover a corpse from the unforgiving river.

Grimm smiled. He elected to use this story to cover his tracks. He sipped the hot tea as he fleshed out the bones of the plan.

After finishing his tea, Grimm stalked through the house gathering bits of Gustav's essence. He went to the room where Gustav slept and picked through the extra clothing the child brought. Grimm paused as he held up the boy's flannel shirt. He put the garment to his nose and inhaled. Gustav's dreams were even woven deep within his clothing. Grimm smelled them; every image left an imprint.

Grimm gathered all of the articles and shoved them into a small leather bag; he then returned to the kitchen. He was satisfied with his plan. Grimm fetched his coat, boots, hat, and scarf.

The winds scraped at the door. To Grimm, it sounded like demons daring him to come out. The scratching was a cloaked taunting message, teasing Grimm into the open. They knew what he was doing, and it was their license to take his soul. Grimm wasn't afraid of them, however. He rationalized that he had done nothing wrong. It was his right to take Gustav, he had been denied too long. He could resist no longer.

The teeth of the north wind bit hard at Grimm. He knew he wouldn't be able to stay in the cold long before being damaged irreparably. In the leather bag, Grimm could feel the essence of Gustav. Slowly, the bag twitched, it became heavier as if the child were stuffed inside. He paused momentarily and dropped the bag in the snow. After looking at the satchel, he finally realized it was his mind playing games.

But then he wasn't so sure it was a game. His heart tugged briefly, falling slightly into the pit of his stomach. Grimm knelt to the bag. In his soul, he felt a twinge of sympathy for the child. Part of him wanted to run back to the workshop, and peel all of the wood away. Gustav would fall into his arms, thanking his uncle for saving him. Grimm would hug the boy, his tears of love falling on his small head.

Grimm inched the bag open. He shoved his hand inside and rummaged from side to side. If there was a beast within, let it take him now. Let it bite his hand off at the wrist, spewing blood all over the clothing that was Gustav's. The blood would be the same, for it would be the blood that traveled Gustav's veins as well as his own. His thoughts journeyed back to the workshop. There, he remembered the blood still coursing through the boy beneath the statue. He was still living. Grimm was certain of that fact.

He looked inside the bag. He prepared himself for an onslaught of hooked tentacles to shoot through his eyes. Grimm imagined that whatever was lurking in the bag was waiting. It wouldn't be satisfied with chewing off his hand, it was going to wait to pluck his eyes like raw eggs.

There was nothing in the leather sack, however. Nothing, at least, that could do him physical harm. He held up Gustav's shirt and inhaled deeply. Gustav filled Grimm's senses.

Suddenly, Grimm realized his foolishness. He laughed to himself quietly and stuffed everything back into the sack. There was no reason for this hallucination, Grimm rationalized. Gustav could not reach him from beyond. Although he was convinced Gustav still lived within the wooden prison, there could be no way the child could reach through time and space. It was impossible for him to transcend the night to attack him psychically.

Grimm was reminded by the icy, knifing cold as to his task. His hands were becoming cold and numb from being out in the elements.

He pulled the bag close and ran through the woods as fast as he could go. Above him, the full winter moon illuminated the night. His own shadow stretched before him on the stark forest floor. Grimm raced the shadow, never able to catch the fleeing phantom. He watched his soul, what was left of it, barely connected to his feet. The rest of it was pulling away from Grimm's body, appearing to no longer desire acquaintance.

The tree branches reached for Grimm. They seemed to assist his shadowy soul's evacuation of Grimm's body. They pulled at his body, tripping him up, slowing him.

The shadow of the bag was growing long, too. Grimm felt the sack suddenly swell and become heavy again. Only this time, it began to kick. Large bulging knots surged the skin of the leather bag. Clearly, there was something living inside the bag. It had to be Gustav. Gustav was stabbing through time, stabbing at Grimm's heart.

Grimm's shadow shortened as he stumbled over a snow-bare hill. He fell to his knees, crunching through the frozen, crusty soil. Pulling himself up, Grimm continued to run toward the river. It couldn't be much further, he thought.

That is when he first heard the voice. Until now, the bag had only gotten larger and heavier. Now, Grimm was sure Gustav was here. His spirit infested the bag. In his head, Grimm heard the voice once more. *Please, help me.* It burned like a drill in his ears. The pain, the pain.

The voice bounced around Grimm's head. He wanted to turn and run. His nephew was trapped, by Grimm's own hand, in a limbo of un-death. Part of him wanted to burst back through the woods, reclaiming the shadow of his soul. That same fraction wanted to go to the boy, free him, hug him hard.

His passion was too great, though. It was like an immense, fathomless addiction; a shark that fed on dreams. The animal wanted to eat; it starved all its life. The river was only moments away. The voice of the child mixed with the swift babbling of the churning water. Grimm fell, stumbling on the shore. He almost fell into the icy water. He screeched to a halt.

Grimm's two halves fought inside. The shadow stretched in the moonlight, thinning as it crossed the rapids. Grimm put the bag on the ground and opened it. The swelling was gone, as was the weight. But the voice buzzed on in pain, *oh, God. Help me.*

Grimm seized the shirt. The smell permeated the night. It was Gustav's odor, not that of the winter. The wind had abandoned him. Right now, Grimm would welcome its bite. But now, all he could feel was the heat and sweat created by his own tormented body.

He ripped the shirt, then tossed it into the river. The water swept the garment downstream. As the shirt vanished, the voice of Gustav hushed to a whisper. Next, Grimm took one of the boots, and pressed it deep into the soggy mud near the bank. The other boot was tossed into the river. In his ears, the whisper was nothing louder than a mosquito's wings.

Then, as Grimm pulled the muddy boot from the ground, the wind restored the usual winter smells. Grimm inhaled, and the cold air stung his lungs and nose. He looked down onto the ground, also. The shadow was so thin in the moonlight, that he had to look hard to see it. Only a sliver remained, a sliver incapable of cutting or infecting.

The shadow ended at the river's edge, perhaps it also washed away. He didn't know, nor did he care. The struggle was over, he had won the battle of conscience.

I ran to the village. In my hand, I held Gustav's muddy shoe. Oh, how the lights came on as I went into town. Hysterical, I was. I think, perhaps, my hysteria was real. I was in shock, not at the loss of the boy, but to the lengths I had gone to ensure he wouldn't be missed. I knew his clothing would wash up somewhere downstream. The river widened up into nearly a half mile across farther along. Even if Gustav really fell in the water, he would never be found.

Anyway, my acting was quite effective. The town mobilized. People came out by the teens, all went down the water's edge and began searching for Gustav. Some asked what the boy was doing down by the water. I told them that he wanted to go out and play. I swore I didn't know where he was. As it got later, I became worried. I told them that I went looking. I said I went to a place where we had fished, and that is where I found the muddy boot.

I was comforted by nearly everyone in town. Word was sent out to Alexander, but it would take some time to locate him on the road. The news would most likely follow the same path and reach Alexander in a week. It would take that long for the return trip.

I was confident that I would have time to enjoy the fruits of my labor before any potential threat returned to my orbit. I went home to wait.

It had been days since I slept soundly. I waited by Gustav, never knowing when things would start to happen. I wanted to be ready. Sleep became a luxury that I experienced in brief glimpses on the workshop floor.

Many times, I woke, or thought I was awake, and envisioned a hazy veil within the room. But then I realized I was hallucinating, probably from my lack of sleep.

When I needed reassurance, I stood by the statue of Gustav. I climbed upon the carousel frame and knelt by his face. I stroked the wood that was once his hair. It made me smile. Then, I thought back to the river. Just a few nights ago, as I was sealing the alibi, I had also killed my feelings of love. No longer would I be haunted by the affection I once had, for now I had something far more important.

Before me was this wonderful fruit tree, and its berries were the dreams I waited so long to harvest. I still couldn't believe that this was how far I'd come. The closeness with this reality made me tremble. My fingers danced down the boy's face. The wood was cool, and it made a fine prison.

Then, as I was fighting the urge to sleep, it began. At first, I was sure it was another hallucination brought on by my exhaustion. The veil was falling again.

The workshop was dark, except for light coming from the stove and two lamps. Long eerie shadows stained the floor. Against the wall, Gustav's shadow loomed like an avenging giant. I tried to focus on the haze; it was most definitely fog. It was lacy, however, like spider webs, but fine as silk strands. I remember the feeling as they brushed my skin. I had never been touched by fog before, I always passed through it. This was different, the filaments burst into condensed water as

> *they impacted me. Before I knew it, I looked as if I'd been chopping wood and was covered in cool perspiration. And if the fog wasn't amazing enough, what followed tore my heart away.*

Grimm hesitated as he felt the first evidence of the fog chilling his flesh. The late evening winds pressed against the workshop door. It jolted and slowly swung open. Terrified of the unknown, Grimm crept from the carousel and hid behind his immense work bench. The fog drifted in, and although the door was open, no winter winds came inside. Grimm could not feel any of the season's breath. He concentrated, because sometimes the coolness was deceptive.

It was no illusion, though. Grimm watched as the lacy fog drifted in from the darkness. The flames in the lamps danced as the air became heavy with moisture. Then, there was the first evidence of movement. Three quarters of the way up the door frame, Grimm witnessed a most unusual sight. Flickering in the shadows, he saw what appeared to be the rapid movement of a large bird's wings. But the shadows occluded his view. Suddenly, he realized what it was. The form moved with no effort. It was like a large hummingbird bouncing from flower to flower. Only instead of being ornithological in origin, the fluttering creature was human. Grimm knew in an instant that it was a winged child, draped in the cloth of the misty veil. The face was like delicate porcelain, and the wings so opaque they vanished on the upstroke.

Grimm gasped. It was true. The dream images were coming. This one he recognized from Gustav's own stories. He described the cherub as the flying baby who came to him one night. Gustav must be asleep, Grimm thought.

The mist crept further. Grimm backed further behind his work bench; he did not want to disturb this miracle appearing before him. A dream, he was having a dream. At long last. Tears ran in torrents from his eyes. He was having a dream, even though it was someone else's.

The tiny angel floated, and his wings buzzed. He was searching, his eyes wandered the entire room. He was consciously seeking something out.

Grimm knew what he looked for. The flying baby looked for his master, just as the *Phuri Dai* had predicted. The cherub was the scout. Grimm thought to himself, what would come next, who would come next? The brain waves washed him in terror, but it was lustful terror that shook him to his soul. He vibrated with energy, his heart swelling and exploding. Grimm felt a certain hardness erupt in his loins.

The cherub had located Gustav on the carousel. He floated down to the child, a troubled look upon his porcelain face. He reached a tiny hand to the boy's face and caressed it. Grimm could see tears in the angel's eyes. His touch went all over Gustav's head, neck and chin.

Grimm hesitated; the child's mouth opened as if to speak.

"Here, little one. What has happened to you?" The flying infant said. "Can you not touch me? Can you not see me?"

Grimm watched the one-sided exchange. The cherub could get no response from the wooden boy. He touched him over and over, begging for a response. He seemed to not realize that Gustav was no longer flesh and blood, at least superficially. The child was a prisoner, petrified. The angelic figure began to back away from Gustav. Grimm read the fear in the figure's face. He reflected doom, agony and pain. Grimm knew the cherub had figured out what had happened to Gustav.

Grimm, in his days of preparation for this moment, drew some of the potion into an old glass eyedropper stolen from Alexander. The rubber tip was cracked, but it sealed enough to be of service.

The child started to rise on the currents of air within the veil. Grimm crept from his hiding place. He stayed hidden in the shadows for several seconds as the dazed cherub fluttered. The face of the infant contorted in pain. He struggled to understand Gustav's pain. He was unaware of the cool potion now anointing his body.

Grimm sprung up from the shadows.

Ator malcuth theraputae.

The words sent the cherub spiraling in the mist, screaming. The potion smoldered upon his skin. The words ignited the fuse, the chain reaction had begun. Grimm leapt up and seized the child before he could fly away. In his hands, the winged baby was washing away in the same brown wood that encased Gustav. It spread like ice forming on a lake and froze the harrowed face of the cherub in time.

Before Grimm realized it, the entire process had ended. He was on his knees, gripping the most intricate wooden carving of a cherub ever to exist. The figure couldn't be larger than a cat, and his wings were frozen in mid-beat. Portions of the fog had been solidified and offered some scraps of covering for the child's pelvis.

Grimm gently laid the cherub next to Gustav's feet. He paused, breathing deep. He waited for reality to bite him. Then, he felt the icy winter wind whipping through the open door.

Grimm turned to the open door. He was afraid to go near the portal, for that is what it now was. The cherub first appeared there, then came in. It was only logical that any other phantoms would come from there. Somehow, Grimm knew there would be no more forms coming tonight. The excitement must have startled Gustav in his coffin, for now only wind blew in. The fog was absent.

He went and shut the door. The lamps stopped flickering, once again standing confident and tall. The breath he drew was long and seemed to take forever filling his lungs. He felt cleansed as he exhaled. But Grimm knew deep inside, his heart blackened to a darker shade even he thought not possible.

I admired the cherub for days. I didn't want to fix him to the carousel yet, I wasn't ready. I remember my fingers rolling softly over the waves of carved curly hair. His features were so much like Gustav. The angel looked incredibly similar to my nephew. The lips were the same, the small hands and ears. But it was the eyes that mostly drew me in. Even as a master carver, I could never capture the emotion in the eyes of either Gustav or the cherub. It was a reflection of hideous terror. Claustrophobia.

I remember the power, also. Using the potion gave me the most intense rush of sheer power I'd ever experienced. Before me, I controlled something. Someone was succumbing to my will. It was the greatest rush, and I couldn't wait for the next dream victim to come along. No one could know the thirst that grew inside. I didn't realize the extent of this lust until I saw Gustav sealed. It was amplified with the taking of the small angel. Now, every time I looked at either, my blood boiled. Streams of raw desire burned me inside and out. I heard the cut open murmurs of my inner self. I no longer had any remorse for Gustav, it was long gone with the river. Now, all that troubled me was the fulfillment of myself.

I remember becoming a machine that was built to consume power. Every touch of the statues fueled me.

But I could not live on dreams alone, that I realized. There was more in the world. I wanted more. I wanted to take for myself what I had been denied, and I wanted to relish in my acquisitions.

I had been haunted by new passion. It was a fresh lust, this time for a woman. I thought about her more and more. I had been wounded through to my heart by Elena, and only she could stop the bleeding. I didn't give any attention to any doubts that she wouldn't want to be with me. After all, she was a gypsy slut who should be rightfully thankful someone was willing to relieve her of such a burdened life.

What drove me now was the fact I was told I was unworthy of a gypsy princess. I knew, though, I would take her for my own. I would deny that arrogant child Sennett of what he thought was already his. I would take it.

Any woman would be thankful to marry me. I was influential with my work, and I was comfortable financially. I had what Elena wanted—a way out of her gypsy existence. She wanted respect and admiration. She would never get that from her station in life. I would give it to her, and in turn take her for my own.

I gathered up my last few remaining coins and marks and decided to journey to the Rom camp. It was time to secure the second part of my life now that I had my dream source. It was time to acquire the woman to be my wife. Alexander would be slain by my happiness.

The forest seemed especially hostile, Grimm thought. As he journeyed the familiar path, he thought about the events of the last few days, and what it would mean to his future. It was late afternoon, but the heavy clouds blocked out any sun that would effectively warm the day. Bundled tightly against the cold, Grimm followed the pathways.

His mind reached inward, searching for words to present to Elena. He wanted to say the right words. He wanted everything perfect, everything to make her agree to be his wife.

The pathway to the camp was not a stranger to Grimm, and he found the compound easy enough. Though, something seemed different about the place. Instead of being inviting, the place loomed large with a sense of doom. No longer was the camp flickering with fires, and women, and song. Grimm then thought, perhaps the camp was dead. The Rom had evacuated the compound and fled for some reason.

Grimm started moving around the camp's perimeter. He searched for the source of the strange new air surrounding the place. He couldn't come to a conclusion, but he felt he was unwelcome.

As he approached the back of the compound, Grimm noticed the first signs of life. He heard what sounded like an animal writhing on the cold ground. Crouching down, Grimm crept forward to get a better view. The Rom often trapped animals for fur and food, perhaps they had snared one in the camp's orbit. There were wolves in the area, not to mention foxes and bears.

More and more, as Grimm listened, he realized that it wasn't animal at all, but human. And there was more than one voice. First, Grimm heard a man's heavy whisper, but could not understand the words. Next, a young woman's laughter haunted the forest. He knew that voice. The gentle lilt, the inflection and passion; it was Elena.

Grimm crept behind a large tree that offered a safe view of the clearing ahead. Elena was there, on a wool blanket tossed on the ground. The man was on top of her, covering her from the cold. Covering him was another blanket.

They were nude. The man, Grimm recognized instantly. Sennett whispered in her ear, and she laughed. Grimm wanted to tear himself away, run for his life, his heart, through the forest. But he couldn't get away.

Their laughter was pure. Grimm watched the two. Sennett pulsed his body, and Elena's echoed his thrusting. The blankets rolled like an angry ocean, and hot steam billowed into the air. She clawed his back, pulling him inside her.

Tears swelled in Grimm's eyes as the man he so hated was having Elena. He wanted to pull away, but it was impossible. Sennett bore deep on her, and she welcomed him with bites and kisses. Sweat poured from the lovers, baptizing them. Their rhythmic thrusts increased in intensity and speed. Elena's wanton moans mixed with Sennett's. Suddenly, Elena began to twitch out of rhythm. She pulled at Sennett harder, screaming between her teeth.

As she was washed in orgasm, Sennett started to display the same behavior. His body was taken with shudders. The muscles in his shoulders and back contracted, as if they were wringing every ounce of sweat and energy from him. He ended his thrusting with three intense pauses, his seed injecting deep within the Rom princess. Almost instantly, he collapsed on top of Elena, and they embraced.

All of this was too much for Grimm. His world, like a piece of glass, was shattered beyond repair. Elena pulled Sennett close; Sennett kissed her face.

Grimm fell away from the tree. He quietly stepped back, attempting to keep his presence a secret. After he felt he was a safe distance, he burst through the woods. He wanted to be away from this place, this place of hatred. The trees pushed at him, the air rejected him, even the very ground he walked upon thrust him away.

Grimm began to circle the camp once again. He tried to grasp the things most important to him. Anything to offer comfort; he remembered Gustav and the angel. Grimm knew he couldn't go back home, not yet at least. He would be confronted with an empty house, a house he hoped Elena would willingly move into. But that wasn't to be. If Elena ever married Grimm now, it would be against her will.

Grimm traveled the cold forest, searching the clearing before him. He wanted to see the *Phuri Dai* again. He wanted some reassurance that things were progressing properly. Even though, deep in his black heart, he knew what she would say: there is no proper progression for such an event; it will go like it goes.

At last, Grimm located the trailer of the *Phuri Dai*. No light came through the window, in fact, the entire camp was somewhat dark. There were no dancing beauties wringing money from the local men, nor anyone moving from trailer to trailer. Cautiously, he stepped into the clearing.

Grimm crept quietly through the trailers. Under the cover of night, he hoped to sneak unnoticed. The menace of the forest no longer troubled Grimm. He felt safer now. As always, the camp seemed alive, a part of the natural world itself.

His breath was hot steam, and it injected into the air. Grimm paused, he listened. For a moment, Grimm thought he heard something. A twig cracked, but when he turned, Grimm saw nothing but the dark forest. He slowly returned to his route.

Suddenly, Grimm was seized, unable to move. A strong forearm wrapped about Grimm's throat from behind. Another fierce grip forced his remaining arm high into Grimm's own shoulder blades. He began to gasp for air. It was at that time Grimm saw the knife. Then, he felt it pressing against his pulsing neck.

"I have no money." Grimm wheezed.

"I don't want your money."

At the instant the man spoke, Grimm knew him. It was the resonant, smooth voice of Sennett. His breath was hot in Grimm's ear. Sennett smelled of Elena. The sweetness of her sweat mingled with Sennett's perspiration, creating the fragrance of hate. Bitterness rose in Grimm's throat, bile almost spilling forth between his teeth.

Grimm knew why Sennett was doing this. Sennett had seen him. Sennett, in the throes of making love, glimpsed Grimm in the forest. He would now take revenge for Grimm's violation of privacy.

"You are a pig, man." Sennett spat in whispers.

"I told you, I haven't got a pfennig." Grimm repeated.

"Your money is no good to me." Sennett pressed the blade firmly into Grimm's neck.

Grimm thought the knife was about to break through his skin, slicing his veins nakedly open. Then, the most bizarre rush came to the carver, all of this action excited him. The adrenaline powered him like a raging river, but he was still too afraid to act. He knew Sennett was much stronger than himself. Grimm had seen Sennett's muscles at work as he peered at Elena and this man coupling in the forest. She clawed him, like an animal, deeper and deeper. Grimm fantasized it was him making love to the exotic Elena. But, in all actuality, he couldn't wipe the handsome face of Sennett away. It was he whom she desired. It was he whom she had given of herself freely. The couple glistened in the light, sweat and semen mingling.

"I've only come to see the *Phuri Dai*, I have no quarrel with anyone here." Grimm attempted to cover up his perverse excitement.

Sennett studied Grimm, he let the knife relax slightly. "What are you? You must be strangest creature I've ever come across. I don't know you, but your heart is black."

"That's very observant of you, Sennett." Elena's voice creased the night down the middle.

Grimm's heart increased its rate. He didn't think it could go much faster, but Elena's presence urged the throbbing to escalate. She circled Grimm once. As her eyes cast down his helpless form, a smile came to her lips. She then went behind Sennett, caressed his shoulder, and started to lick his lips.

This sight was worse than Sennett's knife. Grimm wished Elena's lover would just drag the blade through his jugular, it would be much less painless. He could take some revengeful satisfaction as his blood spurted out, covering them like sticky warm molasses.

"I've come to see the *Phuri Dai*." Grimm said again.

"What for?" Elena backed away from Sennett. "Have you forgotten some detail in your pact with the spirits?"

"I need to discuss some details with her." He hesitated momentarily, "Perhaps, you can help me with my dilemma."

Elena visually prompted Sennett to relax his grip on Grimm. "What is it?"

"Can I speak with you alone, in private?" Grimm watched Sennett as he made this request. It would either be honored, or it would bring the blade crashing down.

Sennett looked to Elena for instruction. "I will be all right," she said.

"I don't think it is wise to be alone with this man, he's no good." Sennett sneered, his catlike eyes narrowing.

"Nonsense, you won't be far. Go to our meeting place, and I'll be along shortly. I don't expect this will take long. I also have some questions for him." Elena looked at Grimm.

Without another word, but with a face full of apprehension, Sennett stalked off into the cold night. Grimm attempted to watch him, but the young man melted away.

"You say you've got questions yourself?" Grimm turned to Elena.

She had been studying his face, "Your jealousy is an ugly mask, mister…"

"Grimm, Edward Grimm."

"Herr Grimm."

"You may call me Edward, if you wish."

She insisted on returning to the jealousy issue. "What do you see in Sennett that makes you so intense?"

Grimm stood silent. Elena pressed on. "His shoulders are so broad; I hang on them when we make love. Did you know he is my lover?"

Then it was true, they had seen him in the woods. Grimm felt powerless in her sphere. Elena controlled, captivated, commanded this moment. What could he do, he thought? Nothing. She would only cut him down with her green eyes.

"I suspected that you and he were intimate, but I wasn't sure to the extent." Grimm coated his lie, hoping there was a slim chance that he hadn't been noticed when the two made love.

"You knew the extent the first time you saw him. I could taste your jealousy, and you didn't even know me yet. Tell me, is it his beauty that makes you jealous? Or is it my beauty and his beauty together? Have you ever embraced beauty, sir?"

"Perhaps." It was all he could say to her.

Elena looked at Grimm, who now stood silent. "Do not worry, Sennett is far enough away not to harm you."

Her words emasculated him.

At that point, it was obvious Elena was an actress of the highest caliber. She wasn't the coy, frail princess she pretended to be. She was a curious creature, and Grimm's fascination took a new turn.

"You said you had questions of the *Phuri Dai*, perhaps I can help you. I know of the spell you have received, but I don't know what price you paid. I know, however, it must be great."

"I don't feel comfortable going into that. I feel it is best to not discuss it."

Elena looked him up and down, "Then, what is it you came here for?"

Grimm hesitated. She was asking him to spill his soul. What if she were trying to trick him, gathering information to destroy him. He had no choice and was ready to take the chance.

"I came to offer you a chance. I want you to be my wife."

Elena's face broke into a wide grin. "You must be a mad man. What reason would I have to marry you?"

Grimm attempted to stay calm and in control, but inside, he was melting away like his father did so many years ago.

"I can offer you many benefits. I have prestige, I am employed by the wealthiest families in Europe. I have money."

"How much money?" Elena didn't care about any of the other marriage promises, only the financial aspect interested her.

"As much as you need." Grimm promised, even though he hadn't any clue as to where he could obtain a regular cash flow. Grimm could see her thinking about the opportunity. "I can take you to the grand balls and parties you desire. Everyone would forget you are Rom, gypsy, despised and looked down upon. I can elevate you to where you see yourself belonging."

"Tell me more," she said.

"But, I can see your apprehension. You have a future with Sennett, is that what you think?"

"Yes, I will be *Phuri Dai* and he the chieftain." Elena answered.

"And still living in a caravan? No servants. No fine dresses from Paris." Grimm had found a weak spot, "How many lovers will he take, and what can you do about it? I know enough to know you have no say or choice, when he tires of you, he'll cast you away. With me, you would have Europe at your feet."

"He would not do that," she said defensively. "Your lies won't blind me like they blind others. You can't hide the evil inside you. Your very aura exudes malevolence and petty jealousy."

"Are you content to live in the forest? Do you want to never see a great castle, and the kings and queens of the world? Name your prize, I'll get it for you." He could see the flower of doubt blooming in her eyes.

She considered her greed for many moments. There were so many things in this world she would love to have. Elena searched her heart and found an empty treasure chest waiting for bounty. She looked at Grimm. She found him unattractive, and unworthy as a prince. In the forest, her lover, prince of the gypsies, was waiting. It would be nice, however, to live in a house, with gold adorning her every limb. It would be easy to find a lover in those quarters as well.

She looked to the forest. "I could scream right now. Sennett would come and cut your heart out."

Then, as if cued, Sennett returned from the forest. "Is everything all right?" He cast a worried glance at Grimm, then at Elena.

"This man was just leaving. There is no more business to be done with the Vitsa."

Grimm's cold eyes fell upon Elena's face, "Some way, you will have a change of heart."

With those final words, he drifted off into the forest, leaving the lovers alone.

CHAPTER 10

I sat in my workshop, staring into the face of the angel. I was sad, even though I had my ultimate goal before my eyes: dreams. Never before had a dream been in front of my eyes. I could touch it, feel it, even taste it. I know, because I had to experience the flavor. I remember licking the wood, just to see how my palate would react. Although it had no taste to speak of, in my mind I reeled in the flavor.

I remember the greatest sigh emitting from my lungs. As I looked at Gustav's wooden features, I recalled myself as a child. Memories I had kept sealed inside now flooded with nothing to stop them. I was just a child of Gustav's age. I must have protected myself mentally, or perhaps God was merciful to me once, and blocked the horrid memory. Perhaps he knew it would make a great torment for me later on in life, and he locked it behind some door in my head. He held it there, waiting for the time I was most vulnerable. And he chose the perfect time. Elena had just spurned my love for some boy made of cat tail fluff. What could he offer her?

Sennett was beautiful, of that she did not lie. He would not remain so for long. Age would ravage him like it did all the gypsies. She would not turn down my offer; Elena was too ambitious and greedy. It was beyond my comprehension that a woman of such potential would be happy traveling the countryside, destined to die in some mud bog.

Perhaps it was this inability to understand that became the key which unlocked God's weapon against me. The weapon was the memories of my own father. For some unknown reason, I could never remember those who were kind to me. I think possibly they were part of my dream state that I used to enjoy, and they were wiped off the world when I couldn't dream anymore. Perhaps, the same despair that killed my soul also killed them, or frightened them off. Often, I would read a book, but I couldn't see the picture it painted. I only saw words, and I understood them for what they were: words. Until it could be set before me in color, shape, or form, I didn't know what it looked like. Surely, if anyone asked me to recite or describe, I used the words I'd seen. That was all I could do.

I loved to touch the image of Gustav. Soon, it was a pleasure I looked forward to. I sympathized with him. I knew he was alive in there. How do I know, because I was there all too often. I wasn't in the wood, but far worse. I was in the clay. I was deep in the earth. I wasn't buried alive, but it would have felt the same. This was the weapon God bore upon me every time I touched Gustav. Perhaps I was comfortable with this pain, and that is why I loved the touch of the statue. It wasn't that I cared for Gustav at all, it was the deeper concept that was drawing me. The claustrophobia of being contained against my will, that was the torture I endured. For so long, I kept the anguish at bay, but now, I was visited often.

I tried to tell once, but that made it worse. My father would attempt to inspire me. He didn't try to nurture my talent or mind. He thought the best way to be inspired to make art worthy of God was to instill the fear of God in an artist. Even if that artist were a little boy.

The first time I remember the wishing well was the winter of my eighth year. I had been bad, or so I was told, and my father proclaimed: it was time to show me the fear of God. I was taken to the old abandoned well that dried up years ago. My father had used it to dispose of all sorts of objects, including animal carcasses from his hunting. After using all that he could, he dumped the leftovers, including the bones, down the well.

This was just after his wife, my mother, had died in childbirth. The baby died as well. I cannot recall if it were a boy or girl, but I was saddened by it. Not that I desired another sibling, I was hoping they would become the target of his brutality instead of me. Alexander never suffered any pain or torture. And he never believed me when I told him.

My father forced me to sit on the special seat he'd fashioned from a board. My rear barely fit, and sometimes I would get terrible rope burns from the suspension. After I was sitting, he would lower me into the well, tie the rope off, and leave. Often, I lost track of the hours I'd been down in the well. While down there, I cried. I trembled because I could see the light so high above me. It looked like a tiny halo, and when my father came for me, I envisioned myself rising into heaven. Heaven stayed above me and out of reach, only teasing me with the promise of a halo above.

Grimm spent many hours pondering Elena. His thoughts of violence and anger escalated. He thought of Sennett; he wanted so much to punish the insolent young buck. But, with so much at stake, he dared not lash out at the gypsy prince. Sennett would be a pivotal piece in the acquisition of Elena. If anything happened to him, all Grimm's plans could fail.

Grimm was spending vast amounts of time in the workshop. He had been caught, almost off guard, by the appearance of the cherub. That was a manageable phantom, but if a larger creature appeared he would have to be prepared to subdue it.

Often, he found himself hovering over Gustav. He was convinced he'd heard muffled sobs coming from inside the statue. At other times, when he had heard these quiet sounds, he rushed to the statue but could never pinpoint the source. Grimm's mind grew paranoid thoughts. He had convinced himself on several occasions that the source of the crying was Gustav. Somehow, the child remained alive. Grimm already knew that. He proved it with the nail.

His fear was Alexander. His brother would return, and he would hear Gustav's cries. Alexander would know what happened, and free the child. Grimm hadn't explored the possibility of freedom for any of his new possessions. If he did free them, how would he do it? Why would he want to?

He heard the sobbing again, but this time it was a distant

echo. Now, Grimm was sure it came from Gustav. He leaned in close to the boy's wooden form. It was at this time, as Grimm scoured the boy's face with his gaze, that he noticed trailing watermarks beneath Gustav's eyes. There were dark stains, as if a constant flow of tears had been there.

It was impossible, Grimm rationalized. Gustav was suspended, sealed away by magic. There was no way he could still cry. But the sounds, the muffled moans seeped through the crisp air.

"No," Grimm whispered, "this cannot be." He was truly amazed as he realized the tiny riverbeds beneath the boy's eyes were moist. "It is impossible." He touched the water, and raised a drop to his mouth.

The taste was bitter salt. There was no mistake to be made, Grimm had tasted Gustav's tears. Somehow, some way, the boy was crying. Grimm suddenly knelt to Gustav's feet and began searching the nail hole for any signs of blood. There was no blood, only the patched hole where the nail once was.

"Gustav, my boy." Grimm stood and touched the tear stains again. "I suppose you can hear me. It is your uncle." Grimm awkwardly addressed the moment.

He had to be sly, there could be no mistakes made. Gustav had to be lulled, and silenced. If anyone got close enough, or if the room were dead quiet, someone could hear the whimpering. Grimm could tolerate no thoughts of failure; he must keep the secret. His dreams now relied on this little child. If Gustav were lost, all was lost.

Grimm suddenly surged with a new idea. The angel came for Gustav, after the boy dreamed him. The cherub was flesh and blood. Would not another figure be real, also? Would what they had with them not also be real?

Grimm rushed to his work bench, and selected a narrow, sharp carving bit. He also took a delicate hammer from the bench and returned to the statue. He inched close to the boy's face. Resting the tip of the chisel near Gustav's eyebrow, Grimm delicately began to peck. The wood was hard, and he had to strike with more vigor to see results. He dared not work the wood too hard, for he didn't want to damage the valuable package contained within.

As he worked his way around Gustav's eye, the chisel moved easier. Sometime, Grimm struck the bit too hard, and the tip returned with blood. In his head, he could hear the painful cries. Every time the chisel went too deep, piercing the boy's skin, Grimm heard a wail. But these mournful cries were all in his head. The mouth was sealed, the child couldn't move his lips.

Perhaps, Grimm thought as he tooled around Gustav's eye socket, it was the boy's soul crying out. Tears also flowed from the crack Grimm caused in the wood. Blood and tears mixed, forming a thin, bright red river that ended in a perfect delta by Gustav's nose.

At last, Grimm completed his circle. The wood had been released around Gustav's eye. Slowly, Grimm maneuvered the chisel tip beneath the puzzle piece. As he looked at the wooden replica of Gustav's eye, he thought of what he was about to see. Would the boy actually be in there? Had death moved in, filling the center of the statue with rotted flesh?

Grimm gave the bit a twist, and he could hear as the wood peeled away from Gustav's skin. Gently, Grimm pulled the small plug of wood away. Beneath the wooden eye, was the real one, blue and darting.

Grimm knew he should feel a surge, a swell of love should be washing over him. But he killed that animal by the river. Grimm only felt that his dreams were safe.

"Gustav, Gustav, can you hear me?" Grimm watched the eye.

Gustav's eye bounced around, taking in sights, and fueling panic. What had seemed like a dream was now a horrible truth. The pupil swiftly enlarged at the mention of Gustav's name. Grimm noticed the reaction, and knew he understood.

"I can only sympathize with you, my little Gustav." Grimm said. "I know how you feel, I've been there myself. No, not as this. I do not know what it must be like to have only a narrow view of the world. But I know what it is like to look out and see only a halo of light. It will pass, and soon you will come to accept it."

Gustav's pupil shrunk, indicating his attention was being lost. "Your father," instantly the pupil dilated again, "will not be coming for you. He left you here with me. It was his plan all along." Grimm knew these lies would devastate Gustav; and, at the same time, empower Uncle Grimm as Gustav's keeper. "I am here, I will take care of you."

Grimm paused for a moment. He had to be cautious, more cautious than ever. Gustav was a slave to him, unaware that he could be dangerous. But now, Grimm thought, perhaps he had a way of getting the things Elena demanded. Gustav could bring to him the treasure Elena desired. But how does one convince a child what to dream of?

"Gustav, there was someone looking for you here." Grimm glanced over at the cherub, but Gustav could not see the form. "I know others will be along soon. I want them to bring something for you. It will be something that will help set you free. You see, there is someone I know who can free you from this wood, but I don't have the money to pay him." Grimm was rather surprised at his lies, and how easily they congealed as they rolled out of his mouth. "I need you to send gold and treasure with those who come to see you. They can help, trust me. Instruct them to bring gold, and jewelry, for only then can I pay the man to help you get free."

Gustav's pupil grew so large, his entire blue eye seemed black. The blood had stopped flowing from his minor flesh wounds, but the tears rolled down the wood.

Grimm held the piece of removed wood in his hand. The image of Gustav's eye was so exact, he looked upon it jealously. This was God's work, beautifully correct. Its precision jolted angry memories for Grimm. This, he realized, was the kind of work his father attempted to drag out of his soul. The muse for beautiful carving like this did not live inside a maggot-infested well, it was given by the kiss of heaven. Heaven had forgotten him; God did not desire to bestow affection or talent upon Grimm.

He turned the piece of wood over. Grimm examined the portion that rested against Gustav's face. Covering the grain, was a thin veil of sticky gel. It reminded him of the fog that contained the dream figures. Perhaps, it was this stuff that kept Gustav preserved, yet living at the same moment. He touched it, smelled it, but dared not taste it. He was afraid to touch it to his lips. This was part of a magic he scarcely understood. Although he was not afraid to exploit it, Grimm feared what it could do to him.

He fitted the piece of wood back into place over the pleading eye of Gustav. As the puzzle piece settled into its proper joint, Grimm tapped it gently with the chisel butt to ensure the fit.

It was as if nothing had been touched. Somehow, the mucous re-sealed itself, and the wood healed. Grimm felt where the scar would have been, but the wood was untouched. Even the grain had been restored.

At that point, Grimm trembled. For the first time, he entertained thoughts of doom. Perhaps, he hadn't realized what his bargain might entail. As he watched the wood heal, the magnitude of the magic's power was all too real. He would be more comfortable if this had been a part of Gustav's dreams. But, deep in his raven heart, he knew this was only a reflection of power he could never comprehend.

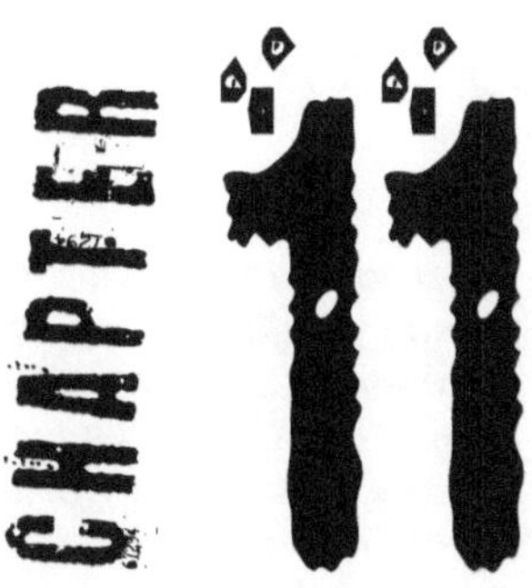

Sleep was my nemesis, orbiting in my mind like a great dark planet. As soon as I tried to sleep, I could feel the animals tearing at me. Was it a dream? There's no way it could have been. I hallucinated from lack of sleep. But I could get enough rest to survive.

At the most, it was anxiety that kept me awake. I was like some drunk, thirsting, waiting for my next drink. Gustav was my intoxicant, rather the creatures that haunted his head. I noticed as they came, they brought with them a rush of energy —a drug on which I steadily became dependent.

I began to sleep in my workshop. I could never be sure when they would come to see Gustav. I had to be there for the visitors. I anticipated every minute until they arrived.

I also noticed a gloom in my workshop, desolation never became more apparent to me. It was always there; I couldn't fool myself. Desolation was my only companion. I was a blind idiot, teasing myself into thinking I was happy in any way. Yes, this barrenness was the only wife I'd ever known. I thought she was good to me, and she was. Until I tasted the pleasures of a dream.

Oh, the sweetness. Almost too rich was the taste. I felt drunk whenever the images came around.

Gustav was the best thing, and the worst, to ever happen. It was a dichotomy I could not deny. I loved the taste, the feeling of the dreams I stole. I hated the boy for showing me how pathetic I was. He showed me my lifemate: desolate misery. I hated him for just being; being a son to my brother, being a nephew to me, and for being a dreamer. Everything he was was a vulgar pointed arrow piercing my eye socket. Somehow, knowing I had him forever satisfied me. I felt avenged.

Perhaps, this is what the place needed, a woman's touch. Elena would be the perfect wife, I was sure of it. She would be obedient; she was trained to be submissive, there was no doubt. The Elena I knew so far was a wicked harlot. She bore into my brain like a worm, her parasitic memory infecting me. She did not need any special magic or potion, she was the kind who had the most powerful spell of all: the magic of a sultry, sexy woman. I resolved to wait and see if she was only wicked to me alone.

Grimm awoke and was greeted by the cold arms of the night. The fire in the stove had waned while he slept. Night still reigned outside, and Grimm had no idea as to the time. Just as the question of time entered his mind, he heard the cuckoo ringing 3 a.m.

He had been sleeping by the stove, drifting in and out of consciousness. Grimm tingled with premonition, he sensed something beyond the house wall. It was in the night, whatever it was, and Gustav was the reason it roamed. Grimm was only now realizing that a child can have nightmares as well as sweet dreams.

Gathering his potion, and a sharp carving bit for security, Grimm crouched in the shadows. He wanted to see what creature now came for the boy. Was it a gentle angel, or would this be a beast? Whatever came, Grimm would not let it leave. This, he vowed.

He watched the door of the workshop. Outside, the curtain of night parted, and a shaft of light descended upon the door. Grimm could see the veil falling with the night. It was like a fine strand of sticky pearls but knitted into an intricate lace. Slowly, the door started to come open under its own power. As the portal fully opened, he could feel the air pressure within the room drop.

The wind was not strong, but surprisingly brisk. Suddenly, his own breath was snatched from his lungs. And it seemed to not be against his will. The breath leapt away from Grimm, longing to sweep into the light. His soul purging, regurgitating any remaining goodness.

Then, in the light, he saw movement. The action was familiar, tiny wings beat like a hummingbird. But as the forms, three of them, moved through the thick fog, Grimm sensed something different about them. His apprehensions were confirmed as they swarmed over Gustav's wooden statue. Instead of having the supple heads of newborns, the cherubs barked and growled through huge, oversized canine mouths. They appeared skinned, with portions of flesh hanging as they bit at each other.

The dog-headed cherubs seemed tangled in the fog, but as Grimm looked closer, he noticed they floated on unseen streams in the lace. In fact, the fog resembled arms of smoke entering the creatures near their abdomens, suspending them in air.

Grimm fell back into the shadows as he saw the creatures. It was unreal, a child could not possibly hatch such horrors. They had to be demons, or worse, previews of nightmares to come. Icy sweat coated him. He was frozen in place, and he prayed that they did not venture into the shadows. Surely, they would be merciless if they caught him. Gustav could have summoned them, beasts to take revenge for the child's unholy prison.

In his hand, Grimm squeezed the vile of liquid. Then, he found new strength. He remembered his vows, his commitment to himself. Nothing would deny him, even if it meant giving his life. Grimm's life meant nothing anyway, for his soul long evacuated his body.

Cautiously, Grimm stood. He kept to the shadows, gripping the potion close. The angels swarmed over Gustav. Clearly, they were turning from playful to vicious. He watched them, hoping they would all settle down. Just for a moment, that was all he needed. Grimm waited, biding his time. Then, as if his wish had been granted, the three cherubs came to a rest at Gustav's feet. At first, Grimm thought they had just settled to rest.

He realized the seraphs had located the nail hole in Gustav's foot. It was seeping blood. Dark, nearly purple blood pooled in a round ball over the head. One of the angels leaned his smashed, skinned dog-face close. His tongue darted into the blood, greedily lapping it up. It made greedy, snorting noises and laughed in halted grunts.

The sight of this infuriated Grimm. He felt violated, as if thieves were stealing everything he owned. And that is what they were doing. Gustav was Grimm's, his heart, his eyes, every drop of blood. These creatures were his, too.

Propelled by anger, Grimm lurched out of the shadows at the cherubs. He surprised them, wildly splashing the potion at them. The magic drops hit two of the resting creatures, and Grimm rattled off the incantation quickly. As they attempted to spread their wings and escape, jagged, grainy wood formed about them.

The one who drank howled as his brothers were sealed in wood. A tremor rushed through the fog as the connection with the two prisoners was broken. The other cherub was visibly weakened, but he still began to fight. His rose up on fleshy wings, bearing his fangs and laughing like a hyena. The lace was channeling itself, feeding the cherub into greater strength.

The lashing teeth snapped at Grimm. He fended off the swift attack narrowly. Suddenly, the seraph lunged for Grimm's exposed throat. The carver rolled away, and as the angel came within a heartbeat of him, he thrust the point of his chisel clear through its body. Grimm's attack was so powerful, the sharp carving bit passed out the back of Gustav's dream figure, impaling him on the carousel frame.

It writhed and squealed in pain. Strange sticky fluid erupted from around the shaft of metal. Grimm recognized the stuff; it was the same solution he discovered while looking at Gustav's eye. It was the same concoction that formed on his cool skin when he walked through the fog. Somehow, all of this lacy fog was intertwined. Perhaps, it was a conductor of psychic energy in which the dream figures fed upon.

At that point Grimm did not care. The painful wail of the

animal was overwhelming. He held up the vial, splashed a modest amount on the creature, and said the words. The wood swiftly formed, wrapping the last angel in a doppelganger sarcophagus. Silence, once again, became his mistress.

Grimm was shaken. He watched as the fog began to dissipate, and as it did, his breath returned. He closed his eyes, drawing back inside portions of him that had been stripped away.

Then, he realized what had happened. It was overwhelming, attempting to comprehend the events of moments past. Demons, fog, it was like a mosquito feeding and unable to disengage her mouth. The pumping heart kept forcing blood inside, even though she no longer wished to feed. Soon, just like that mosquito, Grimm thought he would burst.

His eyes narrowed and focused upon Gustav. He rushed to the statue. Grimm fell to his knees in front of the boy and inspected the nail head. It was scabbed over and looked as if it were never touched. But Grimm saw the dog-headed seraphs, they were licking this wound. Perhaps, they could have been trying to free the boy; however, he would never know the truth now.

Grimm collected the three demon statues. He held one up, its face was that of a grotesque dog. The teeth bared, and its tongue curled between them. Grimm was repulsed. He fetched his hammer and several nails. Then, like a crazed hyena circling a kill infested with feeding lions, Grimm traversed the carousel looking for the best places to nail the angels. He selected three places, at equal intervals, on the canopy. Carefully, Grimm rotated each shape until he was satisfied with their position. Grimm climbed his step ladder and held every angel in place with his left forearm while he positioned the nails. The first two angels were nailed through their wings, and they became a part of the carousel easily.

The final angel had been frozen in quite an unworkable form. He was sealed in mid-attack; his wings curled viciously around his body and head. The mouth was open, and rows of wooden teeth stabbed at Grimm. He positioned the angel as best he could, there was no place worthy of a nail. Any place would ruin the face, and Grimm loved the face on this one. He looked deep into the piercing eyes. They could cut him open if he moved too close.

The only place to put the nail was in the chest. Grimm put the nail against the wood. He twisted it, applying as much pressure as possible. The metal tip ground into the wood, making a nest for the shaft. Grimm raised the hammer and began to strike the head. As the brad slowly sank beneath the surface, the sticky liquid began to ooze forth. It formed a large drop that soon began to run down the angel's swelled belly. The nail moved deeper with every strike. Soon, the head was flush with the body but covered with the tacky solution.

Grimm, suddenly overcome by a wave of nausea, stepped off the ladder, and back from the carousel. The hammer fell away, and the carver gasped to retain his stomach contents. The thought of the angels, more dreams that were now his to own, overwhelmed him. He had seen the liquids of their innards, was this the stuff of angels? Grotesque, oozing phlegm, how could an image of God contain this obscene blood?

Grimm stumbled across the warm room. The heat, along with the rambling thoughts of his mind, drove him into dizziness. He squatted down, attempting to gather his senses together. The fire had cooled to nothing but glowing embers which occasionally licked with a lazy tongue. The heat, however, loomed through the room.

Grimm went from haunches to knees, then laid on his side. He could not keep control. It was slowly leaving him, the power to comprehend. Sleep, Grimm's elusive lover of late, had made her wishes known. His eyes clouded over, the fight with the angels must have exhausted him and now the carver was feeling it.

But he was afraid to sleep. If Gustav's dreams came, would they tear him apart? Would they free the child, and expose Grimm for the monster he was? He didn't care now, sleep made love to Grimm, wooing the man to unconsciousness.

Grimm had stirred awake nearly four hours after falling asleep. He dimmed the lamps and candles and stoked the coals in the stove. His eyes were bleary, sinking away in darkened caverns. The embers were white again, throwing an occasional flame outward. The room was quiet.

Grimm stared into the fire. The single, occasional flame had re-emerged, only this time it did not dissipate. In fact, it had multiplied. Several orange spikes danced, creating shapes that reflected in Grimm's sallow eyes. The heat, which was once oppressive, had gone. The workshop had a coolness about it. He glanced around the place. He felt he was no longer alone. Grimm couldn't understand his feelings. Was it some silly rapture put upon him by an angel? He didn't know, he didn't care, until he saw the fog creeping across the floor.

Suddenly, it was if a blade were inching through the muscles and sinew of his back. He turned as sparks ignited and rose on the eddies of fresh air. The stabbing knife was only the winter. Grimm rose up, and he turned slowly to the door.

It stood open. Through the door, he could see the colors of dawn pushing the stars away. The veil filtered in like stray spider webs flowing in a breeze. Then, he heard them calling.

"Gustav, my boy, where are you?" The voice was feminine, and sweet as honey.

Grimm swiftly went to the shadows; he did not want to be detected. The last time, surprise was his only ally.

"Child?" the voice said.

Grimm could hear the woman, she was just outside. But no one moved beyond the windows. It was if they came through a door unique to them, perhaps a door directly to Gustav's mind.

"Gustav?" the voice questioned again, only this time—it had a harmonious sister.

The voice became louder, for the woman was nearby. The fog grew thick, and within its bosom a figure moved. It was a woman, and Grimm's eyes stared in disbelief. She was the image of Gustav's mother, yet holy. Her hair was golden and appeared to be a halo. The face was serene and pale; her lips pursed as if ready to ask a question.

"Gustav?" she whispered.

Grimm then located the source of the second voice, for directly behind the first woman was another. She was a twin, identical down to the inquisitive mouth. Together, they asked: "Child, don't hide, not tonight."

The sisters moved into the room, their eyes searching like beacons. Still, just as they moved inward, another woman appeared. The two were now three, indistinguishable in shape and form. And, as she joined her sisters, a final sibling appeared. There were now four sisters searching for Gustav.

One thing separated the last image from the rest. All of them had some sort of jewelry on their fingers or neck, but the final woman carried something. Grimm squinted to see what it was, but the fog was sweeping up into them. The veil was part of their clothing, which was bodily part of them. It obscured the object from Grimm's sight momentarily, then he recognized it. The fourth woman bore a wooden box, small yet overflowing with gold coins.

I saw it, there before me, Elena's treasure. Never before had I thought Gustav's dreams would be the source of all my desires. I could smell Elena in my house. She was as good as mine, I had the means to get what she demanded. These four angels were so much like Gustav's mother yet blended with the image of the Virgin. Gustav had always dreamed of the Virgin, but now I know it was only visions of his long dead mother.

I shrank away in the shadows. Surely, if they saw me, they would flee. The fog would consume them again. And I wasn't ready to take the chance. All that I ever desired was before me.

I watched them. The women were oblivious to me. It appeared they were only there for Gustav, they didn't even notice the angels I had already claimed. Unbeknownst to them, I planned to make them trophies as well.

I listened to the women. They spoke in an unending thought that traveled mouth to mouth without interruption. The fog fed them, I watched as ribbons of thicker lace rose upward into their bodies. I was fascinated by all I saw; no dream could ever be this good. Then, in an instant, I considered myself, perhaps fortunate. If I were indeed a dreamer, I would have never discovered such a world in my nephew's head. Suddenly, as if a spasm rocked me, I realized what I was thinking. I was horrified and thrust the notion away.

I returned to my scrutiny of the scene before me. I listened to their whispers of wonder. "Gustav, Gustav," they said. Sappy sickness, pus-flavored honey. I darkened with hate. Even in desolation and limbo, the child received more than I ever would. He got love, he got attention, I had cut my revenge from this cloth.

I watched. The ribbons of fog were thickening, becoming tumultuous clouds. There was a shock wave traveling along this lifeline; the women, in turn were becoming pensive. I sensed time was becoming tight. I readied my potion. Momentarily, I glanced to check how much I had left; there was more than enough to deal with anything Gustav summoned.

The women had started to separate. Their hands and eyes began to explore. A harrowing look of doom caressed the porcelain skin of their faces. As they grew farther apart, I selected them like gazelles. I was the lion watching a herd. These were the strays, leaving the protection of the fold. I was ready to pounce. The first victim rounded around behind the carousel. I played the shadows like a master hunter. She never saw me. I came upon her quickly, her back was turned. I swiftly sprinkled the potion and said the words quietly.

She had started to turn. Her face contorted into a look of horror. As she turned from the waist, her hair flew all around. Then, instantaneously her complexion darkened. It became ruddy with wood grain, and her eyes, hollow fixtures. The golden hair was no longer blonde, but a frozen umber waterfall of windswept follicles.

As the metamorphosis was complete, the foggy umbilical cord was severed. The ripple shocked through the lacy web. I had located the next little lamb. She was not far from the now captured sister. Only she was brave enough to climb upon the carousel. She peered high into the almost finished canopy.

I know she was admiring my work. Perhaps she would be honored to be a fixture on such a work of art.

There she turned her back from me. I used the shadows once again. And I pounced on the sister. I splashed and spilled my incantation. She was transfixed with a look of desolation and surprise. I enjoyed the expression.

The third sister went much the same, only now the fog was incredibly thick. I remember not even a ray of newly risen sun cut through. The last sister was now aware of my presence. Somehow, the ripples in the web had warned her. She was very much aware of me, and I of her.

I knew my workshop. It was my territory—my hunting grounds. I blended in with the remaining shadows. She, however, seemed unafraid even though she knew something horrifying had happened to her sisters.

"Who are you?" she said to me as she crouched to see in the dark recesses.

I knew where she was, though. I watched as she clung to the chest of gold. Rings also decorated this woman fingers just like the others. I wanted all of it.

"Have you come for Gustav?" I asked the last survivor.

"What have you done, foul bastard? Where is Gustav?"

The woman's face was livid, she stepped once backward, however. She was scared of me. Good.

"I have come to see Gustav. This is for him."

She motioned smoothly to the chest. "I think, perhaps lady, this was meant for me."

I reached for the gold.

We both had a hand on the chest, its contents ready to spill because of the action. Fearing an accident, I released the treasure. She pulled it close again.

"I mean no harm," I said. I readied the potion behind my back.

"I just wanted to see what you have brought for my nephew."

*"Your nephew? You have done such an unholy deed to a child
of your flesh?" She backed away, and the fog thickened.
I realized something was going on. The webbing was glinting
like silver, energy was growing around her. I sensed danger,
somehow this woman was going to become the aggressor.
I had to strike like a cobra before I lost any advantage I had.
I splashed the cursed gypsy potion on her.*

Ator malcuth theraputae.

*She screamed as the growing energy in the fog was suddenly
nullified. Fascinated, I watched in splendor. It started to
subside as the grainy coating washed over her body. From
her feet it spread up her legs. Like fire chewing paper, it also
started in her hair. Freezing in place, the golden hair became a
fixture on the newly forming statue. Then, I realized the grain
was spreading toward the treasure. The gold was about to be
lost to the curse.*

*I lunged forward to seize the chest, but just as I grabbed it,
the wood grain consumed it. I let it go, fearing the curse.
Helplessly, I watched as the chest became part of the art.*

*My rage was uncontrollable. How dare any of these
apparitions deny me what was mine. I demanded the gold,
and it came to me. It was mine. I raged around the workshop.
I destroyed things I worked so hard on. I destroyed works in
progress that had been partially paid for. I didn't care, though.
My life was different now. I was the alpha—not Alexander or
Sennett—and surely not my nephew.*

*My anger was like a bolt of lightning ready to strike, and I
aimed it at the figure of Gustav. I leapt upon the carousel. I
addressed his innocent, wood-sealed face: "You see, boy, I took
them all. I did. There's nothing you can do; I have the upper
hand. Now, to show you what can happen to little boys who
seem to not understand this dynamic." I grabbed my nearby
hammer and pick. "Time to get some clarity." I put the pick on
the inside of his ear canal and aimed my hammer truly.*

I knew it was only a matter of time until he came to visit me. I was too lucky. I could take the angels, the demons, anything, perhaps, but Gustav's father: my brother Alexander. The past month was hard on him, and it was my fault. It was actually my pleasure, too. He returned to find his son dead, or so he thought.

Word of Gustav's demise was delivered by the constables of the university. By the time news reached him, it had been almost a week that Gustav had been missing. Then the trip back took several days. I wondered what Alexander thought about when he was all alone in the carriage back from Stuttgart. Did he tell any of his colleagues at the University of Hohenheim that his son was missing and presumed dead? Did he cry? I hoped he cried.

Alexander had been back for a few days. I expected him to come see me first-hand, but he did not. I had heard the talk in town as I went to Resteller's lumber. He was nearly despondent. People said he was gaunt. I could understand that—there was no body to mourn or bury, he did not even get to say good-bye. It was a loss for him, truly. I could not wait for him to come by.

Inside, I would leap joyously as my secret ballooned. Perhaps I'd shed false tears, make my brother think I was sincere. My tears would be rapturous, however.

I would take him into the workshop, and there I'd recount the horrible accident the way I did for the local authorities who passed along the information to the authorities in Stuttgart. My eyes would burn red with tears. If Alexander only knew his child was preserved, possibly alive, only feet from him, if he only knew. I can only describe these vengeful thoughts as tasty.

Grimm prepared for the visit of Alexander. It was only a matter of time before he ventured away from the safety of his wife's family. They had taken him in, loved him like a son, and he valued them equally.

Grimm was the only blood relative left for Alexander, but that was as far as it went. Grimm's animosity was fueled by jealousy. Their father had always shown particular favoritism for Alexander and told young Edward he was nothing in his brother's shadow. Alexander wasn't hesitant in reminding his little brother of this fact. Grimm was sure Alexander did not receive the night visits from their father; and sure, Alexander wasn't put in the well; and sure Alexander always got love.

To pass the time, Grimm worked outside. It was a warm day, for mid-winter. The sun was shining brightly, and a breeze came through the forest. The supply of chopped wood was waning, and Grimm was splitting logs with a wedge and ax.

Some of the snowpack was melting; puddles of cool, clear water were forming in the yard. Grimm only wore dungarees, boots, and a flannel shirt. It was all that was needed on this unusually warm day. Chopping the wood kept him fit and healthy, physically at least. Executing the chore of chopping wood was always a pleasure for Grimm. For as long as he could remember, he envisioned Alexander with the splitting wedge driving deep into his skull. Brains and blood exploding all over the ground, and then father would get his.

Just as Grimm severed a log with an impressive surge of strength, he was aware of a presence near him. The sun was bright, so bright any fog would be driven away. Then, he saw a shadow from behind.

"Edward," Grimm heard his name and turned, "my brother."

Grimm turned to see Alexander standing there. Only, for a moment, Grimm wasn't sure if this were the same brother he grew up with or knew as an adult. He was thin and drawn. The meat on his bones had atrophied, his skin shrunken to paper thin.

"Alexander." Before Grimm had realized it, the sympathetic

utterance has slipped from his lips.

"You didn't know it was me for a moment, did you?" He laughed pitifully, "Neither did anyone in town. They thought I was a stranger until they saw me up close."

Grimm was absent of words, he hesitated.

Alexander saw his brother stumbling for something to say, "Don't bother yourself." He stepped closer, inspecting Grimm with a smile, "You are looking as fit as ever. Whatever you are doing, it agrees with you."

Grimm smiled, "Yes, I think so."

Then, Alexander's face fell. It was if a mask had dropped to the ground, and the visage beneath was borrowed from a sinner. He grabbed Grimm in a great hug.

Grimm felt his shoulders crushing together from the weight of Alexander's embrace. It was also becoming wet. Edward raised a hand to his brother's neck. There he began to stroke lovingly. He wasn't sure if he meant to be sympathetic, or that he enjoyed soaking up his brother's sorrow. For a moment, he forgot the past as this once great man cried on his shoulder.

Soon, Alexander pulled away. "I thought I had no tears left to cry." He flashed a tortured, momentary grin, "Men don't cry, that's what we learned, wasn't it?"

"Yes, it was." Grimm agreed.

"I don't feel very manly, then."

"I understand."

Alexander looked at his brother, "I need to know."

This was the point Grimm had feared. Would the sentiment and tension of the moment be enough to break the secret free? He controlled himself well, however.

"I return to the event every day. I see his face everywhere." Grimm said. Alexander listened intently, "I looked for him everywhere, the river was so fast and high."

Alexander's defeated eyes slowly moved downward. "I know it must be hard. I can't imagine living through the moment. I wished I had been here. I could have saved him, I know."

Grimm heard the guilt in Alexander's voice. Then, he thought perhaps it wasn't the passing of Gustav that bothered Alexander, but the guilt of his own neglect.

"It is all my fault, you know." Alexander sighed. "You don't understand, no one does. I had to be away to work. I couldn't take a little boy away from here, not to the cities. He is," Alexander paused and swallowed hard, "was an angel, an innocent angel. I was protecting him by leaving him here."

"I understand that. You could not have known."

"It's no excuse." Alexander sat on the woodpile.

Grimm thought of the ax in his hand. Alexander sat three feet away, he was waist high. Grimm envisioned his brother's head rolling away like a melon but fought the urge to strike.

He set the ax aside, for another thought of revenge came to mind. "Would you like to come in for a cup of tea?"

Alexander looked up at Grimm, "I would like that, Edward."

The brothers went into Grimm's house and sat at the kitchen table. Grimm measured tea and placed two tea balls inside cups. He put them on the table and fetched the kettle from the stove. He poured water into the cups, and instantly brown stain bled profusely.

Alexander attempted to change the subject, "What have you been doing since I have been away? How did the horse go over?"

"Wonderfully," Grimm answered, "I could not have asked for anything better."

"Did he give you more work?"

"In a matter of speaking." Grimm said vaguely.

"Are you working on it now?"

"Yes, it's out in the workshop."

Alexander's eyes showed a little enthusiasm for the first time. "I would like to see it, is it another horse?"

"It is more than a horse," Grimm hesitated, "it's a carousel."

Alexander was surprised, "A carousel? That's a big order."

"I wasn't sure if I wanted to do it, at first, but when I started, I knew it was the project of my life."

"Indeed."

Grimm sipped tea, and thoughtfully mulled over his words, if Alexander only knew how true they were. "Are you ready to see it?"

"Yes." Alexander started to rise.

Grimm hesitated. He wasn't sure if he wanted to tell Alexander of the statue. Would it be a greater impact if his brother knew about the work, or if he stumbled upon it himself? Grimm decided to let Alexander see Gustav without any warning.

"The workshop is quite full."

They walked toward the door. "I imagine so, with a project like that in there. It is a wonder you have room to move around." Alexander commented.

"Sometimes, I don't." Grimm opened the door.

Spread before Alexander was the canopy and frame of the carousel. Its skeleton was beginning to flesh out. Grimm had been adding touches to the figures he'd been collecting, busy carving grape leaves and birds. He even fashioned faces based on the gypsy people.

"My God, Edward." Alexander gasped.

He moved forward. The majority of the carousel's stage was empty, but there were a few figures upon it. Alexander noticed the dog-headed cherubs instantly and looked up at them.

"Is it all right to walk up here? "Alexander asked before stepping onto the platform.

"Certainly, I have finished most of it. I must find someone to build the wheels, track, and engine before long."

Alexander did not hear what Grimm had said, for he was enraptured by one of the women. He was particularly taken with her flowing hair and chest of gold.

"This is incredible, such detail."

Grimm said nothing as he watched Alexander admire his work. After all, Grimm thought, it was work done by his hand.

Alexander moved from one woman to the next, "Amazing. For some reason, I recognize these women."

Then, over the shoulder of the woman, Alexander saw a small human form. He maneuvered to get a better look and saw Gustav's eyes staring outward. Alexander almost fell off the carousel as he rushed to the statue. His eyes danced with disbelief.

Grimm watched all of this with relish. The agony ruptured from deep inside Alexander. It was like a volcano spilling lava over the earth. He gently caressed the shape, and his tears fell at the boy's feet.

"I made this in Gustav's memory." Grimm lied so well.

"Thank you. Thank you for putting your God-given talents to use." Alexander sobbed quietly.

Grimm wanted to smile at such an absurd statement, it was the forsaking of God that gave him this talent; but he stayed in character as the sympathetic, caring brother.

The only thing that could ruin this was if Alexander heard Gustav's crying. "I thought the king would benefit from such a boy in his presence."

Alexander admired the figure more, unaware that only a thin layer of wood separated him from Gustav. "Now I know why I recognize all these figures." He came away from Gustav, "my boy told me about all of these, these things in his dreams."

"He told me, too." Grimm said, "So I captured them in wood."

Alexander paused and took a deep breath. "My house is lonely, brother." He sat on the side of the carousel, only inches from Gustav. "I don't want to be there much."

Grimm grew nervous with Alexander so close to the boy. What if he heard the crying? What if Gustav began to dream, and something came calling? He stayed in character, however.

"What will you do now?" Grimm asked.

"I think I'll move to the university. I have friends there. There is too much pain here."

"When will you go?"

"I haven't decided." Alexander attempted to change the subject, "But tell me more about this wonderful carousel. You say you need to find someone to build the tracks and such?" Alexander looked to the large empty space in the center, "Why is that area empty?"

Grimm followed his brother's direction. "That space is for a calliope. I have heard word of a gentleman who I think will be sufficient. He is in the north right now, and I am going to seek him out."

"Where at?"

"In Hamburg, he is working on St. Benedictine's. In fact, I plan on leaving in the next few days. I want to catch him before he goes home to Ireland."

Alexander could see Grimm was getting restless. "I think I'll be on my way, brother. I need to do a few things, and some thinking. I am planning a funeral for Gustav, to put him to rest with some compassion. If you leave, I'll wait until you get back. I want to have you there. I know how much Gustav meant to you."

"Yes, he still means a lot to me."

Alexander headed for the door, "I'll see you soon. Please, don't stay away from my house too much."

Grimm became nervous as their eyes met. Alexander looked so much like their father. Grimm was sure his eyes would betray him, but Alexander only offered a gentle hug.

"Good-bye, Alexander."

"Good-bye, brother."

Grimm walked him out through the house and watched until Alexander blended in with the falling shadows. As soon as he was sure it was safe, Grimm returned to the workshop.

The place was empty, seemingly void of life. It was only life interrupted that filled the shop. The carousel was the prison, and the figures were the incarcerated. Gustav was the center of this universe now. Grimm realized just how much he grew to depend on this trapped little boy for everything he held dear.

Grimm walked the rim of the carousel, admiring his own handiwork. The cherubs were nailed to the merry-go-round, the women were fastened to the deck, and Gustav stood among them.

He went to the boy and knelt at his feet. "Are you in there? Of course, you are." He smiled. "Your father was here, as were the women. They all came to see you, but they all think you are gone. Your father is a wreck, he thinks you have floated away forever. But he doesn't miss you, he doesn't miss you at all. In fact, he told me he was moving. He is going to the university for good."

Grimm hoped his words blistered Gustav's ears. He only wished he could see some sign, some visual victory of his torture. Grimm rose up from his position and located the woman who bore treasure.

She was the size of a normal woman, and that pleased Grimm. He was happy that not all of Gustav's minions were vulgar atrocities like the cherubs. His hand fell lightly upon the chest of gold, the pieces were so thick. Then, he pulled away angrily. They were so close, yet unobtainable, just like Elena.

He swiftly returned to Gustav, "If you ever hope to be released, don't play games. Your father doesn't love you, and he is leaving you just like your mother did. I am the only one who cares, so you must help me."

Grimm noticed that the small, stained river delta beneath Gustav's eye was growing wet. He touched the tears; they were real. Grimm, with a fingertip moist with tears, lifted it to his mouth and tasted.

"Tears are so salty."

With those words, Grimm looked to the windows. The light outside was falling, and he still had work to do. He did not like to be alone in the dark these days, the creatures of the forest could no longer be trusted. His pact was made, and that bargain was against all plans of nature. The animals knew that, they could smell it on the wind.

"I must be off. Dream now, sweet boy." Grimm rose up. "I will return shortly."

Grimm headed through the house, locking the workshop. He went back out into the yard, to the woodpile in particular. There wasn't enough wood for the week, and Grimm wanted to be well stocked before he went north. He wanted to return, with all the ingredients in place for the conclusion of the carousel.

Grimm hoisted the ax and began to split logs once again. With every chop, his thoughts roved around. At first, he thought of chopping Alexander to bits, then chopping Sennett to scraps. But soon, he thought of the calliope. Who was this man, Julian Keefe, that he was going to see? What would he think of the work being done?

Grimm was not worried about the money, he felt confident that Gustav could be manipulated into sending it supernaturally. At last, Grimm thought, things were going his way.

The sun had dipped below the tree line, and Grimm paused to catch his breath. Winter was returning with the light's retreat. The moon was a sliver in the sky, and he gazed upon it. The warmth always came before a big snow. He paused for a moment; something caught his eye along the tree line. It was moving, quick as lightning. Grimm wasn't sure what it was.

"Alexander, is that you?" Grimm called. "Hello?"

Suddenly, he heard a low grunt and a growl. Then, he saw the fog hanging like lace in the trees. The crunch of hard packed snow echoed, and Grimm knew it was something large coming closer.

As he turned to run in the house, a woolly, hairy shape thrust up from nowhere. The creature knocked Grimm to the ground with one blow of its strong arms. He looked upward, and his eyes beheld a matted, manlike creature. Its back was hunched; its hands ended in wicked claws. And the face, like the cherubs, was hairless and skinned. Its demonic features were that of a warped bear.

Grimm instantly reacted and used the ax to deflect a blow. The powerful swipe surely would have killed the carver. He maneuvered the ax until the head was below the monster's chin.

With every ounce of strength, Grimm thrust the ax skyward.

The metal crashed into the monster's face, knocking it backward into the snow. Taking advantage of the situation, Grimm scrambled to his feet, grabbed the ax, and burst for the house. The beast had scrambled to its feet and was in relentless pursuit.

Grimm glanced over his shoulder. The creature rumbled closer and closer. It ran almost like a bear. He reached the house, opened the door, and swiftly locked it behind him. He heard nothing outside. Grimm was afraid to breathe, his heart pounded in his head. Struggling to remain silent, Grimm listened for the monster lurking about. He gathered his senses and knew where the monster came from: Gustav.

He had other things to worry about now. The creature revealed its presence. Grimm heard its claws scraping against the door; its awesome fists pounding a way through.

Grimm held the ax tightly. "Gustav, wake up!"

The creature's attack was starting to splinter the heavy door. Grimm thought of the potion as sweat poured down his face. He ran to the door that led to the workshop. Then, Grimm recalled, he had locked it. The potion was in the workshop. If the beast made it through, Grimm would be dead. He pushed at the workshop door. The monster's hot breath steamed through the growing hole. It paused, putting an eye up to the hole briefly, then it resumed the onslaught.

Grimm's struggle paid off; the workshop door was now unlocked. Just as he opened the door, the full arm of the beast smashed the front door. Splinters showered the kitchen as the hairy mass came through. Grimm quickly shut the workshop door.

Its red eyes caught a glimpse of Grimm as he slipped into the workshop. Without any hesitation, the raging beast thundered toward the workshop. Inside, Grimm hid as best he could in the shadows. He had no time to hide properly, much less locate the potion. The vial was on the work bench. He could see the small bottle from where he was. Grimm knew; however, the creature was moments from the door. What would it do once in the workshop? Would it kill Grimm, destroy the carousel, and free Gustav?

The thought pattern was broken as the monstrosity grunted and roared beyond the door. It sounded like a bear, but also like a madman laughing. Grimm knew this beast now. Gustav had spoken about it in the past. What a prize this creature would make for the carousel, if it didn't destroy the carver first.

The horrid creature must be what Gustav thought was a werewolf. It lived on the lacy fog. Grimm looked to the floor by the door, the fog was spilling in like frothy cream. Then, the claws were working upon the door. This portal was not nearly as sturdy as the front door, and its resistance was feeble. Fighting all of his fears, Grimm knew the magic solution was the only hope for survival. Mustering up all his courage to leave the shadows, Grimm rushed for the work bench. As he did, the roaring monster exploded through the door. With thrashing claws, it pounced on Grimm.

Vainly, Grimm attacked with the ax. The blow glanced off the shoulder of the creature, drawing blood from a shallow slice. The thing wailed in pain but did not slow the attack. The work bench was only two yards away, but it could have been a mile. A crisp slicing paw reached for Grimm's leg. And like a razor, it ruptured a clean slit in his thigh.

The carver's painful wail seemed to thrill the beast, and it gave a guttural utterance. Summoning all his remaining strength, Grimm cocked the ax over one shoulder. The monster thrust for a second, killing blow. But Grimm propelled the blade of the ax into the chest of the beast.

The blow was enough to knock the creature backward. It stumbled and fell, blood surging through a deep gash. Taking full advantage of the moment, Grimm seized the potion from the work bench. Spinning around on his good leg, Grimm poised to seal the monster forever in a wooden prison.

A moment of hesitation came. Kneeling on the floor, in a

pool of rich, dark blood was a creature with a familiar face. It was no longer a mutated, skinned bear head looking at Grimm. Instead, it was a man with sad, sad eyes. Alexander looked out at Grimm.

"Freedom." It muttered in an almost indistinguishable growl.

Appalled by this dream figure's utterance, Grimm sloshed the potion upon its bleeding form.

Ator malcuth theraputae.

And the beast was overtaken by the magic wood grain. It crawled from within the wound, spreading with the blood flow. Then, the wood leeched through every fiber, every hair, and even across the skinned face.

The event was so swift, even though Grimm's eyes perceived the moment as an eternity. Quiet settled over the workshop. He dropped the ax that he gripped so tightly. Blood from the blade pooled on the floor.

At that point, Grimm realized his own leg was bleeding. He looked down at the rip in his pants. The cloth was soaking, but he couldn't be sure of the wound's severity. Grimm inspected the laceration, there was plenty of blood, but the wound was not serious or deep.

With the potion in hand, he hobbled past the wooden creature on the floor. He went into the kitchen. Grimm fetched some cloth strips from a drawer, and hot water from the stove. Taking one piece of cloth, he drenched the wound and carefully cleaned it.

He dressed the wound with the remaining strips, packing them around the cut to halt blood loss. His blood had started to clot; perhaps since the creature was now trapped, the wound caused by the magic claws would not get infected. Grimm hoped in his mind that it was so.

The slice was clean, like a razor had moved effortlessly through the meat. He wrapped several long pieces of cloth around his thigh, and tautly secured them. As the cut's two halves were cinched together, the wound practically disappeared. It was such an unadulterated, clean blow. Grimm admired the precision of the stroke, if he could only sharpen a bit to this aperture, his carvings would be just as accurate.

After tending to his injury, Grimm went to his kitchen cupboard. He retrieved a small flask of spirits and removed the stopper. Grimm tipped the bottle, draining it of what would have been several shots. The liquid tingled as it hit his gut. Although the spirits did not totally take away the pain, it numbed him sufficiently.

The feeling of euphoria took him quickly, but Grimm couldn't be sure if the loss of blood wasn't encouraging the sensation. He dismissed the concern and laughed. Grimm sat the empty bottle down, and he raised the vial which he still had.

His eyes reflected in its opaqueness, "What are you?"

He held it so very close to his eye. In the solution, Grimm could see light reflecting like jewels. Grimm tried to understand the power contained in this tiny potion, but it was beyond him.

"There is no way I can ever know what you are, but I tell you this: I regret nothing."

With the vial in hand, the carver returned to the workshop. He located the creature that was sealed in wood.

"You, you look like someone I know." He felt brave as the drunken stupor increased.

Grimm was suddenly hit by a wave of nausea, but he suppressed it. He walked close to the bearlike monster and touched it cautiously. The face was so familiar. He thought back to the heated confrontation, the beast had instantly resembled Alexander. But now, it was just a horrid figure of creation.

"I thought perhaps you had come in the guise of my brother. If you had, and I was sure, killing you would have been a much greater treat." Grimm stroked the knotty fur, "I wouldn't have hesitated a moment if I thought it was you. I would have cut your head off, brother." Grimm smiled, "See this," he held the potion up in front of the creature's eyes, "if indeed you are

Alexander, I wanted you to know I caught you."

Grimm left the beast and located Gustav's form. He knelt awkwardly in front of the child, "See, see, see little boy, this is a situation that I control. Send your dreams, send your nightmares, I'll be here. I was here when the women came, and I was here today when the beast came." Grimm's anger, fueled by the alcohol, erupted. "If indeed, I have trapped your father, then you will be the one to decide if he gets free."

He paused, knowing the boy wasn't listening to him. Grimm was speaking to a piece of wood. The thought of the boy no longer being alert infuriated the madman. What if Gustav's very heart had transformed into a piece of wood?

"Damn this!" Grimm shouted and set the potion on the platform.

Ignoring the pain, he made his way to the ax. Taking the tool of death into his hands, Grimm struggled to move around the carousel.

"Watch me, Boy!" He yelled.

Grimm labored against his own pain. He went from figure to figure, until he came upon the woman with the chest of gold. Scrambling with the ax, Grimm made his way onto the platform. He was nearly a foot taller than the statue of the woman. Grimm gripped the tool with two hands. He extended his arms, lining the blade up on the slender neck.

"Is this your savior? Shall she lose her head?" He drew the ax back.

Grimm started with a slow swing but checked it at the last moment. The ax dropped to the platform, and Grimm laughed.

"My boy, my boy." Grimm smiled insanely. "Nothing can go wrong now."

He ran awkwardly across the vacant areas of the platform until he reached Gustav. Ignoring his wound, Grimm kneeled in front of the statue. He wanted to see Gustav's eye again; he had to know if the boy was still alive. He picked at the wooden eye with his finger.

"Are you in there? I know you are." Grimm's eyes burned with madness.

There was no answer. Grimm really didn't expect one. He lowered himself down to the nail head in Gustav's foot. As he watched, a small drop of blood pooled. But, instead of elation, Grimm fumed even more. The spot of blood was a monument to the fact he still owned nothing. Gustav still lived, and he still controlled the dreams.

"I will not stand for this." Grimm rose to his feet.

He seemed to have a refreshed calmness about him. Grimm returned to the place where the ax had fallen and picked it up. Then, he returned to the woman with the treasure.

Grimm had no doubts about his actions, "If it cannot be given, then I shall take it."

He slung the ax over his shoulder, summoning all muscle strength to the chore. With all the energy transferred to the ax, Grimm sliced the air with the blade. The hard metal targeted the treasure box clenched tightly by the woman's hands. Grimm aimed for the slender wrists, and they cleaved easily with the weight of the ax.

However, Grimm hadn't anticipated the consequences of his rash act. Unlike the fluid inside the angels that surfaced as he nailed them down, the woman was filled with a much different solution. Blood raged from the handless arms. It was as if a heartbeat inside the woman, pumping her blood all over the platform. Splashes of the red, sticky liquid rebounded onto Grimm's legs and body. He screamed in terror as the tidal wave came.

Attempting to control his emotions, Grimm tried to ignore the blood. It was cold, and it smelled of rancid meat and the lacy fog. Somehow sweet, yet stomach wrenching at the same instant. It was cold, cold like the winter breath that waited outside.

Grimm knelt. He rationalized the gore that was taking place before him. He reminded himself of his father, scorched into oblivion in the foundry years ago. His guts rained down, and Grimm came through that with only fond recollection. Though, this was different. The very thing he wanted most was now defaced. A dream was bleeding upon him. Grimm's head swam, and he wasn't sure if it were the invading insanity, or the reality of his actions.

He located the prize of his crime. Grimm picked the blood-coated treasure box and fell away from the scene. The wooden hands were still attached, the box still tightly in their grip. Upon closer inspection, Grimm saw the point where the ax had sliced the hands off. Beneath the thin wood coating, Grimm saw flesh. True flesh and muscle and bone. Remnants of blood and tendon hung like butchered fowl.

She was real.

If she were real, Grimm thought, then what she brought had to be real also. Hope erased the instant recall of the scene on the carousel. Grimm scooted carefully off the platform and took the chest to the work bench.

He placed the treasure box on the table, and pulled up something to sit on. Grimm studied it carefully. The wood was like a glove over the hands and chest. He retrieved several chisels from the back board, and cautiously started to explore.

Grimm picked the flesh at the end of the wrist, until he was satisfied it was real. Then, he began to pick at the treasure box itself. He hadn't realized how ornate it was—the case seemed to be of a rich cherry. The magical coating could be deceptive, however.

Grimm removed the wood piece by piece. As he uncovered the hands, he admired the fairness of the woman's skin. There were no blemishes, nor hair, just alabaster skin. He scraped the spaces where her hands met the chest. The stuff flaked away like mica stone, fracturing in small pieces.

Gradually, after careful work, Grimm freed one of the hands. At first, he flinched at the touch of the cool skin, but then he admired how it worked. Grimm gently moved the fingers, fascinated with their mechanics. Then, he returned to the task at hand.

Beneath where the first hand had been, Grimm was finally able to inspect the chest. Through a thin crack in the covering, a metallic flicker caught his eye. Grimm tooled briefly at the crack until it was large enough to see what it was. A smile crossed the carver's lips as he pulled a gold coin from the crevice. He put it to his lips, and bit to discover the truth. Grimm smiled as the metal bent between his teeth.

With renewed vigor, Grimm removed the second hand. Soon he had the chest completely free. As the lid became free, a wealth of gold coins spilled onto the bench.

Grimm's voice quivered with ecstasy, "Ah, Elena."

*I stopped to see Alexander, as he requested. I wanted to see for
myself if indeed I had killed him in the workshop. Nevertheless,
I was disappointed to find him well.*

*I did stop by with news, however. With my newly acquired
wealth, I felt I was ready to make many moves. First, I was
going to go off to the Vitsa of Casimir Manush. Elena would
now desire me as a husband, I knew it in my mind. If not, I was
sure I could persuade her it was in her best interest. I now had
the means to propel her socially. She would be the envy of all
women, and I the envy of all men. I would have it all. I would
not be denied.*

*As I saw my brother's house, I remembered many things. The
house itself did not jar memories loose, it was the sadness in
Alexander's face. I could not have asked for a greater revenge.
He would be forever tortured by what I'd done. I thought it was
punishment earned, because I hated the fact he never knew the
pain I did. It made me feel good to see Alexander's anguished
face. I only wish it were my father, but this was good enough
now.*

*I told him of my second trip, carefully keeping the first one a
secret. I was ready to seek out the man, Julian Keefe, and begin
work on the calliope. I had mounted the bear on the carousel,
and it took up a large amount of space. It would not be long
until I had enough of Gustav's dreams to fill it completely,
then I could look upon them forever. I also started to think of
ways to finally kill Gustav after I acquired my fill of his images.
This was a prospect that would need more thought, for the
consequences could stretch into unseen directions.*

*Even if I weren't on my way to see Elena, I needed to see
the Phuri Dai once again. The potion was running low, and
I needed more. It seemed to be my only protection against*

Gustav's more dark dream creatures. If it weren't for the potion, I would certainly be dead now.

Alexander was pleased for me. He thought the trip would help me. He seemed to feel I was suffering from Gustav's death still. He felt the trip would be a time of reflection and the settling of my soul. I was happier than I'd ever been. One day, for the final stroke of vengeance, perhaps I will tell Alexander everything on his deathbed. I would confess my sins and claim salvation. That was how it worked.

My brother offered to drop in and check on my house, but I said it was unnecessary. I said I would close everything up. After I left my haggard, worn brother, I started off to the gypsy camp.

As the weather of the previous day had promised, snow moved in with the retreat of the unseasonable warmth. The bitter wind returned. This time its fangs were razor sharp. The gypsy path was a trial. As the gentle sunlight heated the snow and frozen earth, the soil buckled. A field of potholes infected the surface. This made Grimm happy because the wagons of the Rom people would not be able to withstand the jarring. They would fall apart, and the wagons were the lifeblood of the tribe.

He entered the encampment. The Rom men were dressing the wagons for a hard freeze, perhaps the *Phuri Dai* predicted a storm. There was no business to be done on such a blustery day, all the villagers stayed away. No one wanted to be caught in the woods in such adversity.

Grimm passed all the wagons of the caravan until he came to the one belonging to the old wise woman. He needed answers, and she was the one to provide them. Grimm climbed her stairs. He remembered the first visit to this camp. He particularly remembered this trailer door, for this was where Elena's green eyes initially cut him open. Grimm knocked gently.

After several moments, the door slowly opened. The ancient *Phuri Dai* stood before him. She was frail looking, but Grimm knew not to underestimate the power in this withered flower.

"It is you, Grimm." She was not surprised.

"Yes, may I come in. I must talk to you."

She sensed the urgency in his voice but was still unaffected.

"Madame, I beseech you…" His voice trailed away.

"Then enter." The *Phuri Dai* said and retreated into the warm wagon.

Grimm touched his pocket to assure himself the money was still there, then he entered. The wagon was familiar, but not comfortable. He followed her to the table, where she motioned for the carver to sit.

"You do not need to tell me why you are here." She lighted the lamps and candles.

"Then you know why I have returned?" Grimm asked.

"You all return sooner or later."

"I don't understand."

"The magic has consumed you inside and out. You will never be free of it, such is the price I warned you about."

Grimm watched as the flames reflected in her eyes, "It has not become the ruler of my life."

"That is true, you are a different man than all the others."

Grimm wanted to smile. He considered this high praise. "How am I different? Please tell me."

"It is all about you, the madness. Shall I read your cards?" The *Phuri Dai* changed the subject.

Grimm had no objections, and she started to lay tarot cards. She chose a familiar pattern, that of the cross. As she turned the cards over, her face remained unchanged.

"What do you see?"

"Nothing I didn't already know."

"And what is that, madame?"

She sighed and put the cards away. "All I know is the magic has consumed you, but you are its willing lover. I grieve with you in your selfish ignorance."

Grimm was beginning to get annoyed with her rambling talk.

"I am not here to discuss the fate of my soul. I want to discuss this." He held up the half empty vial.

She looked upon the potion. "What about it?"

"I am running out, I need more." Grimm said.

The *Phuri Dai* laughed. "There is no more. You have all that is, all that will ever be. And that will always be enough for you."

Grimm was even more confused, "I don't understand?"

"The potion will always replenish itself when needed."

"It will just magically make more?"

"It is a magic potion, Mr. Grimm." She smiled, "For what you have paid, there will always be enough."

The words satisfied him, "That is all I need to know." Grimm hesitated slightly, "I've come, however, to see Elena. I need to speak to her."

"Elena is here," she said.

"She is here in your wagon?"

"Yes."

With those words said, Elena appeared from the shadowy regions of the wagon. She was beautiful. Her hair was so long and dark.

"It's you." Grimm could think of nothing else to say. Then, he wondered if she heard everything the old woman said. "I… I've…"

The *Phuri Dai* rose from her chair. "I have business with the chieftain. I shall leave you to talk."

"Thank you." Grimm said.

Elena said nothing, she just watched the woman leave the trailer. After she left, Elena sat in her chair.

"Sit down again." She motioned to the chair with a glance.

Grimm sat. "My visit is…"

She cut him off, "I don't care what business you have with the *Phuri Dai*. I heard you say you wanted to see me."

"Yes, I've come to see you."

"And what about?"

Grimm pulled the sack of gold from his pocket and poured

it on the table. "There's more there than you'll ever see in your life."

Elena's eyes brightened. She reached for the money, her hands filtering it lovingly. "Where did you get all of this?"

"What do you care, all you need to know is that I have it." Grimm felt powerful as he watched the woman pawing the gold.

Elena looked at Grimm. She picked up a lone piece of currency. Slowly, she put it to her mouth. Elena closed her eyes, and sensuously kissed the metal. She rubbed it in slow circles on her full lips, then opened her eyes to meet Grimm's staring gaze.

"You could do well by me with this money." She whispered passionately.

Grimm was excited by her response. "Marry me, Elena. The world is yours as my wife."

She smiled and tossed the coin back in the pile. "What would it get me? I see it this way: you get a beautiful woman, but how am I to know this is not all the money you have in the world?"

"I assure you, I have much more than you'll ever know."

Elena turned her back to him. She slightly played with some peppers hanging nearby, "We'll see. I could say yes to you, but what else could you offer?" She turned around, flashing her impaling eyes. "Sennett gives me much more than you could. I please him well."

At the mention of Sennett's name, Grimm's guts boiled with jealousy. "I can give you anything, more than he could. You want parties. You want balls. You crave grand ballgowns—can he do that? I can. He is a gypsy boy."

"Can you give me a night's pleasure? The gypsy boy does— often." She sauntered toward Grimm. "Let me describe what Sennett and I have. He stirs the animal in me, and I in him. He howls and pants, biting me, pulling me onward…"

"Enough!" Grimm shouted and stood.

Laughing, Elena snatched a handful of the gold. "I'll take your money and I'll take your heart, but I will never take your hand in marriage. I am a princess here. I have power. Sennett is destined to be chieftain. You are damned to hell. I don't know what bargain you have struck with the devil, but he has already claimed you." With that, she put the handful of money in her dress pocket.

"You will rethink this, I guarantee." Grimm fumed.

Without further words, Grimm stalked from the wagon. He'd once again been humiliated by this gypsy bitch. The scene replayed endlessly in his brain. She would not get away with this. She was nothing but a woman, a second-rate citizen. No woman should have such power over a man, it was unheard of.

Grimm's thoughts turned vengeful. There was no magic potion to make her marry him, but somehow it would be accomplished. At that point, Grimm looked about him. Across the encampment, Grimm saw the *Phuri Dai* coming from a large wagon. This had to be the wagon of the chieftain. He remembered Elena's boasts about the chieftain being her father. She was in line for authority, power, money.

Grimm took the pouch of money from his pocket. He crossed the tundra-like soil and walked up the stairs. The carver knocked gently.

He heard many voices inside. Just as he was about to knock again, the door creaked open. Grimm did not recognize the man who opened the door, but further in he saw Sennett.

"Yes?" The man asked.

"I have come to see the chieftain," Grimm replied.

The man closed the door without any other exchange. Grimm could hear them talking. Sennett's voice violently rose several times. Many minutes passed before the door opened again. Instead of opening slowly, the door rocketed open, and Sennett burst past. He deliberately tried to knock Grimm off the narrow stairs, but the carver stood his ground.

Sennett disappeared in the night, and the first man returned to the door. "Casimir will see you now."

Silently, Grimm entered the wagon. This trailer was vastly different from that of the *Phuri Dai*. On the walls hung many masculine things: weapons, flasks, medallions, and skins. Grimm scanned the trailer with curiosity.

"Leave us alone." said a mature voice from one corner of the trailer.

Grimm located the man. He was elegant, a true gypsy king. Casimir, chieftain of *Manush*, *Manouches*, and *Sinti* proudly stood. He was a sturdy man, bearer of obvious physical strength. He wore a mustache and beard highlighted in white.

"What can I do for you, sir?"

Grimm was instantly intimidated. "I've come to discuss something of great importance with you."

"Then sit, sit," Casimir said.

"I've come to ask for Elena's hand in marriage."

Casimir did not reply immediately. Instead, he pondered the possibility.

Grimm could see him thinking and sweetened the pot. "I have money, I am able to care for her well. I love her, chieftain."

"You love her?"

"Yes, I do."

Casimir looked at Grimm with scrutiny. "You have money? Who are you?"

"I am Edward Grimm. I am a master artisan woodworker. My carvings have pleased kings, popes, and American presidents."

"I have heard mention of you around these parts." Casimir thought about his offer again.

Grimm, in an attempt to prompt a decision, took the pouch of gold to him. "This is for you, a gift for your blessing of marriage."

Casimir took the sack. He reached in and pulled out some coins. He studied them momentarily but was obviously impressed with the gold.

"She is yours. Consider this marriage arranged."

Grimm was surprised at Casimir's quick decision. He expected it to be a trial, he anticipated much resistance. Then, he remembered the place of a woman. To Casimir, Elena was just another commodity to be traded. His daughter was his property, and now she had been sold to Grimm.

Casimir called the attendant's name. The man who answered the door returned. "Yes?"

"Summon Elena. Tell her I wish to see her." Casimir waved his hand, dismissing the man. He returned his attention to Grimm, "There will be much planning, much celebrating. It is not often a *Gadje* marries a princess."

"I look forward to marrying Elena. I love her very much."

"So you say." Casimir said flatly.

Both men turned as the door creaked open. The attendant came in first, followed by Elena. At first, her face was puzzled, but as soon as she saw Grimm in the room, she knew something horrible had happened.

"Yes, papa?" Elena's eyes fell to the floor.

Grimm was fascinated at the transformation he'd just witnessed. The brazen woman he knew was cut in half, reduced in age to a humble maiden. She was submissive in her father's stare. Grimm hoped this was the woman that would come home with him.

"My daughter," Casimir began, "you know this man, he has come to me for your hand in marriage."

Elena started to protest, but one blow from her father's paternal stare drove her back down. "Yes, I know him."

"I have accepted his agreement. You shall be his wife, and I welcome my talented new son."

"No!" Elena burst into tears. "I do not love him."

"Elena, I am a man of honor, and your father. You would not go against me." Casimir's voice was stern.

Elena lowered her eyes again, humbled in the great man's shadow. "No father."

"It is settled." Casimir smiled. "We shall prepare for a wedding."

Grimm then remembered his impending trip, "With all due respects, I have a business trip that I must take. I wish I could put it off, but I cannot."

Casimir looked at Grimm with slight disapproval. "You ask for my daughter's hand, then you want to postpone the wedding?"

"I am in the middle of an enormous project for a Scandinavian king. The only person who can perform the duties I need is set to leave for Ireland soon. I must catch him before he leaves."

"A king, I suppose that is important." Casimir seemed convinced. "My new son—artist to kings."

"As soon as I return…" Grimm started but was cut off by Casimir.

"I say we marry you now. I am the chieftain." Casimir thought momentarily, "We can postpone the celebration until you return, Grimm. You shall introduce yourself to the courtiers as the son of Casimir, the Chieftain of *Manush*, *Manouches*, and *Sinti*."

Grimm realized it was useless to argue the point, and meekly succumbed. Casimir pulled the attendant aside, quietly gave him instructions, and sent him into the night. Elena silently wept nearby.

Sennett was the first through the door. Again, I had exacted revenge on my enemies. Sennett's eyes could not lie, he loved Elena, but I now owned her. The attendant must surely be aware of Sennett and Elena's feelings and told them of what transpired.

The Phuri Dai also came in. She was helped by two women I'd never seen before, but they didn't matter to me. There were more than enough witnesses to make this wedding real. I told her she would be mine, one way or another.

The brief ceremony was filled with words I didn't understand, and some that I did. All of the cordial phrases brought no comfort to Elena. She cried through the swift nuptials. I knew she didn't love me then, but that would change. She would never want for anything. All I knew was, for the first time in my life, happiness wasn't too far away.

I had something to tell Gustav upon my return from the troupe. He would be happy to know a woman was coming to live here. I couldn't be sure if he heard me at all. I did not even know if any more dreams would come. Perhaps, the boy died of loneliness in his confinement, but that was the least of my worries.

I had a most unexpected visitor, someone potentially more dangerous than any creature Gustav could dream: Sennett.

Grimm was in the workshop when he heard footsteps in the crunchy snow beyond the door. At first, he thought it was a creature come to claim the boy. He wasn't up to the fight; the carver was drained of all energy. Grimm was too exhausted to struggle right now, but if it was a creature, he could accept it as a sign the boy was still alive.

Grimm turned to face the door. As it opened, a look of astonishment crossed his face. The dangerous beast was there, but it was human. Sennett stood in the doorway. He looked like a wounded animal, the most dangerous kind of animal there was.

"I have no quarrel with you." Grimm said, realizing he was no match for Sennett's youthful strength.

"But I have one with you." Sennett closed the door behind himself. "I am not here to fight you or kill you, not yet at least."

The statement eased Grimm to a point, but still kept him off balance. He studied Sennett, attempting to see what was inside. Grimm knew he was bothered, but the depth of his trouble was masked in harnessed hatred.

"Then, why are you here?" asked Grimm.

Sennett was also studying his foe. "I am at a loss. I don't know what you want from her. She doesn't love you. She loves me. Why must you take that?"

Sennett's feelings were honest, and the naked emotion thrilled Grimm. "I do love her. I must have her."

"You don't love her. You want to have her. You want to own her, and I guess you have accomplished that."

Grimm defended his position, "I have done nothing that hasn't been done for centuries."

"Why a gypsy?" Sennett asked, "You have nothing to gain, and everything to lose."

"What do you mean by that?"

Sennett moved in from the doorway, "Your people will shun you. You won't be worth the shit of a dog for marrying a gypsy. Don't you know?" Sennett's voice dripped with sarcasm. "Gypsies are thieves, dirty people who live in the woods. Uncivilized. Your own people will talk about you, you will be persecuted beyond belief. No one will buy your art. Word will spread all across Europe. Remember, we gypsies are everywhere."

"You lie." Grimm said defensively. "I will propel her away from her life. I can give her wealth, luxury, a home."

"At what price?" Sennett said. "You'll make her an outcast among the Vitsa. No one will accept this marriage to a *Gadje*. Her life will be just as horrible."

Grimm listened to his words, but then it was his turn to talk. "I never thought I would see you snivel. What you say may be true, but I think you are just here to persuade me to relinquish my claim on Elena. I won't do it. Even if I did not love her, I would keep her because I know it causes you pain."

Suddenly, Sennett was seized by rage. He lunged for Grimm and knocked the man against the carousel. Sennett's strong forearm pinned Grimm's neck to the platform.

"Just know this," Sennett sneered, "She may be your purchased wife, but I made love to her last night. That is something you'll never change. We'll always find a way to make love. I can give her something you could never give her because she would never want it from you." Grimm was starting to gag so Sennett let him up. "You just remember that as you sit here and carve your toys."

With those words, Sennett stormed across the workshop. Grimm visually followed the stalking young man. He remembered the display of strength experienced just an instant ago. Sennett could have snapped him in pieces with just an extra push. Perhaps, it was this strength that Elena found so appealing.

Sennett paused before leaving, "Remember this whenever you look at Elena: I am the one who makes love to her."

"I'll have you arrested for adultery." Grimm's brittle threat was ineffective.

"Like I said before, you are an outcast. Your own people look down on you. They don't care what happens where gypsies are concerned, so tell anyone you want."

Sennett was swallowed into the cold day. Grimm watched as his nemesis trudged off through the snow. The elements seemed to welcome Sennett, unlike their total rejection and attack of Grimm.

He shut the door quietly. Grimm walked over to the carousel, he recounted Sennett's words: sit and carve your toys. He rubbed the wound on his leg. It was a reminder of the struggle with the bear. If Sennett only knew the secret about Gustav, the women, the bear, the cherubs.

"He doesn't know, how could he." Grimm spoke to his creations. "He will find out differently. I promise on my grave, he will."

I will always remember the driving rain. It followed me from the start of my trip. I think perhaps it was a curse delivered on Sennett's behalf. The elements seemed to enjoy his presence, and they were out to punish me for taking away all he held dear. Still, I didn't feel any price would be too much to pay.

I hired a man to take me north to Hamburg. I knew of him, and he knew of me, but that was the extent of our relationship the entire trip. I couldn't recall his name which is unimportant. I had other things on my mind. I worried about Gustav; I knew I would. My fear was that Alexander would go to my house, and somehow figure out his child still lived.

I took the best precautions I knew how. I sealed the entire body of Gustav in wax. If any creatures came for him, they could not locate him by scent. Then, I covered Gustav in canvas and bound him tightly with rope. I was sure he would be undiscovered.

I had entertained the thought of letting go of my desire to provide music for my dream machine. But I found myself overwhelmed with the thought of being eternally entertained by my dreams and the music. I elected to go through with finding this man: Julian Keefe.

Since my driver was less animated than a forest mushroom, I found myself thinking of this man often. Julian Keefe. Would he be sufficient for the work I needed? I considered my taste more precise than that of a simple king who desired excess. I expected so much more from the world than that.

I knew nothing of Julian Keefe, and he certainly had never heard of me. I hoped the amount of money I brought would be enough. If not, I would bargain, telling him it was merely a down payment, and I had the means to pay him well.

I wondered if he were young or old, and if he were handsome or offensive. Those facts were of no consequence because it was the talent that mattered. Music to dream by, that was all Julian Keefe needed to provide.

The first day of travel was a nightmare. Although the weather was quite agreeable, the duration of the journey's first leg was extreme. We made it into Freiburg well after dark. I found lodging at a nearby hostel. I don't know where the driver stayed.

The entire night I slept perhaps two hours. My mind was still in the workshop. For some reason, I felt the presence of visitors in my house. I hoped Gustav wasn't freed.

I didn't waste time thinking of excuses in the event he was liberated, my greatest fear was of his death within the sarcophagus. I was also haunted by my first meeting with Julian Keefe.

I attempted to shift my thoughts from topic to topic, but I seemed to always return to speculation. I had attempted to prepare the spare bedroom for my visitor, even though I was unsure if he was even going to come.

The reason it was hard was because Gustav had always stayed in that room. He slept there, and I watched him many times. I pretended he was mine. I remember the horrible visits from my own father, and I saw Gustav's angelic face on the pillow. I cried at the thought of ever doing those evil deeds to him. How could my father do those things to me and not to Alexander?

I tried to push the memories of Gustav from my mind, but somehow they always returned. Bitterness stained my tongue. I tasted my spite for Alexander, my spite for the world.

Day two was marred by a cold wind that brought sleet as we followed the Rhein to Offenberg. The night was spent in a drafty inn, but I was so exhausted from the trip I fell into a deep sleep. The driver woke me before dawn because the winds let up. He wanted to make Karlsruhe before the storm strengthened again. We were blessed with good conditions for the next two days. We made good time through Mannheim and Wiesbaden. I noticed a distinct shift in dialect as we moved northward toward Hamburg. The people spoke low Deutsch,

*and some spoke such strange hybrids that I was often unable
to communicate with them. I didn't care to communicate with
them anyway. For the first time, I had contact with truly poor
people. I realized how much better I was; I had no desire to
converse with them. Although my affluence was meager, I
was a king compared to them. The driver, however, got along
famously with them.*

*The fourth day of our trek fell on a Sunday. We had made it to
Cologne, and our place of lodging was near a gothic cathedral.
There were so many lovely churches I can't remember which
one it was. I only know it had originally been Catholic, but
the Lutherans had since occupied it. Their style subdued the
grandeur that was once a glamourous temple. I thought it was
a perfect irony to my worship.*

*I listened to the priest delivering his sermon. I found no
comfort in it, only humor. God wasn't merciful. God was
spiteful, taking pleasure in my agony. I laughed inside. I
struggled to contain my cackles.*

*These peasants that surrounded me made my stomach
roll. Such hypocrisy. I could see it in their faces. One day of
worship was automatic forgiveness for six days of sin.*

*I looked about me at the angels on the wall and above the nave.
They seemed perfectly superior in their posture. The angels
knew the hierarchy of God's children.*

*We were the slime at the bottom, and they floated so clean.
I was content to be among the peasants for now. I knew
where I belonged. In my home, in my workshop was the door
to heaven. And I was the only keeper. I started to cry. And a
peasant bitch gave me a comforting smile. Little did she know
my tears were a joyous celebration of my own superiority.*

*The remainder of our journey saw us through Dortmund,
Bielefeld, Hannover, and Wolfsburg. Eventually we ended up in
Hamburg by the tenth day.*

Grimm paid the driver and let him be on his way. The driver
offered to remain with Grimm until he was ready to return, but

the carver declined the offer. He was unsure of his schedule.

With that said, the driver left Grimm's service, and Grimm located a place to stay. It was a small inn with only a few rooms, but he found it sufficient. Grimm had been frugal the entire trip to save money for Julian's anticipated fee.

After settling in, Grimm went walking. The sun had just dropped from the sky, leaving only a swatch of leftover color. He wandered the streets, taking in Hamburg's industrial smell.

Grimm located the Elbe River and walked its banks. He slipped into a quaint tavern where, over a beer, he was told the whereabouts of St. Benedictine's. As Grimm consumed the last swallow of brew, he smiled. He was a step closer on his quest for music to dream by.

CHAPTER 16

Morning, for the first time at the inn, was memorable. I can't remember when I had a more refreshing night of sleep. It was the last, I fear, I would experience for a while.

I was served hard sausage and kraut for breakfast. I paired some tea with my meal. I loved having tea, it seemed to cleanse me of sour feelings. One of the keys to the morning's happiness was the fact I knew where the church was. As luck would have it, St. Benedictine's was just a few streets over.

The innkeeper was a further source of pleasure for me. The man and his wife attended St. Benedictine's. He was more than happy to share information about the place. Then he said something disturbing to me. He mentioned the great pipe organ was now in place, and the talented craftsman who made it was gone.

My morning which started out so precious and jewel tone was now muddy and gray. I had wasted my trip. I left Gustav unattended. Certainly, this was a prophetic glance at what was to come upon my return home. I feared Gustav had been discovered. But it was worse than that, he was probably dead and stinking.

I decided that I must see the man's work, though:

I could drown in self-pity as I looked upon the shimmering pipes. Then, I would be ready to go home and witness my fate.

The streets of Hamburg were alive with activity as Grimm made his way to St. Benedictine's. Children played in the crisp air. Grimm enjoyed the scenes that played before him as he crossed street after street. Nearly everyone nodded and wished him a good day.

Soon, the carver reached St. Benedictine's. At first, he was overwhelmed by the sprawling cathedral that reached for heaven. But upon closer inspection, Grimm noticed the state of disrepair the building was in. He tried to envision what the place looked like just after completion, but he remembered that the capacity to dream was beyond him.

St. Benedictine's became a reminder of his quest, an agent of despair. Grimm climbed the stairs and pulled the heavy oak door open. He was consumed in darkness as the doors of the church closed behind him. Inside, his dilated pupils made him blind. After a few moments, he began to see the cathedral's heart. Inside the basilica, Grimm viewed once glorious artwork that had been neglected for years. The craftsmanship was exquisite. The atrium, as he passed through, was dark yet he could see traces of fine woodwork.

St. Benedictine's was smaller than many cathedrals, and Grimm doubted any true relic of the saint was on the premises. When this church was built, people were desperate for any shard of hope. Someone probably found a swatch of dirty cloth and claimed it belonged to Saint Benedict of Nursia, perhaps it was a handful of dirt from the Holy Grotto. It did not matter what relic rested below, all that mattered was the fact the people found something to renew their faith. Grimm wished he could find something here to renew his faith, but he feared it would not be today.

Slowly, Grimm made his way through the narthex and down the nave. It was at this point he first saw the glamourous brass pipes reaching for the sky. Grimm was unfamiliar with most religious practices and was unsure of the importance of music in local worship. Then he really did not care at all. He was not here to give God any prostration or sacrifice. He was not here to even mutter his name. As Grimm walked closer, he saw the instrument become clearer.

"May I help you?"

Grimm heard a voice and turned to see who addressed him. The man Grimm perceived as the church's patriarch had come forth from the shadows.

"Welcome to our house of worship." He repeated.

"Thank you." Grimm replied.

"May I help you with something?"

"Yes, as a matter of fact, I think you can." Grimm moved closer to the old man. The shadows erratically separated his face, "I've come from a long way to see your new pipe organ. I have heard it is a wonder to see."

The old man's face wrinkled into a smile, "Indeed it is. It is a source of pride for us all. The organ is helping bring the people back into the church."

Grimm glanced over his shoulder at the organ, "May I get closer to it?"

"Yes, yes by all means."

The patriarch accompanied Grimm to the apse which was much smaller now that the instrument had been completed. Stray sunlight filtered down through breaks in the clouds, slicing in colorful arcs past the stained-glass biblical scenes. These rays glinted off the tubes of shined brass.

Grimm felt as if he were in the presence of God himself. If this was not God then it was his voice. The carver's touch slid along the keyboard. Inside himself, electrical flashes re-ignited the passion of owning dreams.

"Of course, it is unusable right now."

Grimm really didn't hear the comment. "I'm sorry, I did not understand your question."

"This great piece of work is unusable right now. The steam has not been connected."

Grimm's hopes, once tattered, now lived again. "You mean it is flawed?"

"No, sir." The patriarch proudly smiled.

"I don't understand," Grimm stated.

"Everything you see is complete. The pipes have all been tested and sound wonderful. The steam engine has to be completely installed, however."

Grimm could barely contain his pleasure, "Does that mean the creator of this fabulous machine is still here?"

"Mr. Julian Keefe," the old man said, "yes, he is still in Hamburg."

Those were the words Grimm wanted to hear. "Is he in the cathedral, right now?"

"No. He is presently in town searching for something, I am not sure what, to cut down on the flow of steam into one of the pipes. I don't understand the young man well, but he is talented. He is far more talented than his father."

"His father?"

"Yes, Angus Keefe. He also makes such beautiful musical instruments. His brass work is sought after by the great symphonies of Europe. 'Used to be' is what I should say." The patriarch smiled. "You know, sir, I do not know your name. I am Father Gunther Schnell."

"Father, forgive me. I didn't recognize you without a collar on."

"It is understandable. I have been doing some extra work around here. We are going to unveil this masterpiece at Sunday Mass. That is why Mr. Keefe is in a rush to finish. He ran into some last-minute problems, and it put him behind schedule. I understand he was on his way back home to the Isles when the unexpected came about."

Grimm realized he had not revealed his identity. "I'm sorry, I am Edward Grimm. I am an artist, a wood carver. I create works for kings, aristocrats, and American presidents. I am surprised you have not heard of me. I have done much work for the churches as well. I have sought out Mr. Keefe for a project I am working on."

"Is that so?"

"Yes. Do you know when he will be back?" Grimm asked.

"I'm not sure, but it should not be long." The priest was cordial, "Why don't you come back later on in the day. I'm sure he will be here. All of his belongings are here."

"They are?"

"He stayed here at the church while working on this gorgeous instrument." The holy man gestured with a withered hand.

Grimm's eyes were led by the movement back to the pipe organ. He went to touch it, feel the molecules vibrating beneath his fingers. The metal was cool to the touch, but an aura of steam spread from where Grimm's fingers rested.

"This is indeed a beautiful instrument." Grimm smiled.

"Well, Herr Grimm, I must be on my way. I have other duties." Father Schnell said. "I look forward to seeing you later. Until then, I bid you good-bye."

Grimm returned the courtesies. "I appreciate your time and help. I will come back later to see Mr. Keefe."

The patriarch bowed and quietly made his way toward the atrium. Grimm watched him carefully. As soon as he was alone, he scanned the chapels for activity. He was unsure if they were occupied. Grimm so wanted to explore this Basilica and find Julian Keefe's belongings. A man could learn a great deal about another by examining his possessions.

The urge passed soon enough. Grimm looked once more upon the organ. He touched it again, stroking the black and white keys. The organ was so sensuous to Grimm. He could feel the pulsation of elements making up the brass. Soon, very soon, the instrument would sing only for him. And his newly acquired dreams, too.

Never was a day so long. What a ridiculous journey that I must endure. All my dreams were just a breath away, but my vision stood incomplete. God found a way to deny me what was owed to me. I did not have the skills to complete the calliope.
I could have let that urge pass. After all, the carousel would be exquisite in its own right.

I had to consider what the difference was between a vision and a dream. I had no dreams. I was unable to dream. My father ripped that from me, and God rubbed it in my face consistently. But a vision: I had those. Visions did not require imagination just perseverance. And I was not going to give up. I had the vision on how to beat God. I would realize that no matter what.

Hamburg did not have enough interests to keep Grimm's mind from anticipating his first meeting with Julian Keefe. Although he wandered the city and admired its sights, the eye of his mind was focused on this encounter. He reviewed each shred of information the priest had given. From this, Grimm attempted to piece together an image of Keefe.

What would he be like? Talented yes, but what of his disposition? Would he even be interested in Grimm's offer? Grimm solemnly thought of this possibility.

He had circled the block St. Benedictine's rested upon several times. It was as if he expected someone to rush out and proclaim the man had returned. He chastised himself mentally each time he passed the steps. But he could not stop this action.

Finally, Grimm had the nerve to go back inside the basilica. It had been a few hours, surely Keefe had returned by now. Slowly, he climbed the stairs. Each one seemed to be made of caramel, or worse, molten iron.

As Grimm reached the door, he heard the sound of metal being hammered upon. Panic shot through his heart as his imagination created horrendous scenarios. The worst thought was the pipe organ was being disassembled.

Swiftly, Grimm crossed the atrium, passed through the nave, and paused at the cancelli. He could still hear the banging, but the source could not be located. Then, as Grimm zeroed in on the sound, he saw a pair of legs protruding from beneath the pipe organ. They were encased in dirty work pants, and worn leather shoes bound his feet.

Grimm knew this had to be Julian Keefe, it could be no other man. At last, the banging stopped. The man started to slide from the narrow opening. He was slim, but as Grimm watched the man slowly emerge, his strength was evident. Confident hands reached out from below, looking for the edge of the pipe organ base. As they gripped around the base, he moved further outward. Now, Grimm could see the man's thick torso, narrow at the waist and wide in the shoulders.

Finally, his head emerged.

"Hello." he said to Grimm while wiping dirt on his red cotton shirt. "I didn't know anyone was standing there."

Grimm looked at his face, it was fair with a broad smile framed in shadowy stubble. Julian's hair was dark like Elena's. He stood several inches over Grimm, also.

The familiar feelings of jealousy came to Grimm. Suddenly, he was reminded of Sennett even though these two men were barely similar, only the fact he felt diminished by the mere presence of both men.

"Hello." Grimm replied.

"You wouldn't happen to be that Grimm fellow, would you?" Keefe said. "Good you speak English because I don't know any German."

Grimm could hear the accent in Julian's smooth voice, but

could not place it as Irish. He only knew it originated somewhere in in the British Isles and was typical of someone who traveled quite extensively.

"Yes, I am." Grimm said. "My father insisted that both my brother and I learn English. He said it would make good men of us." In Grimm's mind, that scenario only happened to his brother as he watched on—ignored.

Julian extended his hand. "The priest told me someone came looking for me."

Grimm found Julian's grip warm and friendly against his own cold hand. "Yes, I've heard a great deal about your work." Grimm removed his hand from Julian's and gestured to the pipe organ. "If this is typical of your work, then I am in the presence of a master."

Julian's boyish face flushed red. "Oh, go on with ya. But thanks for saying so. I try to do a good job."

"That you do."

Keefe's eyes narrowed as he looked at Grimm with slight suspicion. "Is there a particular reason you came to see me. From what the priest said, you came quite a long way to find me."

Grimm affirmed his statement, "Yes, that I have." The carver paused to carefully select his next words. Only the proper phrase would hook this fish. "Like you, I am an artist. I am a carver."

"What do you carve?" Julian asked.

"Just about anything anyone wants, but wood primarily. I love to work in wood. The feel is so natural, not like stone or clay. It is far too cold." Grimm's brain fished for words, "I usually carve for kings, queens, and churches, much like this one here."

"Well, this is the first church I've done." Keefe warmly smiled.

"Really?" Grimm looked at his young face. "Yes, I thought you were quite young to be so accomplished."

"I suppose it runs in the family. My father used to be a tinsmith, that is what I started out as. He made musical instruments on the side, eventually he made a pipe organ for a local church."

"And he taught you."

"That's right." Keefe seemed to be enjoying the conversation. "I haven't got to talk a lot around this place. Everyone is so damned quiet. Sorry about the language. I believe in God, but I don't think I'll go to hell for using a word."

Grimm listened to this young man talk. Julian Keefe was brash and impulsive, a man that was very hard to read. Grimm felt uneasiness fill him. He found himself at a disadvantage with people like this. They were capable of eluding Grimm's cognitive process. People who lived with passion disturbed Grimm. Julian Keefe disturbed Grimm immensely.

"That is very interesting." Grimm said. "You had started to say this is the first church you've worked in. How many instruments have you made altogether?"

Keefe thought momentarily. "Counting this one?"

"Yes."

"I've made four of them." Keefe said modestly.

"There's no need to be shy about your work, be proud about your work." Grimm said.

"You misunderstand me, sir." Keefe corrected Grimm. "I am proud of my work, damn proud. But I also know the value of humility. Boasting is for those who aren't good at what they do. Those who love what they do know it, and do not need the words of others to convince them otherwise."

Grimm understood the intensity of Keefe's words. As the young man passionately spoke, the accent of his Irish homeland peppered his inflections. At this point, Grimm was unsure if Keefe was insulted.

"I am sorry, I didn't mean to offend you." Grimm said.

"It's all right." Julian calmed down. "Those are my father's words."

"He is very wise."

"Aye, that he is." Julian's eyes sparkled with love when he spoke of his father. "That Angus, yes. A wise old ass, he is."

Inside, Grimm sneered at Julian, but outside he wore a false smile. This man had one virtue that made him uneasy: passion. Now, another, fouler trait joined in fueling Grimm's contempt. A son who loved his father, a father who loved his son, Grimm was repulsed. He could never entertain pleasant thoughts of his father. The only thing that came to Grimm's mind when thinking of his father was the well.

"You must have loved him a great deal," Grimm said.

Surprise crossed Julian Keefe's face. "I still do. The old man wouldn't die if God himself came and took him by the arm."

"You say you've made four pipe organs?" Grimm reminded Keefe. "Where at?"

Keefe looked at the pipe organ like a lover, "This one is the first I've made that hasn't been in England. The other three are organs in theaters. One is in Palace Hall in Maidstone, have you heard of it?"

"No, I'm afraid I haven't."

"You never said how you heard of me," Keefe asked.

Grimm saw the element of suspicion in Julian's eyes again. It was the only trait Grimm enjoyed thus far.

"I carved a carousel horse for a king. His men told me about you."

"King Leopold, yes." Recognition showed in Keefe's eyes. "I have been approached by him. I haven't decided if I can work for him or not. I want to go home. I haven't been home in months because of this project."

"My ambition isn't as grandiose as King Leopold's." Grimm said. He moved away from Julian and went to the keyboard of the pipe organ. "I need a steam calliope constructed for a carousel."

Julian wasn't sure if he heard the man correctly. "A calliope, a steam calliope?"

Grimm turned to face Julian. "I know it sounds absurd." He raised a hand and touched the shining brass, "It's the greatest project of my life."

"Somebody must be paying you a pretty pound to make that," Keefe commented.

"Yes, I am being paid well for it." Grimm smiled at his clever statement. If Keefe only knew the true cost of the carousel, he would rethink his theology.

"Who is buying it from you?"

"It is not important. All I need to know is if you would be able to come to my workshop and fashion the calliope."

Keefe did not immediately answer. Grimm looked at the young man's face, he was weighing the idea. Grimm feared he would turn down the offer. He made it perfectly clear earlier how he felt about going home. His father was very important to Keefe, Grimm hated that trait, too.

At last, Keefe reacted. "I am honored that you came all this way to see me, but I really must return home. My father is getting old. I want to spend as much time with him as possible before he passes on."

The words were sharper than any knife. Grimm felt the wound go deep in his heart. "I sympathize with your decision, but you don't seem to understand my situation." Grimm attempted to woo him, "It is the most magnificent piece of art you have ever seen. The calliope would be your contribution to history."

"As I said before, I am flattered…"

Grimm cut him off, "If the promise of historical immortality does not entice you, perhaps this would."

Grimm reached into his jacket and produced a bag full of gold coins. He handed them to Keefe. "Here, take this."

Julian opened the sack and pulled out one coin. "There's a lot of money in here, sir."

"Of course," Grimm replied.

"To have this much, the calliope must be important to you." Keefe returned the coin to the sack and pulled the drawstring closed.

The look of contemplation once again came to Keefe's face. He was torn. This was more money than he'd ever seen, Grimm knew it. Keefe is just a young man. No matter how old and mature Keefe tried to act, his passion gave away all claims to rational adult thought. Money could steer a young man's heart, but Grimm feared it would not be enough to buy Keefe's loyalty. Grimm was too close to let him slide away so easily.

"Consider this a down payment for your services. You'll never work again." Grimm sweetened the offer. "You can buy a house, live in luxury."

The new proposal confused Keefe even further. "I don't know. I have to think about it. I'm not one for luxury, and I do love what I do."

"You could give your family everything they've ever desired. You could even go to America."

"America?" The word inspired Keefe's thoughts.

He'd heard tales of America. Many of his family had gone to America in search of a better life. From the letters written home, some had found it. Some had not been heard from again.

Keefe felt the weight of the gold in his hand. It was so much. This was more money than he'd ever thought existed. Only kings and nobles had this kind of wealth. And this was only a down payment, Grimm said. How much more could there be? One thing was clear to Keefe: this could only be his if he went to Grimm's workshop.

"I still don't know."

Grimm felt Keefe slipping away. "Then, may I have my gold back."

He hoped the absence of gold in Keefe's hands would spark greed in the young man. Everyone had greed, the only variable was the degree of the sensation.

As Grimm wished, the money had started a chain reaction in Keefe. "Well, sir…"

Grimm immediately shoved the sack into Keefe's hands, "Feel it, son. It's all yours."

Keefe reacted by pushing it away, "I can't be sure. I don't know how right it is."

"What's right?" Grimm didn't understand him. "All I am doing is hiring you to build a calliope. I only hire the best, and you are the best."

"I haven't been home in so long. I have a girlfriend back there, not just my father."

"With this much money you can marry her, and never be hungry. No one in your family would ever go without." Grimm could feel Keefe taking the bait.

At last, Keefe struck. "All right. I'll do it. It's against my better judgment, but I will do it."

"Excellent." Grimm was pleased. "You won't regret any of it."

"I warn you here and now if I have to leave to go home I will," Keefe strongly stated. "Another thing, I've never built anything as unique as a calliope. What I do is what you pay for."

"Agreed," Grimm said. "I can expect no less of you, I suppose."

"I'll need a few days to make arrangements."

"If you would like to ride with me back to my workshop, I plan on leaving in the morning," Grimm said.

Keefe thought about the offer but declined. "I need some time to myself. I still have a few adjustments to make here before I'm ready."

Grimm could see he had pushed to Keefe's limits for today. "Very well. I will drop by here tomorrow morning and leave instructions to my house. Any driver can get you there."

"Well, I guess I'll see you when I get there," Keefe smiled.

"Yes," Grimm echoed.

I returned to the inn, wondering if my own greed hadn't taken me too far. What if this man was nothing but dandelion fluff, incapable of any thoughts except those of his family? I had no patience for his values, I found them stupid and unimportant. Any man who loved a father that deeply disturbed me. Which brought me around to thoughts of Gustav again. I worried a great deal the entire trip. Once, I even entertained the thought that it was paternal concern. This soon passed as I found the notion quite distasteful.

I was very apprehensive of Julian Keefe. He was not at all what I expected. But then again, I had no expectations in the first place. All I was interested in was his talent. I never thought that the bearer of that ability would be so young, so opinionated, and so innocent.

As I stopped by St. Benedictine's for the last time, I tipped my hat to the cross. I felt it was only fitting that I was getting everything I had wanted. Slowly, I was realizing that desires and dreams were sisters.

After delivering instructions to Keefe, I found a driver and carriage to take me home. I wisely kept enough money from Keefe to pay for my return trip. This time, the journey was much more difficult. The wound in my leg had started to heal well enough, but I feared infection had set in. The joint stiffened in my knee, and walking was impeded by a limp.

The weather was also disagreeable. At one point, we lost a day because of heavy snows. But eventually, we made it home.

The journey was tedious, and it was good to be home.

The house seemed different to Grimm as the carriage driver pulled up. The ground was still frozen, and ice coated the trees, but something was not right. Grimm realized it as soon as he looked at the chimney. Smoke from a stout fire billowed freely in the cold air.

His first thought was someone had taken refuge from the winter. All around him, Grimm saw evidence that a major storm had blown through the region. Perhaps, a band of thieves moved in to occupy his home and would kill the carver upon entry. He didn't care, someone could be in the workshop. Someone may have discovered Gustav.

Grimm stepped from the carriage cab. "Please bring my things to the house."

"Very good, sir," the driver said.

Grimm walked carefully toward the door. The entire area was slick and shiny with a coating of ice. Every footfall emitted a crunch. Grimm didn't care if anyone was in the house. All he cared about was if someone went into the workshop. That was forbidden. To him, the workshop was a church, and the carousel an altar. He picked up the pace.

Grimm paused before going in. He looked back at the carriage. The driver was taking the luggage off the top. Surely, if anyone killed Grimm, the driver would be able to escape for help. That would be even worse, he thought. If Grimm died, the driver would return with the law. The carousel would be discovered; all his dreams would fall to ashes. It would be better if everyone died, then no one would come.

He looked back at the door. Grimm focused on the new door which was replaced after the beast's attack. If he could face that danger, common thieves would be nothing but a nuisance. Taking a breath to engorge his courage, Grimm opened the door.

The sight was very different than expected. Although Grimm had been an adequate housekeeper, the dwelling looked especially clean. The house had been left in shambles. Grimm barely had the strength to gather himself together for the trip to Hamburg, much less clean house.

Then, he looked over to the fireplace hearth. She sat in a chair and was mending the torn curtains. Grimm never expected Elena to live so contentedly in his house.

"It's you," Grimm said with disbelief. "What are you doing here?"

"I am your wife, aren't I?" was all she said.

He noticed a difference in her. Elena appeared defeated. She had traded in her beautifully feminine dresses for diffused, dark hued clothing.

"I mean, I didn't expect you here, not yet at least."

She set her sewing aside and stood. "What happened in this place? I come into my husband's home and find it in shambles.

The door can't even keep the cold out."

"Nothing happened," Grimm said. "When did you get here? How long have you been here?"

"So many questions from a man who wanted me here so desperately," Elena said while moving past Grimm on her way to the small kitchen. "I've been here three days."

"Three days," he echoed.

She filled a tea ball and fetched a cup. "I am your wife, and this is where I live."

Grimm was unsure of her feelings. She seemed so different than the wild vixen of the Rom. Elena's attitude was like her clothing, subdued and subtle. Even though the fire in her soul seemed extinguished, Grimm could sense a smoldering cinder deep inside.

"So, you've accepted it," Grimm said.

She poured water into her cup and floated the tea ball liberally. "I did not say I have accepted it. I only said I am living in my husband's home. This is where I'll live until he dies, or I die." She turned to him with the cup of steeping tea, "Here, I've made you some tea, husband."

Grimm cautiously took the cup from her. Elena's green eyes watched with anticipation as he raised the tea to his lips. Grimm smelled the tea, then cautiously he sipped.

He found the tea refreshing, "I thought I would struggle to get you here."

A knock sounded on the door, and the driver poked his head in. "Where do you want these things?"

"Just put them by the fireplace." Grimm instructed.

The driver ignored Elena and Grimm, but Elena did not ignore him. He struggled with Grimm's luggage, and Elena took it as a sign that the driver verged on exhaustion.

She shot Grimm a vindictive look, then went to the driver. "Sir, you look very tired. Those bags must be heavy."

The driver was surprised at her forwardness. "Yes, they are a bit of a burden."

"Please, let me help you." Elena purposely brushed up against the man as she reached for a bag.

Jealousy erupted inside Grimm, but he controlled the explosion. "That will be all," he said to the man.

The startled driver was responding to Elena's lingering presence. "Yes, sir."

Elena looked at her husband, but addressed the driver, "Thank you very much." She pulled the bag slowly from the man.

Grimm took the last few coins from his pocket, and swiftly went to the driver. "Thank you very much for your help. If I ever need a carriage again, I will not hesitate to seek you out." He shoved the money in the man's empty hand.

Elena smiled as she turned away from the men. She went to the fireplace and listened to the pleasantries being spoken. Soon, the man left.

Grimm said nothing for several moments. Within his soul, the jealous dormant seed came alive. The thought of a mere cab man thinking of his wife in a sexual way. But, he reasoned, she brought it on. She taunted Grimm by flirting with the man, wielding the powerful sword of human jealousy.

After letting his rage subside to common anger, Grimm went to Elena. She stood with her back to him. Looking down, her eyes focused on the licking flames.

"What are you looking at, my lovely?" he said sarcastically.

"I'm looking at your face, burning in hell," Elena said pleasantly. There was no anger in her voice, but her message was clear.

It was as if Grimm had been sliced with a blade made of candy. Elena had such venom for him; she was not shy about letting her feelings known.

He sighed sorrowfully. "I regret that you hurt. I know that right now you do not love me."

"At last, you speak the truth."

"But," he continued, "in time, you will grow to love me."

"There isn't a clock that will run that long," Elena said.

As he reached to touch her small shoulders, Elena grew rigid. "I can give you everything you need. I can give you a home, money, a child."

Elena turned to face Grimm. Her eyes were blazing angrily. The words caused her hate to deepen.

"Look at me," she said. "Look at me long and well. I despise you. The thought of having your child sickens me. I would kill it at birth, just to deny you a child. You will never know what it would be like to have a wife that loves you. Or children. You stole my life from me, so I shall return the favor in the brightness of day and the deep dark of the night."

Grimm's mouth fell open. Genuine surprise reflected in his eyes. All his life, as he understood it, women lived to have children. It was their destiny, their one want in the world. How could a mother think of murder?

"Oh, do I surprise you?" Her smile unfolded like the razor he first saw in the wagon of the caravan. "Your fate is me, and I am a terrible fate."

"I thought that…" Grimm found himself wordless.

"You thought I would just move in, see the light, and fall on my back with my legs spread wide for you?" Her laughter was a stabbing dagger.

He wanted to strike her, but he was immobile. Grimm had never heard words like this come from a woman. He thought it was impossible for a woman to speak with such foul depravity. "Insolence. You will change your mind. I will make sure of it. I know your type all too well."

"You don't know me at all." The razor closed.

Then, Grimm found his voice as many questions suddenly blossomed. "If you feel this way, why did you come here? Why didn't you put up a greater struggle? Surely, a princess like you is not without influence."

She had no immediate answer for him. Elena turned away. "You cannot know about loyalty and tradition, you are *Gadje*."

"What do you mean?" he asked.

"It is forbidden to go against the chieftain, much less my father. His word is law. By tradition, I am your wife." There was defeat in Elena's voice.

Her words pleased Grimm, "Then you have accepted it."

"I accept nothing, as I have said. I am here out of tradition to my father, and chieftain. We shall see how long it lasts, and if either one of us survives."

Grimm moved close to her, intimately close. Elena did not react, she waited to see what the carver's true intentions were. As he raised his arms to embrace her, Elena pulled away.

"I am here out of obligation, don't press me."

Grimm was getting angry with her, "You are my wife."

"I am nothing more than property. I am not your lover." She managed to slip away.

Grimm followed her, "Where are you going?"

Elena moved through the house, "I love my new living space, husband." She went to the workshop door and paused while grabbing the knob. "I especially like where my husband works."

"Have you been in here?" Grimm referred to the room just beyond the door.

"Why yes, my husband's work is very important to me." Elena twisted the knob.

Grimm was overcome with dread, "What have you seen in there?"

She said nothing to Grimm and opened the door. He followed as Elena crossed the room's threshold. She walked confidently, almost defiantly, through his territory. Elena knew this was the most important room to her husband, like a tiger's hunting grounds, no trespassers would be tolerated.

But, to his wife, the one creature he bartered for, was this the truth? Elena walked to the carousel, pausing to catch Grimm's worried expression, and then stepped onto the platform.

His eyes danced around the carousel. Grimm took a visual inventory of the workshop, the women, and most important was the statue of Gustav wrapped and bound in canvas. He sighed with relief. The canvas seemed untouched.

"I did not know how talented you are, husband." She flirted through the characters sealed in wood. "They are so lifelike."

Elena's complements fueled Grimm's anxiety. The carver fought off panic as her words echoed around his skull. Had she somehow discovered the secret of the carousel? After all, she is a blood relative of the *Phuri Dai*, and the old woman could have revealed his secret. If she did know anything, Grimm thought, she would never say.

This kind of information would be the greatest weapon Elena could ever hope for. Perhaps, she had uncovered Gustav, and rewrapped him before Grimm's return. Grimm decided to wait and see, she would reveal herself soon enough.

"Tell me," Elena paused by the bear, and stroked the finely detailed claws, "Do you plan on painting this carousel? The pieces look so naked."

Although Grimm had never thought about the prospect of painting the individual characters, it took no measurement of time to decide on the issue. "I would never paint them. It would detract from the beauty of the grain. I think the grain is more attractive than any paint."

She seemed confused, "I've never seen an unpainted carousel. All I have ever seen are bright green dragons, majestic horses, colorful sleighs to ride in. Has someone specifically requested this particular carousel? They must be unusual to desire no color at all." Grimm did not answer her.

"Another thing, shouldn't there be a place to sit down on a carousel? There are no animals with saddles, no seats, swings?"

"Perhaps, it isn't a carousel for physical pleasures."

Elena paused to digest his words, then laughed. "My husband the poet. You are full of little surprises, aren't you? I have another question, what is that one." She pointed at Gustav's covered likeness.

Nervously, he answered. "That one had some jointing problems. I used a special glue on it. The canvas promotes a better seal. I would like you to come down from there now."

Elena attentions turned from Gustav; she went to one of the women, the one with no hands. "I have been meaning to ask you, why does this woman have no hands?"

"I've asked you to come down from there." His tone was insistent.

Elena realized she had pushed him to the limit and elected to dismount. Grimm's eyes never left her. He read her actions, her breathing, the way her head tipped. He waited for her reactions to betray what she knew.

"I will tell you this, right now." Grimm approached her. "This is my place of work. This is where the money is made for you to have everything you've ever wanted. It is also forbidden to you. I do not want you to come in here anymore unless I ask you to."

Contempt rose in Elena's eyes. "I do nothing for your pleasure."

"It is not for my pleasure, my lovely." Grimm said. "The workshop can be a dangerous place, and I do not wish anything to befall you."

She turned away from his gaze, "What happens if I disobey you? Will you send me back to the troupe? Turn me out? Return me to the arms of my lover?" Elena glanced over her shoulder, hoping to see an instant of pain on Grimm's face.

Grimm changed the subject, "I would like you to prepare the guest room."

"Are we having visitors?"

"Yes. A gentleman by the name of Julian Keefe will by staying with us for about a month. He is going to make a calliope for the carousel."

"How fascinating." Elena took a last look at the carousel, "You have never said who this carousel is for."

"As of now, there is no buyer."

Elena turned to him, a look of utter disbelief upon her face. "Is this the way you do business?"

"I know what I am doing. I will not be questioned by a

woman. Now, go prepare the guest room as I have asked."

Elena hesitated, but then left the room without further dialog. Grimm sighed. His temper had been pushed to the extreme by Elena. He questioned his decision to claim her as his wife. Then, he thought of her rapier-sharp eyes, the mesmerizing hair, and her extraordinary beauty. She may prove to be the most expensive prize in his possession, Grimm thought.

Moments after Elena left the room, Grimm started to assess the workshop. He wanted to know what she had touched, and what she knew. Did the fog visit while he was away? If any creatures came, was Elena able to see them?

Grimm went to the work settee. Beneath the bench, Grimm located an inconspicuous lump of cloth. He pulled it out and examined it carefully. It, too, had been untouched. As he began to unravel the cloth, the stench of rotting flesh burned his nose. Slowly, the woman's severed hands were revealed.

Grimm experienced relief. Then, he realized these hands were unsafe so close to Elena's curious eyes. Although he ordered her to stay away from the workshop, Grimm knew she would come in here whenever the chance presented itself.

He quickly rewrapped the hands and went to the outside door. Grimm left the workshop, trudging through the crunchy snow. He deliberately went around the backside of the house to avoid the front windows. Grimm did not want Elena seeing him.

He went near the edge of the woodpile, and quickly dug a small hole in the snow. Soon, Grimm was satisfied with its depth, and he placed the package inside.

"This will do until I have more time to take care of them properly." Grimm filled the hole in with snow, and rapidly made his way back to the workshop's outside door.

On his return trip, Grimm noticed how warm it seemed outside. He was sure it was warmer than when he came home but couldn't be sure. In any case, the warm air moving over the snow gave rise to a thin fog.

Dismissing the sensation, Grimm returned to the warm

workshop. He shut the door and paused to gather his thoughts. Even though the carver relied on the dream figures for the bulk of the carousel's images, there was work to be done that no dream could complete.

Sighing, Grimm moved to the carousel. He looked skyward into the canopy. The skeleton was nearly finished. Only a few more spines had to be installed, then the entire merry-go-round would be ready for the colorful canvas top. Grimm was pleased with how far things had progressed.

He remembered the confrontation of moments past. Elena chastised him, claiming he was crazy for building a carousel no one had bought yet. Sheer lunacy, she suggested. Grimm laughed at the memory. She knew nothing of the matter. It would be more than Elena could grasp, Grimm thought. She was only a wife, secondary to the man. Elena had her place, and Grimm would make that clear to her soon enough.

Grimm's thoughts returned to the heat. The workshop seemed warmer than usual. Grimm noticed the haziness from outside had manifested inside now. Then, he realized the lacy fog was beginning to fall.

"No, not now," Grimm pleaded.

He feared Elena would come into the workshop if any strange noises were heard. But the fog's web-like threads were falling all around the workshop. Grimm was unable to stop the process.

In a matter of seconds, the fog was all around him. Grimm could feel its sticky fingers lingering, but something seemed different. The haze was distinctly peaceful, quite different than the frantic energy of previous visitations. Grimm hesitated. He looked around the room. Perhaps his prayers had been answered. There would be no strange creatures coming, and Elena would not discover his secret.

Then, he thought perhaps something was wrong with Gustav. Had the boy lost his ability to dream? Did the figures abandon him for a dreamer they could visit? The intrusive fear was unacceptable to Grimm. He was not ready to trade the dreams for Elena.

Slowly, Grimm began to back away from the carousel. Something was going on, but he could not figure what it was. Grimm retreated cautiously. His eyes danced around the room, attempting to sense any changes in its environment. Grimm was left empty.

As Grimm backed deeper into the workshop, something stopped him. His body came in contact with an immense form. It was warm, and pulses of hot breath raged upon his neck and head. Fear seized Grimm in a contracting fist. The fog swirled all around and seemed to concentrate behind Grimm.

He wanted to turn; he wanted to be face-to-face with the dream. But he was without the potion, and would be no match for its fangs, claws, or weapons. Suddenly, a sense of limited mortality infected the carver. For the first time, Grimm felt death behind him.

"Why don't you kill me? Take my head off," Grimm whispered.

There was no reaction to his words, no blades sliced through his neck, no claws impaled him, and no teeth crushed his skull. Grimm felt he had no recourse, but to turn and face the beast. He could feel sweat from the beast's warm skin pressed onto his back. He began to turn.

Surprise met Grimm's eyes. Instead of some wild and wicked behemoth, the carver stood before a large black horse. He raised his eyes to meet the gaze of the stallion. Its eyes burned red, but there was no anger, no violence in them. The creature was quite content to stand stoically.

Grimm looked the horse over, somehow the beast was familiar. The bridle, the colorful leather saddle, the flowers, all of these features were known to Grimm in the past. Grimm realized the horse was totally unaware of his presence. The stallion looked elsewhere; its eyes focused well beyond Grimm.

Grimm traced the racer's gaze, and revelation overtook him. "Zoltan."

Grimm inched slowly away from the horse. He did not want to spook the beast. At this point, no one was aware the horse was here. Silence was Grimm's ally. Unlike the other images, Zoltan proved to be peaceful.

Grimm's heart trembled, it quivered as if it would instantly stop. Zoltan was here, and alive. It was more than he could ever dream of if he had the ability to dream at all. A smile crossed his lips. Grimm did have the ability to dream. Gustav's dream power was now his to command as long as he was sly. A small laugh squeezed through Grimm's lips.

"Zoltan, is this what you look like alive?" Grimm's eyes drank in the stallion's calm beauty.

Grimm's mind raced. Every cell was searching for any memory of the potion. He had to have the horse on the carousel, and the magic liquid was the only way the task could be accomplished. Where was it? He could not remember. Had Elena found the vial? Then, he vaguely recalled storing it in the work bench.

Grimm's cautious pace increased. He gauged the horse's reactions, to establish what action to take. But the stallion did not move from its stoic vigil. His powerful black frame stood in a protective posture, watching over Gustav's prison.

Grimm reached the work bench. Soon, the memory became clear, and he located the vial. As he turned to see the horse again, something was different. The atmosphere was changing. The fog was beginning to break up.

"No." Grimm whispered vainly.

Zoltan had started fidget. The stallion anxiously shifted its weight from foot to foot. Grimm hastened to capture the beast. He uncapped the potion as he rushed forward. Zoltan reared violently upon it powerful rear legs. The muscles rippled, and detailed lines erupted. The horse remained silent. He made no noise of protest.

Grimm prepared to anoint Zoltan with the liquid, but the horse was no longer flesh and blood. As the fog dissipated, Zoltan also faded. His form became more vaporous.

"I said no." Grimm shook the valuable drops of potion at the vanishing steed.

However, there was nothing solid on which the potion could cling. Helplessly, Grimm watched the tonic trickle to the dirt floor. As the liquid disappeared into the soil like so many drops of rain, the last traces of Zoltan vanished.

"It can't be." Grimm fumed angrily at his loss.

He looked to the wrapped statue of Gustav, then back at the empty space where, moments before, the horse stood. Grimm recapped the liquid. He returned to the work bench. In his mind, Grimm recalled the events that had just transpired. Gustav must have returned from slumber. As the boy gained alertness, Zoltan must have retreated into the dream world.

Grimm spoke aloud as he pondered the solution. "That must be it. It must be."

He placed the vial on the work bench and started to dig through his miscellaneous tools. Grimm selected a pair of heavy shears and a small saw. Then, he walked to the carousel and mounted it.

Grimm walked along the platform until he was in front of the boy's enshrouded statue. "Now, to see how you have weathered in my absence."

Starting near the feet, Grimm cut the heavy, wax laden cloth with the shears. When he came to a spot that resisted the scissors, Grimm used the small saw to make progress. Slowly, the figure of Gustav was revealed. First the ankles and feet were imparted, followed by the knees, thighs, and abdomen. Grimm was pleased to find the wood in the same condition as before. Then, just as Grimm freed Gustav's chest area, he heard Elena's voice from behind.

"I thought I heard something in here." Her voice expressed curiosity.

Grimm turned to her, "How long have you been standing there?"

"Not long," Elena said. "I thought I heard some strange noises."

"What kind of noises?" he asked with concern.

"I'm not sure," she replied.

Grimm then realized she had entered the workshop without permission. Her trespasses enraged him. "I told you to never come in here, never." He searched Elena's face, attempting to detect any nuance that would betray what knowledge she held. She was too skilled in deception, however. "Have you prepared the room for our guest?"

"I'll see that it is done in enough time," Elena said.

"See to it now," Grimm snapped.

Elena remained silent only for a moment. "You have a way with women." She refused to be belittled by Grimm and knew the way to cut him down. "So does Sennett."

Grimm could not think of a reply. The man's name was an ax. Although the carver attempted to deny Elena's words, he knew they were true. Sennett gave Elena what Grimm could never bestow. The revelation sliced deeply into Grimm.

"Please, leave this room," Grimm said in defeated whispers.

Without further words, Elena left him on the carousel. He watched as she disappeared into the main part of the house. Grimm collapsed around the feet of Gustav. He reached out and caressed the wood. The grain was cool to the touch.

"One thing I know is that you are mine."

Grimm rose to his feet, and slowly pulled away the remainder of the covering. Gustav was intact and untouched. None of the dream creatures had gotten through, and that made the carver content.

Grimm reflected upon the image of Zoltan. The horse showed him how far away the dreams really were. Over the past months, Grimm grew more confident with every image he captured. But when the horse appeared, Grimm realized how powerless he was. Gustav decided what visions came, and Grimm had to deal with them. The entire sphere Grimm had constructed, the illusion of power collapsed.

What had begun as the greatest triumph of my life, fell apart in an instant. But my hopes could not be shattered that easily. I took the hit hard, and depression almost captured me.

I would not give up that easily. I had to divide my attention in different directions now. Elena was proving to be a greater challenge than I ever imagined. Breaking her would be delicious, I savored the thought like a rare vintage. She would be the wife I wanted and give to me everything I desire. As for Gustav, I still had him, and it would always be that way.

The snow had frozen the flesh of the woman's hands. It was amazing what the cold could do. I located the hidden hands and took them secretly down to the river. There, I tossed them far into the churning water. I watched as they sank from sight.

Elena did not suspect anything. She was busy preparing our home for our guest, and we expected him any day. I had received a letter from Keefe. It said he stopped at a town along the way that supplied the proper formulation of brass he needed for the calliope. He would be delayed a few days, but I didn't care when he arrived. I only wanted him to get the calliope finished.

Something was in the air on this day, and I expected Julian Keefe to be at my door by nightfall. I was wrong, he came much earlier. I was away, and Elena was home alone.

Elena tended a pot on the stove. Although she despised Grimm, some of her duties as a wife were a welcome change from the constant motion of the Rom. She liked it when her husband was away. Elena dreamed as she stirred the gruel on the stove. Her mind wandered far from the house of Grimm, and to the forest where she made love with Sennett.

She fantasized that he would come to the door. His boots would be soaked from the snow and cold. She would bring him in from the elements and warm him by the fire. Elena fantasized that she would slowly take his boots off, then rub Sennett's cold feet. Her hand would wander up his legs, until it rested upon his groin. There, she would find Sennett's interest peaking.

Suddenly, a knock at the door shattered Elena's dream world. Instead of being cautious, she hoped her dreams had somehow become reality. Elena raced to the door, praying Sennett would be just outside. But as she opened it, she was greeted by a stranger.

"Hello, is this the house of Edward Grimm?" His voice was smooth and resonant, and an accent peppered his inflections.

Elena looked upon his face: the confident eyes; the strong jaw line shadowed with at least four days growth; the pleasant smile on his lips. She thought about Sennett, and the man before her now. They were very similar in physical attributes.

Elena smiled and hoped the stranger did not catch her staring. "Hello, you must be Julian Keefe."

"That I am," he spoke.

"Please, come in." Elena stepped aside and watched him enter. She looked him over and paused as she saw his boots.

"It must have been a long journey. Are you cold?"

Julian looked around the small house. "Yes, I am cold. And yes, it was a long journey. I thought I would never find the place. Your husband didn't mention how deep in the woods he lived." Julian then turned to Elena. "Is there a place where I can put my bags?"

"Certainly. Why don't you just set them down over by the fire. It will give them a chance to dry out, and I can make you a cup of tea."

"Wonderful." Julian strode over the fireplace and put the luggage down. "I hope you don't mind, but I would really like to take off these wet boots."

"Please, feel free." Elena tasted the irony in the moment. "You will be staying with us for a while, please treat this as your home."

"I appreciate your graciousness."

Elena went to the stove and stirred the contents. "Are you hungry?"

"No, thank you, but the tea sounded good." He unlaced his huge leather boots and started to remove them. Elena was aware of every motion Julian made. Even though she did not look directly at Julian, no nuance went undetected. She prepared a cup of tea for her guest, then placed some more water on the stove. Gently, Elena floated the tea ball, and removed it.

"I expected you to have more things." She took the hot beverage to Keefe.

Julian removed his wool socks and placed them on the stones of the hearth. "These clothes are all that I own." He patted the bags that sat nearby.

She handed him the tea, "I meant in the way of tools and brass, for the calliope."

Keefe smiled. He was surprised at her knowledge of the project. "You're the first wife I've met that knew what her husband was working on. Usually, they just don't care, or the husbands will not tell them about it."

"That's very interesting." She focused her eyes on Julian's face as he sipped tea. She felt a tingle, deep inside, and it slowly began to spread. "How is the tea?"

"Just right," Keefe said.

"I had asked you about your tools and metal."

Keefe gulped down the tea in his mouth. "Oh, yes. I'm sorry. I had it shipped, and I'm expecting everything to be delivered in the next few days." He paused, then changed the subject. "So, where's your husband?"

"He left early this morning. He said he had some business to take care of."

"When do you expect him back?"

Elena looked at the cuckoo clock over the mantle, "Anytime, really."

As the conversation lapsed, they found their eyes had locked onto one another. The silence seemed to push the two forward, their gaze lingered. Elena felt the tingle, it spread like wildfire through her belly and pelvis.

Julian took note of Elena: she was so pleasant to look at, her hair was so black, and her face so sensual. In his head, Julian had to remind himself that this was another man's wife. Elena was off limits, but that did not erase the fact he found himself in a state of arousal.

He had to break eye contact before things went too far. "What do you know about this project?"

"Not much." Elena was frustrated as Julian glanced away. "Would you like to see what the calliope is for?"

"You mean the carousel, certainly." Keefe said.

"It's right this way, follow me."

Julian watched Elena as she turned. Her hair was like a shadow, hugging every curve of her body. He started to follow Elena, ignoring the warning signals sent by his own brain. He was intrigued by the carousel, and an opportunity to steal a glimpse was too good to let pass.

Something inside, however, told Julian that Elena was trouble, and to follow her would lead to despair. The urge to flee grew, but he was able to suppress it. Disregarding his own sensations of doom, Julian's hesitation was brief. He followed Elena into the workshop.

Although the room was dark, Julian could see the immense silhouette of the carousel. Elena went to light the lamps, and Julian cautiously approached the platform. He mounted the carousel, investigating the bog-headed cherubs nailed to the walls. Even though he knew these creatures were recently crafted, something about their look made Julian think of antiques. The wood grain was stained, and patches of shadows danced on their faces.

"These are just incredible." Julian said, unaware that Elena had also mounted the carousel.

"Yes," she startled Julian. "I'm sorry, I didn't mean to frighten you."

"Oh, you didn't. I just thought you were over there." Julian motioned to the stove.

"Maybe this will add enough light for you to see by. It's usually very bright in here with all the lamps lit, but I didn't think we needed them all." Elena handed him the small oil lamp.

Julian started to move on to the next shape, and Elena followed. She watched him in the flickering candlelight, the way he moved and adjusted to objects around him. The light illuminated Julian's face, and Elena made no attempt to conceal her analysis. For the first time since their meeting, she realized how handsome the stranger was. She watched his eyes focus on one of the women, they were so intense in their scrutiny. Elena hoped one day he would look upon her that way.

"What do you think?" Elena asked.

"As I said before, I've never seen anything like it. All these carvings look antique, and the detail is like none I've seen before."

"Yes, he is talented." Her voice fell.

Julian turned to her, "So, how long have you been married?"

Elena hesitated. She sensed an opportunity to manipulate Julian. "Not long." She purposely took a haggard breath. "Not long, at all."

Julian did not sense her trap and fell into the web. "Really, is something wrong?"

She artfully turned away. Elena dismounted the carousel and listened for Julian's trailing footfalls. She stood for a moment and heard nothing. Elena was unsure if her talents of manipulation were working on the stranger. Slowly, she turned to see what was distracting her victim.

Julian knelt in front of Gustav, scrutinizing the boy's face. He reached out and touched the tear stains just below the boy's eyes. Elena looked at Julian's face and saw sadness in his eyes.

"You better come down from there. My husband will be home shortly." Elena said.

Keefe did as he was asked and dismounted. Just as his boots impacted with the hard soil, the outside door opened. Edward Grimm stood within the frame, steam from the warm work shop billowed around him as it contacted winter's breath. He did not look happy.

"Elena." Grimm said with a tempered voice.

"Look, husband, your guest has arrived," she seethed.

The air was so thick with mutual animosity, Julian felt as if he were about to be caught in an enormous explosion. He attempted congeniality, "Hello, again. I must compliment you on such fine craftsmanship. I had no idea that…"

"I know you did not intend to come in here without my permission." Grimm cut Keefe off in mid-sentence. "But she knew better."

Elena attempted to calm Grimm, "I apologize, husband. I thought he would like to see what he would be working on. You were not home, and I saw fit to entertain our guest with a small tour of our home."

Grimm moved across the floor to the couple. He looked at Julian Keefe, then at Elena. She smirked. Elena knew Grimm's own jealousy would rot his mind, and all she had to do was provide the slightest insinuation that something may have happened. All it took to provoke such thinking was a glimpse, a glance, a dramatic expression. He fought the urge to strike the both of them in a jealous rage.

"Thank you." Grimm said to Elena.

She glanced at his shaking hands and knew she had scored another victory. "It is the least I could do."

The tension forced Julian to take a cautious step toward the house door. "I think I'll go and unpack my things. It has been a long journey, and I would like to clean up."

"We'll be eating dinner soon." Elena said as Julian backed away. "I'll bring you some fresh water and a few towels."

"Thank you."

Grimm waited until their guest had returned to the main part of the house. After Keefe was out of sight, Grimm turned his attention to Elena. His eyes raged, but he seemed to have control of the feeling. Elena sensed the amount of strength Grimm's efforts consumed.

"I will never ask you again to stay out of my workshop…" he paused, "next time I will punish you."

"Punish me? How?" Elena flared, "Being married to you is punishment enough."

"Good, then I know I am the cause of your unhappiness. If you can't be happy, I want you to be the most miserable woman on earth."

Elena pulled out her sword of manipulation, "Perhaps, one day I will be happy with you."

Even though Grimm doubted the hopes Elena planted, he could not ignore their promise. If there were a remote chance Elena would be his happily wedded wife, Grimm would endure the wait—and her punishments.

"If only I could believe it," Grimm sighed.

"You must, because it may come true," Elena said. "Now, I have a house guest to attend."

They had nothing more to say to each other. Elena left Grimm alone in the workshop. He waited until his wife was clearly gone before mounting the carousel. The carver walked to Gustav and knelt to see the boy's eyes.

"Dream for me," he whispered. "I need a dream."

CHAPTER 20

Julian sat on the edge of his bed. It felt firm, and he thought it might be too hard to sleep. Julian missed his bed at home. The mattress was made of feathers and was covered in soft linen. Julian remembered his mother tucking him in at night, and the church bells ringing. They were so soothing, Julian felt as if the very eyes of God were looking down. A touch of sadness came to Julian as he unpacked his things.

On the top of a small dresser, Julian found a small chamber pot, a pitcher, and a bowl. He looked inside the pitcher, and noticed it was full of fresh water. It was cold, however.

Julian started to pour some into the bowl, "I can't wait forever for that hot water. I stink to high heaven now."

Julian unbuttoned his shirt and draped it over the unstable chair that was also in the room. The extensive traveling made his body tired. He really needed a long restful sleep, but somehow was unconvinced he would get it in this house. Julian located one of his bags, and dug out his straight razor, a cake of lye soap, a mug and brush, a comb, and a toothbrush. He placed his toiletries neatly on the dresser top.

Attached to the rear of the dresser, was a faded mirror. Julian could see his reflection, only it seemed marred by fog.

He smiled, looking at the stubble covering his face. The faint hair looked like soot.

"She promised hot water."

Julian cupped some cool water in his hands and distributed it through his dark hair. The water was soothing upon his scalp. Next, he let another fistful of water fall across his chest. Julian caught the dripping water before it soaked his pants, and forced it back upward to wet his stomach. His hands lingered and massaged his sore abdominal muscles. Long journeys always distressed him. Perhaps having a lot of money could make that a thing of the past?

Then, he paused. Julian felt the eyes of another on him. He looked in the mirror and saw Elena's reflection. She stood in the doorway with towels and steaming water.

"How long have you been standing there?" He asked.

"Long enough to see the trip has left you full of knots." Her footsteps were like whispers as she crossed the floor.

"Yes, I'm afraid traveling doesn't agree with me." Julian gave his arm a therapeutic kneading.

She placed the towels on Julian's bed, and the water on the dresser. "I have some oil you can use. It works wonders."

"Thanks." Julian was leery of accepting her gift. "Maybe I'll put some on just before bed."

Julian averted his eyes. He was uncomfortable in Elena's company. She was very attractive, and it had been a long time since Julian had entertained a young woman. He glanced at the mirror and saw her reflection. Elena's waist was small, and her black hair was like a shadow. Julian stole a brief glimpse of her breasts, and momentarily fantasized about their shape, texture, and softness.

"I will leave you alone so you can finish cleaning up." Elena was fully aware of Julian's surreptitious scrutiny. "I am ready to serve our evening meal."

Julian smiled as he watched Elena leave. Then, he scolded himself for thinking lustfully about another man's wife. As she pulled the door closed, he noticed her eyes lingered. Lust was also in her eyes.

Julian looked in the mirror, searched his image for some kind of guidance, but there wasn't any. Blue eyes stared back with the same lost look. Julian finished his grooming and went into the kitchen.

Elena and Grimm were already seated at the small table.

Julian smiled and scanned the food. There were traditional German sausages and other specialties.

"Sit down," Grimm invited, gesturing at an empty chair.

"Thank you." Julian sat. "Everything looks so good."

"There's plenty to eat. You'll need to keep your strength up with all the work that's ahead of you." Elena took Julian's plate and began filling it.

"Elena has turned out to be a fine cook." Grimm attempted to compliment his wife, but she gave him a look of cordial distaste.

Julian could feel the tension rising again and attempted to disarm his dinner companions. "Being able to cook is wonderful, I ruined my father's kitchen."

"You cooked?" Elena asked while serving her husband's food.

"I like to say we survived." He smiled warmly as a fond memory surfaced. "My mother was a tremendous cook. Oh, she was the best."

"Really? Why did you cook, then?" Grimm said, pouring glasses of white wine.

Julian sighed, and his eyes dropped slightly. "She died many years ago. From then on, it was my father and my three brothers."

Elena asked, "You had no women to cook for you?"

"Every now and then—yes." Julian reflected. "On holidays and such. But we all worked such strange jobs. Two of my brothers were in the army, and the other was with the government. My father and I were craftsmen and traveled all over the British Isles. So, you can see we were not a very settled family."

"That's very interesting." Grimm took a drink of wine.

Julian also drank. "I wanted to apologize for earlier. I had no idea of your wishes. I am so amazed with your talent, sir."

"Thank you." Grimm accepted the compliment.

"Who taught you such craftsmanship?"

Elena smiled. "The Devil."

Grimm smiled, but it was only superficial. Deep inside, his paranoia erupted. She knew the truth, the *Phuri Dai* had told

Elena everything. No, Grimm told himself, the *Phuri Dai* could not betray her own vow of trust. Elena was just being sarcastic, but could he be sure?

"My wife has such a wit," Grimm said.

Elena kicked out an obviously false laugh. "Yes, he really learned it all from his father."

Julian looked down at his plate, he was unaware that so much food had been consumed. "I'm so tired. I think I'll head to bed. I'm sure tomorrow will be a long, long day."

"So am I," Grimm stated.

"I want to write my father a letter before I go to sleep." Julian rose from his chair. "Thank you both, dinner was wonderful."

"You are more than welcome," Elena replied.

"Good night, young man," Grimm said.

He waited until Julian was in his room, and the door was closed. Then, he turned his attentions to Elena, who was clearing the table. Grimm drained the wine from his glass and poured more.

"He's a nice man," Elena said while shuttling plates to the sink.

"Yes, very nice." Grimm's eyes covered Elena's body lustfully. In his pants, an urgent pressure made itself known. "You know, we've not yet had time to consummate our marriage."

"I know." Her tone was cold.

"Now that I am back, I think it is time to do so." He moved closer to her.

Elena avoided him; the thought of his touch was revolting. "I have dishes to clean."

"Those can wait." Grimm pressed his body against Elena's, trapping her against the sink.

"What makes you think I want to make love to you?" Her tone was venomous.

"You are my wife."

"I am your property."

Grimm spun her around. "Then, I'll take what I want."

Elena never realized he was so strong. She couldn't get away. "I'll never love you, never. Now that there's a real man in the house, who knows what can happen? First Sennett, now Julian."

Grimm angrily snarled. It was as if he was no longer in his body, he watched as his hand struck Elena's face. She shrank away in pain, and Grimm realized what he'd done.

"I'm sorry."

Elena looked angrily at him, his eyes were becoming red. "I'm a princess, the chieftain's daughter, you can't do this to me."

"You aren't a princess any longer." He eased back so she could move around.

Elena walked to the kitchen table and resumed her work. "No matter what you say or do, I will never love you."

"You have a lifetime to grow to love me. I can give you anything want."

A smile came to her lips as she thought. "Give me something, then."

"Name it." He did not hesitate.

"I will make love to you, as a wife has to do, for a ring. I want a ring of gold, with a huge precious gem."

Grimm smiled. He knew where to get such a ring. "You make it too easy."

"Really?"

Grimm moved closer, but she backed away. "You said you would make love."

"Get me a ring."

Her words were a knife. She teased and manipulated so easily. Grimm's anger rose once again, but he did not want to risk killing her. He stormed from the room and went into the workshop. She laughed.

Orange lamplight bathed Julian as he lay in bed. He could hear their bickering but was unable to understand specifically what they argued about. The covers were pulled only halfway up, and paper rested beside him. Julian was writing to his father.

Dear Father,

I have arrived at Edward Grimm's house, and hope to get started tomorrow. I had dinner with him and his wife tonight, such a strange pair. I don't know how things are going to work out, I still have many reservations. Something doesn't seem right around here, but I'll heed your wise words: I'm here for finance, not romance.

Although Edward is an unusual, paranoid man, his wife is just as intriguing. I don't know what it is about her, father. You should see her. Her name is Elena. She has green eyes like none that I've seen before. Her hair is so black, blacker than any Irish woman's hair. She is so beautiful, and I try to not think of her. I cannot help but think of how she would feel in my arms.

Tis wrong, I know. She is another man's wife. He doesn't treat her well. He tries but doesn't know how. It's not like you've taught me, the way you and mother were.

I can't explain it.

Yes, father, I am confused. I just want to get done here, and come home. Give everyone my love. I'll write again soon. Please write back, I'll need to hear from you to keep my sanity.

Love from your youngest, Julian

CHAPTER 21

I'll never forget that night. Elena, to my surprise, gave little resistance to sharing my bed. I did not need to remind her of her duties as a wife, she knew them from her childhood. Rom women knew their place, even the princess who lay next to me.

As she slept, I watched her. Elena's breathing was effortless and full of beauty. It was at times like this when I realized what a gentle creature she could be. This is the woman I wanted as my wife. Once, I thought I wanted the fire and radiance, but now I knew other men could see that glow, too. I was a fool to think other men had never seen it, but now I wanted them all to go blind if they looked on Elena lustfully.

I could also hear Julian sleeping in the next room. The gentle timbre of his snore permeated the thin walls of my house. I wondered if Elena heard him, and also wondered if it sounded like music to her. Did she dream of making love with him? She seemed to befriend Keefe from the start.

I asked myself many questions before bringing him into my home: Would Elena find him attractive? Would Julian Keefe desire my wife? Would I have to kill him?

I drifted in and out of light sleep. I was used to it by now, because of the erratic appearance of the dream creatures. I had to be ready to jump up instantly or lose my advantage.

I hoped Gustav would dream soon. It had been so long since I had seen a dream. I grew accustomed to the chase and capture, even addicted to the sensation of taking a dream for myself. It gave me a sense of power, which I savored like fine chocolate.

I was uncomfortable with this new man in my house. I did not understand him. I told myself it would take time to get to know him, to become acquainted with his habits and ways, and accept and trust him. Then, I realized he wouldn't be around that long. Julian Keefe would only share my house for the remainder of the winter at the longest. After that, I wanted him out.

My thoughts drifted to aspects of dreaming again. If Gustav summoned a creature, would Elena or Julian hear it? Would I be able to capture the creature, or would it slip away like Zoltan? I dwelt on Zoltan for the moment. Never before did I want to capture a dream so. I created Zoltan, but from another man's illustrations. But I gave him form, I could touch his mane, I painted his eyes, and I alone carved his face. Perhaps, I did dream of Zoltan. Bitterly, however, I realized I was only a mirror to another's imagination.

Maybe, that is why I am surely insane.

Grimm's light sleep was shattered. Quietly, he sat up in bed. At first, he thought Elena had gotten up, but she slept effortlessly beside him. Then, Grimm wondered if Keefe was up, exploring his house by moonlight.

Grimm eased out of bed and crept from the room. He gently closed the door. He turned to go down the hall, but paused to allow his eyes to adjust to the dim light. Grimm squeezed his eyes shut, attempting to produce tears. The room seemed cloudy, and he attributed it to the veil of sleep that hung about his eyes.

As Grimm opened his eyes again, he realized the fogginess was not in his eyes. The room was filled with gentle mist. He cautiously scanned the house as he crept forward. Light from the fireplace was diffused and dreamlike. For a moment, Grimm wondered if he were walking in his sleep, but dismissed the notion.

The fog was so delicate, like a frail piece of threadbare lace. It spiraled outward from underneath the workshop door. An uncountable number of luminous fibers knitted their way from beneath the door, and through any crack that allowed passage. Grimm recalled the configuration. He remembered when the dog-headed cherubs appeared, and the women, too. A web of lace identical to this marked their entrance into his world. Grimm also remembered the sensation of breathlessness. That, too, returned. He could feel his heart leaping and heard its thunder in his ears. The pounding drove him to the door.

Cautiously, Grimm eased the door open. He tried to prepare himself for what was beyond, but there was no way of knowing who, or what, lurked in the room. He had never seen the fog so thick. Grimm strained to see the carousel, and even though it was only yards away, the shapes upon it were only shrouded silhouettes.

Something, however, was in the fog. Grimm could feel the energy; it sucked at his lungs. Everything was so quiet. Then, Grimm heard the soothing sound of crickets. They chirped harmoniously as moonlight streamed through the workshop windows. But, as the moments passed, the fog grew more and more impervious. The walls, doors, and fixtures were fading from view, and the moonlight was blotted from sight.

Grimm also heard leaves rustling. Nearby, trees swiftly manifested in the fog. Strange outlines of their twisted branches could be seen in the remaining, dim moonlight. The trees thickened and were soon as dense as the forest outside. Grimm trembled with anxiety. The dreams were delicious, but he knew terror waited.

As Grimm attempted to move safely in the fog, a new sound echoed. Galloping hooves. The sound was all around. Grimm moved off in one direction, hoping the carousel was nearby. He groped the creamy mist, wishing his hands would contact anything familiar.

As the blind carver moved around, another strange vibration cracked through the air. It was a low growl, and obviously belonged to a beast with a deep, seemingly bottomless throat. Grimm turned to the direction from which the sound came. He wanted so desperately to see the creature.

He did see something in the sea of white. An eddy rushed

through the fog as if a fish were passing just beneath the surface. Only, it was no fish. Grimm watched the disturbance and heard the growl again. Something brushed by his legs. Fear screamed inside Grimm. His eyes swelled in their sockets as pressure from his squeezing heart tried to blow them out. But he couldn't give in to fear, not now, not ever.

The creature brushed by Grimm again, but this time it passed behind him. He turned to watch the wake, and saw a long, long coil of green scales break the surface, then pass under again. Grimm thrilled at the sight. He couldn't manage the emotions rushing around inside and burst into tears. He was lost in his own house, unable to escape.

Suddenly, everything grew quiet again. His ears thundered, and tears burned his face. Grimm tried to regain control of himself; he willed away the fear and welcomed the sweet seductive illusion of Gustav's dream.

Once again, Grimm could hear the hooves in the cloud. They were slowing to a trot, then finally to a walk. He knew they were close, so close he could feel the animal's hot breath just behind him.

Grimm turned as the image of Zoltan came into view. On his back, a small figure rode. The person was in heavy battle armor, and it shone brilliantly. The polished silver glinted like a jewel in the sun.

"Who are you?" Grimm cautiously asked the stranger.

The little knight stopped Zoltan and lifted his visor. "I am the man who would be king."

Grimm gasped. Gustav looked from inside the silver helmet. It was him, his eyes, the twinkling smile, everything. Yet, this dream figure did not seem to recognize Grimm.

Grimm realized he was in the middle of one of Gustav's dreams and savored the richness. "You are the king?"

"Soon, after I find the castle of the green dragon."

Grimm remembered the story, Gustav told it as he sat upon Zoltan for the first time. "What is your name, brave knight?"

"I am Sir Gustav, and I've come to kill the green dragon."

"You have a magnificent horse, he's so strong."

"Yes, his name is Zoltan, and he's the finest horse in the land."

"Suitable to help kill a dragon?" Grimm said.

"Yes, but I've no time for this chatter, peasant. Have you seen the green dragon?"

Grimm looked into the boy's eyes, "Yes, he's here. I've seen him."

"Where?" Gustav looked around.

"Everywhere."

Gustav gave Grimm a disgusted look, "You are a stupid old man, you know nothing. I've no time for this, I must save the queen. Then, all this land will be mine."

Grimm felt around in his pocket. He searched for the small vial of potion. The carver hoped an opportunity such as this would come around and came prepared.

Just as Grimm located the potion, Zoltan reared violently. The mysterious wake surged by in the fog. Then, an enormous green coil lurched from the cloud. Gustav struggled to maintain control of Zoltan as part of the dragon's body surfaced nearby.

"There!" Gustav shouted and drew his mighty sword.

The dragon circled, and Grimm was unable to determine how large it was. Suddenly, an immense green, almost black, head rose from the wake. The dragon's head was long and narrow, with a tuft of white hair on its chin. His eyes burned red, and vertical yellow pupils adjusted to the light. Along the crown of its head, there was a row of three large black spines. He seemed to laugh—a low rumble churned deep in his throat.

"At last!" Gustav shouted.

The dragon arched his head and neck, as if preparing for a tremendous shock. Then, like a geyser, sticky flames rushed through its teeth. As it opened its mouth to let the flames pass, Gustav directed Zoltan from the fire's path. Gustav then charged the green dragon. The beast turned but was too slow. Gustav's sword sliced a large wound in its neck. Bright, hot, orange liquid oozed from the cut as the dragon screamed in agony. It was not a mortal wound, however, and the serpent turned to attack again.

Grimm backed away from the battlefield. As the dragon moved, the wound on its neck spilled more liquid. To Grimm, it resembled the molten iron that killed his father so long ago. The liquid splattered, and where it hit, fire erupted.

Grimm watched the battle rage on. Gustav scored direct hits, and so did the dragon. But each burst of flame torched the dense dream forest. The trees were burning, and now it was almost out of control.

Grimm panicked; the dragon's burning blood flowed in the fog. He could faintly see its glow. The small streams ignited the dream trees. He backed away from the approaching liquid, again groping for the carousel. He feared the liquid would catch the carousel on fire.

"Gustav!" Grimm shouted.

The fire now roared out of control. Grimm ignored all caution, and frantically searched the cloud for the carousel. The liquid inched closer; the fire reached higher. Suddenly, Grimm made contact with solid wood. Instantly, he recognized the carousel, and leapt up onto the platform. As he became oriented to the surroundings, Grimm could see the fire all around the carousel. He wondered if the house, itself, was on fire.

"Gustav!" Grimm screamed again.

The sound of battle merged with the fire's roar. Grimm rushed around the platform until he located Gustav's statue. The boy's image was stoic.

"Gustav! Stop this!" Grimm shouted above the noise.

The battle still raged. Thinking quickly, Grimm fell to his knees. The carver located his hammer, which he'd left there the day before. Grimm groped Gustav's foot until he found the patched nail hole. He dug at the nail head with the hammer's claw. Grimm finally worked the claw's teeth beneath the head and used leverage to force the nail to emerge. The nail scraped against the wood, and the imprisoned flesh of Gustav's foot. Slowly, the pain of the nail woke the child.

The din of the battle subsided, as well as the fire. The trees retreated into the fog, and moonlight became visible once again. There were no sounds of horses, nor of growling, flame-spitting dragons. Even the crickets drifted back inside Gustav's head. As Grimm looked around, the workshop emerged from the dissipating fog, it was as if nothing ever happened.

Grimm began to sob.

CHAPTER 22

Dear Father,

My first night here was long. I struggled with myself, not about sleep, but whether I should just come home. I feel a little sad, but the money is so good. I know what you will say, money is not all that matters in this world. Jesus was not a rich man, but a man who had love. I know that is right, but the money will make things easier for the family.

I want you to know I'm thinking of you, and the rest of the family. Tell everyone I'll be home by spring, then we'll all have a nice holiday. I wish I could be there with all of you, now. Please take care of yourself, I know you haven't been feeling well. I'll be home soon, and everything will be fine. Please write to me as much as you are able.

Love your youngest, Julian

Julian folded the letter and prepared it for mailing. He looked out his window and saw the sun's morning rays bounce through a cascade of icicles. Julian thought they looked like teeth clamping down on the house of Grimm. He shook off the feeling of doom, the young craftsman had no time for it when work had to be done, and it was work he wanted to complete as soon as possible.

As he rose, there was a gentle knock on his door. "Yes?"

The door opened effortlessly, and Elena stepped in. "How did you sleep?"

"Well." Julian smiled at her, but it wasn't true, and he did not want to offend his host.

"There's breakfast." She cocked her head coyly. "I thought

you might be hungry before you started work." Elena then noticed the letter in Julian's hand.

Julian tracked her gaze. "I'm writing to my father. He's been feeling poorly, and I like to keep in touch."

"You must be a good son."

"I try to be, he's been good to me." Julian pushed the letter into his pocket. "I'll try to mail it later."

"It's a warm day, and town isn't too far. Perhaps, we can walk there later?"

"Maybe, but I've got a lot of work to do."

"Oh." Elena looked away. A shade of rejection purposely colored her words. "I'll get you breakfast now."

"Thank you." Julian said and followed her from the room.

Quietly, Julian sat at the kitchen table, and watched as Elena served him some warm oatmeal. The moment became tense as she moved about. Elena purposely moved in mysterious ways, she wanted to be enticing to the houseguest.

She came to the table and placed the bowl in front of Julian. "Would you like something to drink?"

"Yes, water would be fine." Julian said as he lifted a spoonful of the warm grain to his mouth. He savored the bite and realized how hungry he was. "This is good, thank you."

"You're welcome," Elena said while pouring some water for Julian. She placed the beverage in front of him, then sat.

"Where is Edward this morning?"

She watched him eat. "I don't know. He was not in bed when I awoke."

"Is everything all right? Do you think something happened to him?" Julian seemed concerned.

"No, he probably went to town, or he's working."

"He may be in the workshop?"

"Yes, I suppose," Elena replied.

Julian then remembered Grimm's fierce words of warning about the room. "I hope he's in there. I'm ready to start work." Julian swallowed the last bite of food, "I still haven't been able to assess the workspace. I hope it's big enough to suit my needs."

Just then, the workshop door opened. Looking beaten and tired, Grimm emerged from the portal. Elena looked her husband over, then turned her disinterested eyes back to Julian.

"Good morning," Grimm said as he approached the table.

"Good morning," Julian returned the greeting.

"Good morning, Elena."

"Is it?" She smiled, "Can I get you anything?"

Grimm smiled, "No, but I have something for you."

Her curiosity piqued. "Really? What?"

Grimm extended a closed fist and slowly turned his hand. As his fingers unfolded like flower petals, Elena saw the first glimmers of a shining ring. Her eyes ignited as the jewelry became fully visible. It sat there in Grimm's calloused, pale, sweaty palm: a magnificent jewel on a circle of gold. Elena carefully picked the ring from Grimm's palm. She studied its beauty.

"Is it real?" She was breathless.

Grimm savored the selfish passion in her eyes. He realized this was the way to her heart. "Truer than the morning sun, the greatest emerald I could find."

She slipped the jewel onto her finger.

"A wife who performs her duties admirably is equally rewarded," Grimm stated.

"So she is," Elena replied.

Julian could not believe the ring's beauty. "I've never seen such an exquisite ring in all my life."

"Then, you've not seen much, my friend." Grimm smiled. "Come, Julian, let us go to the workshop. I know you are eager to get started."

"That I am." Julian rose from his chair.

Elena said, "Don't forget, Julian. You wanted to mail your letter. I would still like to walk into town later." She twisted the ring.

Grimm fought the surge of jealousy. "Why don't you take it for him?"

Elena thought of the ring on her hand. If there was more of this to come, she didn't want to push him away. "I could do that."

"Thank you," Julian said, and retrieved the letter from his pocket. "The other one is on the dresser."

"Well, shall we?" Grimm gestured to the open workshop door.

Julian followed the carver's hand and entered the room. Grimm seemed uneasy with Julian in the workshop but knew he would have to allow some measure of trust. He watched Julian carefully, and Julian's eyes went directly to the carousel.

"I still can't help but admire all your work."

Grimm was touched. "Thank you."

"It looks nearly finished. Will you put more figures on it?" Julian asked.

"Yes, eventually."

Julian started to climb onto the platform, but hesitated. "I'm sorry, is it all right to go up on it? I have to measure the workspace."

"Certainly."

Julian continued his ascent. He moved to the large column, which occupied the center. Above him, vast arms of timber supported the canopy. Julian noticed Grimm had started to paint it, and the artwork was consistent with the rest of the carousel's quality. The colors were vivid and contrasting. Grimm had a fondness for shades of red.

Julian located the door of the central support pillar. He studied the narrow, but tall, hinged door. Grimm had painted it also. He chose a mural of intertwined trolls and demons. They cavorted sensually. Julian stared at the image, but then returned to his original course.

Again, Julian studied the hinges. "Is it all right if I take this door off? It would really help."

Grimm's eyes peeled Julian's skin to the bone. Who was this man wishing to take liberties with his device of dreams? Grimm wanted to strike out, dismiss Julian from his house forever.

"Certainly."

Julian smiled as permission was granted and removed the holding pins. He carefully removed the door, then propped it against the nearest figure: Gustav.

"Please, not against that one!" Grimm said.

"Oh." Julian looked around to see where he'd left the door. "I wasn't paying attention, I'm sorry." Julian laid the door on the platform.

Grimm sighed with relief. "So, tell me what kind of space you will need?"

"Not much, really." Julian said while inspecting the exposed cavity. "I need a place to set up a smithy, just for some heating and forming. Most of the brass I can buy in sheets."

"How much room will that take?"

"None at all, in here. I'll clear a small space outside for that. I can use your work bench and anvil."

"Fine." Grimm was pleased with Julian's apparent expertise.

"There are a few things I might need." Julian climbed out of the hollow pillar. "I'll need some special couplings to fix the calliope in here. It's narrower than I thought. I'll only be able to fit three octaves of pipes in here, I hope that will be adequate."

Grimm thrilled as he anticipated the calliope's completion. "How long do you think it will take to finish it?"

"Looks like two months of work, right off hand."

"I'm in no hurry." Grimm smiled.

"Perhaps, I will go to town after all. I can look for the hammer I need. I think I'll be able to make all the other things right here."

"Elena has already left. I saw her pass by the windows about five minutes ago," Grimm said.

"Maybe, I can catch her before she gets too far." Julian went to the windows and looked out over the snowscape.

"She's on foot, and already on the path." Grimm attempted to dash Julian's hopes of traveling with Elena. "Besides, you will need to follow the roads. You are a stranger, and the woods are full of gypsies."

"Gypsies?" Julian seemed amused.

"Yes, bitter thieves, all of them."

Julian succumbed, "Very well, it's the road. I hoped there would be a quicker way, but I guess you probably know best."

"It isn't that far," Grimm said with assurance.

"I'll get my coat and be off." Julian started to walk into the main house.

Grimm stopped him, however. "Go to Resteller's. I have credit with him. Tell him who you are, and he will be more than happy to arrange for everything to be delivered."

"Thank you." Julian smiled and went to get his coat.

Elena knew the trails and roads well. The Rom had traveled these paths for generations, it was their way. She swiftly navigated the paths leading to the village. Elena thought of the letters in her hand. They burned her fingers. Julian's thoughts were in her hands. The closer she got to town, the hotter the words became. They were like branding irons in the snow, hissing their secrets.

Elena paused to rest. The unsealed letters called to her. Succumbing to their seduction, Elena unfolded one of the letters. It was the first one Julian had written. At first, the words made Elena angry. The descriptions of herself and Grimm were less than flattering. But then Julian wrote of his desire. She was intrigued and read the second letter. He wrote of money, and how good it was.

Julian also mentioned Jesus, and his longing for home. The main thing that enticed Elena, was the issue of money. Her husband made good money, although she did not have any idea where such amounts came from. If he were paying Julian, then Julian was worth knowing. But there was more to it, Elena thought as she refolded the letters. Julian was attractive, and if he had money…Elena smiled and returned to her journey.

Soon, Elena approached the village. She crossed the wide dirt streets and made her way to the post collector. He was the butcher, and he had a small booth. This is where all mail for the village and surrounding area traveled.

Elena approached the butcher shop. She pushed the heavy door open, and bells announced her arrival. Pungent smells of meat and sausage greeted her. Overhead, other meats hung for sale.

"Hello?" Elena called.

There were no customers, nor a vendor. She casually looked at some of the fresh meats in the case. On top of one of the counters, there was some sliced ham. Elena moved in close, taking in the wonderful aroma.

"Can I help you with something?" A man stepped from a back room. He was dressed in a bloody apron.

Elena looked at him. "I need to send some letters."

The man suspiciously scanned her. "You weren't stealing from me?"

Elena was insulted. "I don't need to steal, I'm a rich woman."

"You're a gypsy."

"May I mail my letters please?" She was fighting anger.

He cast her a look of superiority. "Over there." The butcher gestured to the small postal area.

Elena followed instructions but remained silent. She attempted to keep her cordial smile, but her mouth quivered with the strain. Elena placed the letters on the table.

He said nothing and prepared the letters for travel. She watched as he weighed, calculated, and placed proper postage on the correspondence. Every now and then, the butcher glanced up with contempt.

"How much will it be?" She asked.

"One moment, I'm not finished." The butcher did something else, then addressed her, "It will be 3 Reichsmarks."

Elena pulled the amount requested from her pocket and handed it over. "Here you are, sir." She attempted to be regal, mirroring his superior attitude.

"You are a gypsy," he said as he took the money. "I know who you are, you ruined a respectable man's life. How did you do it, I wonder?"

Grimm was well known in the village, even considered someone of importance. Elena wanted to strike back, it was her way, but she knew better. Gypsies were not favored in this area, and men had no respect for Rom women. They wouldn't hesitate to beat a gypsy woman, and the woman could do nothing in return. Elena ignored his bait.

"Thank you for mailing my husband's letters." Elena made sure the butcher knew these were not hers. If they were, she had no way of knowing they wouldn't be read or mailed at all.

"It's my job," he replied.

"I will stop by if any mail comes for Julian Keefe. He is working for my husband, and he asked me to pick up any letters from home."

"I'm sure he did."

Elena wanted no more words with him but couldn't resist. "I also needed to buy some sausages, but I saw nothing of quality. I think I'll go across the street. Good day."

Before the butcher could reply, Elena left the store. Although her words probably hurt him, it was nothing compared to the way he made her feel. She made her way back to the paths and headed down the familiar Rom trails.

Her mind swam, echoes of loneliness returned. Elena despised her husband. He could only give her money and status. She needed more. Elena remembered Sennett as she went down the trail. The trees whispered his name, and the ground thumped with the rhythm of his heart.

Elena decided she must find Sennett. It had been too long since she reveled in his strong arms. She hadn't been to the camp in three days. The last time was just before Grimm came home.

Elena closed in on the campsite. She detected no movement or activity. Surely, on such a pleasant day, people would be moving around, gathering wood, and performing other chores before the cold returned. The wind licked Elena's ears as she approached the clearing. Her heart fell, and she nervously scanned the empty space. She stopped. The family had moved on.

"Sennett?" Elena frantically called. "Anyone?"

She moved about the clearing, looking for any sign of her people. Elena scanned the muddy soil. Tracks and hoof prints led off down the path, and Elena realized she had been abandoned.

"It is me, Elena!" She fell to the ground, weeping. "Oh, God, please!"

Sennett was gone, and she felt like a lost child. How could he abandon her? Why, when they made such passionate love?

"Sennett." Her whispers were choked with tears.

Julian was able to find his way around the small village; he followed Grimm's instructions and located Resteller's. The place seemed deserted as Julian entered. The fire burning in the stove was the only sign of life. He looked at the high stacks of lumber. Row upon row of rough timber lined the walls and floors. Julian looked around for brass but could not locate what he needed.

"May I help you with something?" a voice said from behind.

Julian was startled, and gasped.

Resteller reacted with a smile. "I'm sorry, my boy. What can I help you with, today?"

"I've come looking for some brass sheeting, and some iron couplings. I also need a hammer."

"It sounds like you are taking on a big project." Resteller looked Julian over. "I haven't seen you around these parts, are you from here?"

"No, sir." The young man proudly said, "I'm from Ireland."

"Ah, I should have heard your accent. My old ears don't work very well, I'm afraid." Resteller walked toward the warehouse. "Everything you might need is this way."

As Julian followed, he commented, "I've never seen such an immense storehouse. It seems as if you have everything in here."

"I bargained with all the local millers and such to sell their wares. In return, I take a share of the profit."

"That is a good idea," Julian said.

"Thank you, but sometimes it is a little difficult dealing with some of the people."

They paused in front of numerous sheets of hand-hammered brass. Some were ragged and irregular, while some were oval. All of them were tarnished with age.

"I suppose brass isn't popular around here," Julian commented as he inspected the metal.

"Demand for it comes and goes," Resteller said. He watched the young man inspecting the malleability and quality of the brass. "You never said what brought you this far from home."

"I'm doing some work for Edward Grimm, he's the one who sent me here." Julian looked back at Resteller expecting to see a pleasant face but was greeted with a look of mild distaste. "Is something wrong?"

"Grimm, eh?" Resteller was unsettled. "What are you building for him?"

"A calliope for a carousel."

Resteller digested Julian's words. "Listen, boy, be careful in that house."

"What for?" Julian was genuinely surprised.

"He's always been a strange bird, but rumor has it he married a gypsy bitch."

Julian was shocked at Resteller's harshness but hid it from the merchant. He didn't know what to say. Then Resteller removed the burden by continuing. "She's been around town, showing off her money like some harlot. I tell you again, be careful around a gypsy woman, she'll cut you open if she thinks you swallowed a pfennig."

Julian was uncomfortable with the conversation and attempted to switch subjects. "But," he flashed his charming grin, "is his credit still good?"

"That it is."

"Good, then I'll deal with the other things when they arise."

"One thing I can say about Edward Grimm: he is a good customer who settles his debts on time."

"Great," Julian said, "I'll take the whole lot of brass, now let me see a nice, heavy hammer."

I waited until Julian was down the road, and I could see him no longer. At last, I was alone. It was a calm time, and I found I needed a diversion. That, I decided, would be Gustav. I had to speak with him.

I was angry with myself, and dwelled upon the other night. I'd had such a wonderful opportunity to capture Zoltan, an image of the child and a formidable dragon. I hadn't understood what was happening to me—I was mesmerized.

The images were like no others before. The fascination overwhelmed me, then came the fear. I was a fool, but there was no one to punish but myself. I only prayed I would get another chance to see Zoltan.

I went to Gustav and knelt at his side. I spoke of his long dead mother, and of Zoltan. I told him his liberators had come for him, but there was no gold to pay for their services. I also said this is why they left him. I bade him to dream of gold. It was the only thing that would set him free.

I stroked his wooden face. It was wet again, and I thought I heard a distant sob. It was true: I heard weeping, but it was a woman. I listened intently, attempting to focus on the sound's direction. Then, I realized it was coming from inside my own home. As I traced the source, I quietly peeked into the house. Elena was home, and she was sitting at the kitchen table. I heard the crying again. For some reason, the sound pleased me. I was seeing her vulnerable side, and I liked the helpless aura she emitted.

I found myself wanting to go to her, hold her, and comfort her. But I knew that would be hazardous. She was a viper, and one move would bring the bite of death. Her guise of feeble female must be a ploy, a trick to get more treasures. And I still had to collect my fee for the ring.

Grimm watched the scene at the table but elected to return to the workshop. Gustav was more important to him than Elena. Elena did not dream for him, she only offered a shallow promise. But there were different needs and different dreams Elena represented, and as time advanced, Grimm vowed to fully explore these realms. Until then, Grimm wanted to concentrate on Gustav.

As Grimm returned to the workshop, Julian came in through the opposite door. Grimm went to the carousel and pretended to be deeply involved in artwork.

Julian greeted him with a friendly smile, "Thank you for such good instructions."

"You're welcome." Momentarily, Grimm relaxed his charade. "Did you find everything you need?"

"Yes, certainly. He was vague about when the brass could be delivered, but that was the only drawback."

Grimm came down from the carousel. "I'm pleased."

"Now I need to set up the smithy and fire it up." Julian moved toward the door. "It is all right to set it up just outside this door?"

"Yes. Feel free to use anything you find around here for your needs."

"Thank you. I noticed you even have a healthy supply of coke under a tarp by the woodpile." Julian then opened the door. "I'll see you later."

"If you need any help, just come in and ask for it."

Grimm simmered. It was becoming more and more difficult to pretend Julian was wanted. Jealousy clouded Grimm's mind.

Grimm moved to the opposite side of the carousel. From there, he could see Julian through the workshop windows. The carver pretended to work in case Julian's eyes wandered. The more he watched Julian work, the more he wanted to kill him. However, Julian was the link to the dream's completion. Without him, there would be no music.

Julian moved rocks and wood about, crudely fashioning a

place to heat brass to a malleable state. The fire did not have to reach melting temperatures, it just had to warm the metal enough for manipulation. Julian's skill impressed the craftsman in Grimm, but jealousy washed any compassion away. Julian's eyes glanced momentarily at the window, and Grimm averted his own gaze. He pretended to be hard at work carving details.

As he watched Julian, he could hear Elena's faint sobbing. Suddenly, the crying stopped. After a moment of silence, Grimm turned to see Elena standing in the doorway.

"Ah, Elena," he said. "You frightened me."

"Did I? I should be more careful, or I might scare you to death." She scanned him. "What are you?"

"What?" Grimm was stunned by her question.

"I don't know you. I don't understand you." She moved closer. "I certainly don't love you."

Grimm smiled wryly, "Yes, but you're mine. I have you, there is no one else for you." He watched as his words made Elena hesitate. "There's no one else for you? Has the troupe moved on, leaving you to the *Gadje*?"

He came down from the carousel and approached Elena. She was vulnerable, unable to fight back. Had she been abandoned by the *Vitsa*?

"Sennett left with them, didn't he? You are alone."

Elena looked up into Grimm's face. At first, she was a defeated little girl, but then she looked into her husband's eyes. They were empty, lifeless, and loveless. He had no passion. He was nothing to her. Suddenly, the dimming fire rose inside her. Elena's passion returned, feeding on her hate for Grimm. The viper returned.

"Sennett?" She straightened her back and stood proudly.

"Sennett has moved on."

"I know, I heard you crying. I hope he is gone for good."

"How will that help you?"

"He was distracting you from your good fortune. The hay-seed is gone and will not cloud you so. Now, you will want to love me. I've given you plenty, more than any gypsy woman could dream of."

"Dear husband." Elena stepped closer to him. "That is the greatest mistake you have ever made."

Grimm was confused. "What?"

"I'm not a gypsy woman." She rubbed her warm body against Grimm's, "I'm a gypsy princess."

Just as Grimm reached out to embrace her, she pulled away, laughing. Grimm seethed with anger. He watched as she flirted away like a fickle butterfly. Then, Elena went to the outside door. Just beyond, Julian worked at his smithy. The queen was using her pawns now. Elena opened the door and went to Julian.

Grimm quickly returned to the carousel. He watched from the windows as Elena talked and smiled and fawned. Faint words echoed from outside. Grimm heard her say: ...*muscular... you must be sore...you're very talented...*

Jealousy joined with anger. Grimm attempted to shift the blame to Elena for she was the source, but Grimm only saw Julian. The young man could take it all away from him: the music, the woman, the dreams.

Elena placed her hands on Julian. He smiled, unable to mask his feelings for her. Julian wanted Elena; it was blatant as the summer sun. He fought his passion. He knew it was deadly. But she was so tempting.

Elena's touch was fleeting, and she moved away from him. The cold was driving her in, or so she said. She asked Julian if he wanted to come in; he said no. She told him to call if he needed anything...anything at all.

Elena closed the door.

"I wonder where Sennett and the family have gone. No matter, I think I can be happy here." She paused as she walked past Grimm, "He's a good, strong worker, husband. I think he'll do a fine job on your silly toy." Then, she continued into the main part of the house.

Even though the night was quiet, Julian could not sleep. Moonlight danced on the snow and reflected into the growing icicles outside his window. He watched them glow in the light; they looked like monstrous canines clamping down on prey.

The house was silent. Only the faint crackle of the fire could be heard. He focused on the day that had just passed. Julian's body was physically tired from all the work, but his mind raced with incredible vigor. He saw images of Elena, her breasts taut from the cold. Julian felt his penis swelling.

Then he remembered the change in his host. Grimm was no longer helpful and accommodating. He had turned aloof, avoiding any questions or casual conversation. Perhaps he had seen Elena with Julian? Could Grimm read his mind? Perhaps, Julian thought, this was the devil's house.

Suddenly, he heard the bedroom door creaking open, but, as Julian turned, he could see it was Elena, carrying a flickering kerosene lamp.

"What are you doing in here?" Julian said apprehensively.

She moved over the floor like a sensuous ghost. "I can't be alone, not tonight."

"You aren't alone, what about your husband?" Julian consciously kept his voice low, even though he wanted to shout at her.

"Don't worry about him, he's not going to wake up just to search for me."

"Oh, no? If my wife suddenly got up in the middle of the night, and a strange man was staying in my house, I'd be getting up."

"If you could."

Elena's words led Julian down many paths. Had she killed him? Was Julian next? "This isn't right. I think you should leave. I promise it'll never come up again."

Elena set the kerosene lamp on the dresser. Julian gazed upon her skin. Shadows danced across her face, and her green eyes stripped him to the heart.

"Julian," she maneuvered closer to the guarded man, "please, I need a gentle touch tonight."

She rubbed against him. Julian wanted to run. The only escape was the window, but the teeth of ice would cut him to ribbons. What was worse, he thought, dying in the claws of an unknown creature, or dying in the clutches of a wanton mistress?

"Don't you want me?" She taunted Julian with sweet kisses of venom. "You can't say no, because I know you do."

"You're another man's wife."

"I'm a slave. Free me, Julian, free me."

Then Julian kissed back. It was true, he did want her. Their saliva mixed; their tongues twined like serpents. He could no longer deny his passion.

Julian's hand searched for Elena's breast. He caressed it, and she responded. Elena's hands frantically raced over Julian's chest and shoulders. Their kisses grew intense, so savage Julian thought the room would burst into flames.

Julian's sensibilities still tried to stop him. "Your husband… this is wrong…what if…"

"He won't bother us. I gave him something to help him sleep."

"You drugged him?"

"Yes, now make love to me."

Elena's words of assurance destroyed any defense Julian had. Elena's wandering hands found Julian's organ and massaged it. He, in turn, began to undress Elena.

They awkwardly went to the bed. Julian laid Elena down and removed her clothes. He paused momentarily to drink in her beauty. Then, he disrobed and climbed in on top of her.

Elena drew him near. Moments later, Julian was inside. Elena pulled at his sweaty shoulders, urging him deeper and deeper. The only thing she saw in her mind as Julian thrust strongly, was Grimm. Julian pumped faster, harder, and deeper. He rapidly approached orgasm. Elena wouldn't let him stop now. She, too, traveled the same road. The feelings whirled like a tempest, building to climax. She felt Julian twitch, his thrusts became erratic and unpredictable.

This was when she smiled. Julian groaned like an animal as his seed spewed into Elena. She saw Grimm's face in her mind. The dagger to slay him had just been delivered.

Dear Father,

I've been waiting to hear from you. I hope you are well. I miss home more than ever these days. I guess when you're away, you realize what is really important. To me, you are the most important, and I want you to know how I miss and love you.

The days are becoming longer, and my work is progressing well. You would be so proud of the calliope. At first, I questioned myself. Would I be able to do this? I was so unsure. But now, I realize it is probably the best instrument I've ever built. The carousel Mr. Grimm is building is the most incredible thing I've ever seen. The detail in the figures are overwhelming.

I hope you've gotten better in these warmer days. News comes slowly to this little town, and I heard there was quite a storm in the Isles. I trust everyone made it through safely.

Father, I'm very confused. I've committed a grievous sin, and I wouldn't be surprised if God hated me forever…

At that point, Julian heard his bedroom door open. Elena stood like a cobra in the doorway. Her black hair draped her shoulders, and she calmly folded her arms across her chest.

"What are you writing?" She came in. "Another letter to your father?"

Julian put his pen aside and folded the paper. "Yes, I like to keep in touch with him. I wish he would write soon."

"I'm sure he will, Julian." She stalked over to him. "Thank you for last night. I needed someone I could trust."

Julian hushed her and scanned the doorway. "If your husband hears, he'll kill us both."

"He's not here." Elena held Julian's hands close to her mouth. "He left for town thirty minutes ago." She kissed Julian's fingertips.

Julian nervously tried to retract his hand, but Elena was insistent on showering them with attention. "It's wrong, this is wrong."

"You didn't seem to think that last night." She slid his index finger deep inside her mouth.

Julian tingled as he felt the pressure on his digit. The sensation tumbled across his shoulders and fell like water down his spine. He was again being swept up into the spider's web.

"What were you writing about?" She sucked on a different finger.

Julian found it hard to concentrate, his body was responding to Elena's stimulation. "I told my father I loved him. And that…I miss him."

"Love." She moved Julian's hand to her breast. "I know what love is."

"Do you?" Julian wanted to pull away from her, but passion was controlling every move. "What do you love?"

"I love never wanting anything."

"Do you love your husband?"

"I'll let my kiss answer that question."

As Elena promised, her lips sought Julian's. They pressed together, and Julian received his answer. No woman could love her husband and kiss another man that way. Raw fire penetrated every pore. Julian struggled against his emotions. His heart yearned for touch, for compassion, but his mind warned this was a poisoned well.

"No." He was able to break the bond. "I can't do this. This is wrong. I don't care if you don't love your husband, I cannot commit this great a sin."

Elena recoiled. "Sin?" She pulled away from him. "Do you

think being sold into marriage is not a sin? I hate him. I've no reason to love him, or you, or any man, for that matter."

Julian looked at her with surprise, her anger was so vivid. "I don't understand."

"How could you? Did your father give you to the highest bidder? Did your family leave you behind? You can't understand." Julian stood silent, and Elena went to him again. "I do have some power, though." Then, Elena grabbed Julian's face and kissed him. It was a hard, forceful kiss that lacked any feeling. She backed away. "I know you want me. Your eyes told me the first minute you walked into this house."

Julian looked away.

"Don't worry, no man can hide it. They are all the same." She turned and headed for the door.

"Wait," Julian said. "You never told me what you love."

She stopped and faced Julian. "I'd love for my husband to go to hell." She took a deep breath and regained her composure. "You know, he talks of dreaming all the time. Well, I'll tell you the dream I've had about him. Every night, I dream he is a tree, an ugly, obscene, immense tree.

So, he can never touch me again, and I can have everything I want. I'd sell him to the devil if I could, then he would know how it feels."

Julian heard a knock at the door. They looked at one another, and Elena went to answer the door. Julian followed.

She found Grimm's brother at the door. "Hello, come in."

Julian watched her transform into a loyal wife in front of her brother-in-law. Her performance was flawless, she lived the part.

"I hope I'm not troubling you," the elder Grimm brother said. "I stopped by to see how everyone was doing."

Alexander moved near the fire, and Elena went to the kitchen. "Would you like a cup of tea? You look tired."

Alexander noticed Julian. Julian scanned the man; he was dirty and unkempt. Julian smiled, however, and Alexander returned the greeting.

"Alexander," Elena said while fixing the tea, "this is Julian Keefe. He is helping my husband on his carousel."

Something in that phrase made Alexander glare at Julian. The young craftsman felt his frosty stare.

"Hello, nice to meet you."

Alexander mumbled a brief greeting, then turned to Elena. "Is my brother here?"

"No, he went to town." Elena brought Alexander the tea. He accepted the cup but set it on the table. Then, Alexander grinned. "Is it all right if I go look at the carousel? I enjoy looking at it."

"Certainly, I don't think my husband would mind."

Elena followed Alexander to the workshop door and unlocked it. Alexander disappeared inside. Elena shut the door.

Julian walked over to the untouched tea. "Who is that?"

"That is my husband's brother. He was once a proud man. His son was his life, then Gustav, his son, fell into the river. They never found the little boy's body."

"That's terrible."

Elena continued, "Gustav disappeared while Alexander was away teaching, and he never forgave himself for not being here to save the boy."

"It wasn't his fault."

"No, it wasn't," Elena said. "To him, though, it doesn't matter." She paused to gather her thoughts. "After the death, he tried to go on. I think he even left the area, but he just fell apart. Now, he comes by occasionally and looks at the statue on the carousel."

Julian looked at the cup of tea again. "I think I'll finish my letter."

Elena watched as Julian returned to the bedroom. She took the cup of tea to the sink and dumped it out.

Dinner time was especially quiet that evening. Elena haunted the room. Her spirit was uneasy, and she hovered near Julian.

I watched her linger, then wondered why she was paying him such close attention. I watched them both. Julian was as uneasy as she, and nervously played with his food.

Perhaps, she was getting to him. Then, I would have a justifiable reason to kill Julian—but not before he finished the calliope.

"Would you care for more potatoes?" Elena said as she settled down in her place at the table.

Grimm observed Julian's plate. "He hasn't eaten the ones he has, my love."

"That is because they are probably cold." She sweetly stroked Julian with a glance.

"Nonsense," Grimm said, "you just served them."

"Perhaps some more sausages, Julian?" She started to rise.

"No thank you, I'm quite full."

"You've hardly touched anything on your plate," Elena said. "A strong man like you needs nourishment. What if some young lady came and stole your heart? You would be so weak you couldn't perform your duties."

Julian nervously looked at Grimm, then at Elena. "I'm very tired and not very hungry."

Elena's face wrinkled into an expression of concern. "Are you sick?"

She stood and moved to Julian. He was sweating, but he

couldn't be sure if he was indeed ill. Elena paused just behind Julian's chair. She touched his forehead from behind. Grimm watched, seething inside.

Her hand slid down Julian's nervous face. "You seem warm." Elena drew her hand sensuously up Julian's face again, "Does my hand seem cold to you?"

Julian was in her web. The more he struggled, the deeper he became entangled. "I'm not sure. I don't think I'm sick." His voice shook.

Grimm studied them.

"You need a woman's touch." Elena deliberately brushed the back of his head with her breasts as she moved away from him. "A cup of tea will make you feel better."

"I don't want any tea, but thank you." Julian desperately sought to change the subject. "I met your brother today, Herr Grimm. I'm sorry to hear about the loss of your nephew."

Those were the last words Grimm expected out of Julian's mouth. He was stunned. Grimm's eyes bore down on Elena, and she seemed to squirm as if tacked to the floor.

"You didn't tell me Alexander stopped by."

Elena swiftly regained her composure, like a cat that fell a short distance. "I'm sorry, husband. It must have slipped my mind."

"Did you give him any money?" Grimm drank some ale from his stein.

"I had none to give," she said.

"If he comes around again, I'll make sure there's some money in the house for him." Grimm guided his attention to Julian. "Thank you for your sympathy. When I…when we lost Gustav, it devastated the whole town."

"I can imagine."

Grimm sniffed the air. Julian's choice of words burned in his nostrils. "Can you imagine, Julian?" He glanced past Julian; his eyes remained unfocused. "Can you imagine what it's like at all?" Grimm noticed Julian's uneasiness. "You know, you have done an incredible job on the calliope. You are very talented."

"Thank you."

Elena could sense Grimm's bitterness subsiding, and she moved to stoke the fire. "It takes a strong man to do what he does, husband. I've seen him work, he's very strong."

Grimm recognized her tactics, and he was too weary to fight her. "Yes dear, it does take a strong man."

Julian sensed Elena's antagonism, and knew it was only a matter of time before she ignited his fury. He also knew he would be the weapon she used, indirectly or directly. Julian decided to remove himself from the looming battlefield.

"Hard work also makes one very tired." Julian said as he rose. "I think a little extra sleep will do me good. I start work on the valves tomorrow, and I need to be alert. It's very delicate work."

Elena watched Julian start to walk toward his room. "I hope you feel better, and your fever doesn't get worse."

Julian paused in the door frame, "I think I'll be all right tomorrow morning."

"So do I," she said as he closed the door.

Julian braced his back against the door, imagining he was keeping all the strangeness of this house at bay.

"I have to get out of here." He looked around the room. "I don't even know who I am anymore."

Julian slowly moved away from the door. He fell to the bed and buried his head in the covers. Then, Julian turned over. He remembered the letter he'd started earlier and pulled it from his pocket.

Carefully, Julian unfolded the paper. He located his pen and returned to the correspondence.

I wouldn't be surprised if God hated me forever. I miss home, and I miss everyone. I only pray I make it home soon, father.

Love your youngest, Julian

Julian woke early and slipped quietly from the house. Even with the Grimms asleep, tension scratched at the walls. He contemplated packing his bags and leaving, but he had no money left. Julian had sent what he had been paid home to his father and counted on the final wages to pay his way home. As the sun rose, Julian walked to the river's edge. Thoughts of Gustav echoed through Julian's confused mind. He watched the river churn. It looked so cold.

He thought of the little boy lost somewhere beneath the unforgiving water. Such a horrible way to die. Julian sighed as the notion passed.

Then Julian knelt by the shore. He could hear the water talking, telling secrets in its special language. He desperately wanted to know what it said. It was frustrating.

Julian's mind wandered home. He thought of Ireland and remembered the sea. It also told secrets. Only the fortunate could understand her words, and many perished when they learned too much.

The sun had now cleared the horizon, and the air started to warm. Julian unbuttoned his coat slightly, and stood. It was time to finish the project and get home. There was nothing for him in this land. He had grown to hate it. He hated the smell, and the barren hills, and the secretive river.

He turned and followed the path through the forest. Julian attempted to clear his mind. He wanted to keep focused on the task at hand. All he thought of as he walked was home.

He opened the door and witnessed Elena floating around the kitchen. Grimm was nowhere to be seen.

"Good morning," Julian greeted Elena.

"You're up early."

"I couldn't sleep and went for a walk." He took off his coat and hung it nearby. "I had to clear my mind. I'm ready to finish the calliope and had to re-focus my thoughts."

"Almost finished, are you?" She turned to him, and he noticed a slash across her nose and cheek. "Care for some breakfast?"

"What happened to you?" Julian looked at the angry wound.

"It was time to make good on my payment." Her eyes fell downward.

Julian had never seen Elena look so defeated. Her energy was gone, her fire extinguished, bitterness stained her face. Julian reached to touch the blood-encrusted cut.

Elena, however, shied from his touch. "I'm fine."

"Where is your husband?"

Julian attempted to sort his feelings for Elena. On his arrival, Julian felt attracted to her, then he feared her. As he looked at the cut, Julian realized there was another dimension to his feelings. It wasn't love, but pity for her loneliness. On the other hand, he couldn't help feeling she deserved all her pain.

"He's in his damned workshop." She spat the words venomously.

As Julian entered, he heard Grimm mumbling quietly. The carver didn't notice Julian at first, but hushed as he sensed the young man's presence.

Julian momentarily glimpsed Grimm's face. On it, he saw a multitude of scratches and claw marks. Julian knew Grimm's wounds were far worse than Elena's, and his soul smiled. Her fire wasn't gone, she hid the flame on purpose to exact a longer, sweeter revenge.

"Are you alright?" Julian pretended naivete.

Grimm sighed and returned to the carousel. "I fell in the woods."

"Thank goodness you weren't seriously hurt." Julian said as he looked over Grimm's latest figure.

Grimm noticed Julian's curious eyes. "It is beautiful, isn't it?"

Julian reached to touch the figure. The woman was identical to the others already in place on the carousel's platform, but only one other did not have any hands.

"She's incredible." Julian pondered her missing hands. "May I ask you why she," he pointed to the other handless woman on the carousel, "and that one has no hands?"

Grimm smiled, he seemed content and victorious. "My young friend, I wanted them to represent the greediness of women. Take away their hands, and they can take no longer."

The words confused Julian, but he pretended comprehension. "I see."

Grimm could see in his face that he didn't. "Ah yes, take from them like they take from you."

Julian leaned closer to the figure. Her face was distraught and tragic. He reached to touch her surface and was surprised to find it warm to the touch. Julian couldn't explain the sensation, so he dismissed it as imagination.

Then he noticed stains on the wrists where the hands had been severed. The blemishes were rusty in color. Grimm's nerves twitched as Julian curiously continued.

"The glue's not dry," Grimm suddenly retorted.

Startled, Julian retracted his hand. "I'm sorry."

"Just be careful." Grimm watched through narrow eyes as Julian stepped away from the carousel.

"Well, I should get to my work." Julian smiled at Grimm and walked to the door, then glanced back at the figure. Her face was maligned, contorted in fear and pain. Only a madman could depict a woman in such anguish, Julian thought. He went to the smithy.

It was now bright and sunny outside. The sun glinted like a jewel, and contact heating melted some of the snow. In the air, familiar smells of wet earth and mild breezes hinted to warmer weather just weeks away.

Julian retrieved a nearby shovel, and put some coke in the small, makeshift furnace. Luckily, the fire had not completely gone out. Julian fetched a set of bellows. As he pumped oxygen into the fledgling conflagration, the coals turned white with heat. Gradually, the fires grew.

Julian set the bellows aside. He checked the furnace heat a few times, but it was still not hot enough to be effective. As he opened the door a final time to add coke, the coals began to pop. Water must have seeped into the coke, and now the expanding steam was blowing pieces apart like popcorn. Just as Julian hurried to fasten the door, a large chunk of flaming coke sailed from the oven. It impacted on Julian's forearm, searing his coat and flesh at once.

Screaming in pain, Julian knocked the hot material away and scrambled to the nearest snowbank. He shoveled snow on the area, but the coat prevented the soothing precipitance from reaching his burned arm.

Julian ripped his coat off and tossed it to the ground. He squeezed his eyes shut, hoping to shut off the pain. The burn was small, but intense. The wound was no larger than a tea ball, but its borders were blistered and fierce.

He packed snow on the burn. The pain subsided. Julian calmed himself. The heat of his skin and the burn melted the snow quickly. Julian piled more on his arm.

With his free hand, Julian dug in the snowbank for fresh relief. Suddenly, his hand impacted an object with strange consistency. At first, Julian thought it was a stone. He started to uncover the object in the snow.

As more snow was moved, Julian realized there were two objects. Before him rested two slender human hands, severed at the wrists. The surrounding snow was brightly stained with blood.

Julian was stunned. He had never encountered something so grisly and was unsure of how to react. It must be a mistake, was Julian's first thought. These weren't human hands; they were something else entirely.

But somehow, he knew they were real. Julian also believed

they belonged to the woman on the carousel. *She was wood*, he told himself. *She's not human, these cannot be her hands.*

Some way, his mind said, somehow these were her hands. *Don't be fooled*, a voice in his head cried. Julian reached to touch the skin. Perhaps, they weren't there at all. His mind, distraught with recent events, was creating this illusion.

That explanation shattered as he touched the clammy flesh of one hand. They were all too real. Julian's confusion continued. He rationalized the existence of the hands.

Strange things had been happening in this house, but Julian was unwilling to be involved in what could amount to murder. It was time to leave this place, penniless if need be. If Grimm wouldn't pay him, Julian thought, he would steal the money. Sins were nothing now. Julian felt he'd already broken one, so another would be inconsequential.

He piled snow on his burn, pushed the hands back into the bank, and covered them. Julian wanted no part of this place, or the Grimm family. He would deny any knowledge of these hands. He just wanted to leave.

Julian calmly walked into the house, with his new secret tucked away. His head swam with nausea, as he saw Elena standing in the kitchen.

"I burned my arm."

Elena came to inspect the wound, "Let me see."

As she peeled Julian's hand from the wound, she diagnosed the burn. She gently inspected the blistering, redness, and charring.

"Can you feel it?" she asked.

"It hurts terribly." Julian answered.

"I think you will live." Elena commented. "Sit down at the table, I'll get something for it."

Julian observed her carefully. He watched Elena's hands, she still had two and that comforted him. She returned with cool rags soaked in water and tea leaves, and some sort of poultice. Gently, Elena fastened the cloth strips on Julian's forearm.

"Does that feel better?" She asked.

"Yes, it does. Thank you."

Julian wanted to tell her about the hands he just found. He wanted to tell anybody. So many confusing emotions swirled in Julian's mind. It was possible Elena could be involved; she could be the murderess. As he reviewed Elena's character, Julian knew it was completely feasible.

He fought the urge to spill his secret. Julian appraised his desire to leave; it was more powerful than any inclination to confess finding the severed hands. He had to get out, get away, as soon as possible.

"Will it get infected?" Julian asked.

"I'm not sure."

As the conversation lulled, Grimm entered from the workshop. Julian carefully assessed the carver. Grimm calmly moved, he appeared to have no evidence Julian had discovered the hands. Then, Grimm noticed the bandages on Julian's arm.

"What happened?" Grimm asked with genuine concern.

"The coke was wet, and it popped onto my arm." Julian explained.

Grimm looked at Elena, then at Julian. "Is it bad?"

"He'll live long enough to finish your damned carousel." Elena touched the cut on her face.

"There's no danger of infection?"

"I don't know." Julian answered.

Grimm quietly thought, then addressed Elena. "Please go to the village doctor and get him some salve. I don't want anything to happen, not when we're so close."

Elena resented Grimm's orders, "Certainly, husband. Perhaps you could use some on your face. Human scratches are the most dangerous of all, so *Phuri Dai* used to say."

"Go now," Grimm ordered.

Elena whirled away from the men. She went to her room, and swiftly re-emerged. Without uttering any words, Elena left the house for town. The atmosphere lost its edge as Elena vanished on the path. Grimm sighed.

"She won't be long," he said.

Julian was nervous now that he was alone with Grimm. In front of him, stood a man that could possibly be a murderer. He was so confused, but not about his decision to leave.

"I think I'll lay down until she returns. I don't feel well." Julian said.

"That sounds like a good idea." Grimm went to the kitchen and poured some water. "I almost forgot what I came in for." He downed the fresh water. "If you need anything, I'll be in the workshop."

"Thank you." Julian watched Grimm as he returned to the workshop and closed the door.

At last, the Grimms were gone. This was his chance to escape. Julian paused momentarily and listened. Every sound heard was familiar and proper; fire in the stove and fireplace, water dripping in the warm sunshine. There were no signs of Elena returning prematurely. Julian could hear Grimm's hammer creating new patterns in the workshop. Now was the time to locate money—and flee.

Julian backed toward Grimm's bedroom door, all the while keeping his eye on the workshop door. He would only have a few brief moments to locate some money, and to get his things together. Julian opened the door quietly.

Julian made sure the door was open so he could hear the workshop door if it opened. He thought to himself: where would money be hidden? Attempting to think like Elena or Grimm; Julian tried to think of good hiding places.

He went to the dresser and pulled the drawers open two at a time. There were two columns of four drawers. Julian swiftly rifled through their contents, producing a few stray pieces of gold. It wasn't enough to hire a driver to carry him ten feet.

Julian paused to listen. He could still hear Grimm hammering in the workshop. Nervously, Julian scanned the room. He focused on the bed and remembered where his own grandmother used to hide money: under the mattress.

Carefully, Julian went to the bed. He knelt, and thrust a hand between the box spring and feather bed. Suddenly, Julian noticed the house had grown quiet. He could no longer hear Grimm's pounding.

Fearing the worst, but unwilling to stop, Julian continued his search. His hands ran across paper, and he pulled it out. Then, his other hand discovered a flattened bag. Julian also drew that out.

Clutching all of his prizes closely, Julian stood. He was relieved to hear the pounding of hammer and chisel resume. Julian looked about the room once again. He pushed all the drawers back in the dresser and straightened the bed's linen and quilts. Then, Julian left the room of his host.

He safely scouted the hall and house as he exited. Julian crossed to his room and shut the door. His heart pounded like Grimm's hammer, and seemed to pump sweat through every pore of his body. The salty perspiration lubricated Julian's burn, and it stung.

Julian went to his bed. He laid the bag's contents out on the blanket. There was quite a bit of gold and silver in front of him. He counted the pieces. Realizing there was more than enough, Julian took what he needed, and shoved the rest under his pillow.

"There, they'll find this after I'm gone." He wiped his forehead.

Julian sighed. He gathered his thoughts and calmed himself with reassurances of home. He looked to his window.

The dripping water and warm sunshine eroded the animal-like icicle teeth.

Julian returned his attention the collection of treasures on the blanket. He gathered the money into a small pile and placed it in his pocket.

Then, he noticed the sheets of paper he had taken in haste. Julian was tempted to shove them under the pillow without looking at them, but they were so familiar. The paper was just like that he'd brought from home, the paper on which he wrote letters to his father, the letters he entrusted to Elena.

Julian selected one of the pieces of stationery. It was his, he could tell by the feel. As he unfolded the paper, revulsion and tears flooded his eyes. Julian looked at his own writing and read his own words; his tears smeared the ink as they fell on the paper.

Every letter written rested before him, every letter except the first one. Julian unfolded each and arranged them by date. She must have mailed the first one but kept the rest. It was beyond all reasoning to Julian. Why would she keep these letters? They meant nothing to her.

Julian then realized Elena knew every thought and desire he put to paper. She armed herself well. Anger surged through Julian as he comprehended Elena's manipulative tactics. She used every scrap of information like a warlord, she plotted, attacked, pitted, and now destroyed him.

But that was not the final blow, Julian noticed an envelope on the bed. He snatched it and examined the address and return labels. It was from Ireland. It was addressed to Julian Keefe. He tore the envelope apart and retrieved the enclosed message. As Julian read, his heart sank.

Dear Julian,

We miss you dearly and await more letters. I hoped you would be home by now, but I understand how busy you must be.

I have terrible news. Father died late last night. We were all with him, but all he asked for was you. The doctors said he didn't suffer, and he was now free of his burdens.

Please come home soon. We're together and miss you painfully. It's not certain how long Daniel will be here before returning to America. I will be staying only two more weeks. There's nothing at home for us anymore. We want you to come with us, but we can talk about that later. All our prayers are with you, brother. We hope to see you soon.

Love your brother, Aaron

Julian could barely see through his tears. They burned, flowing like the melting icicles outside the window. He located the envelope and examined it. Julian found the postmark; it was only a week old. Aaron and Daniel would only be home another week.

He took the letter in his hand once again. Julian erupted into heaving, yet silent, sobs. Angus was gone, the man he loved and worshipped, the only man worthy of his respect.

She took it from him, everything. Elena ripped from Julian the only thing that mattered in the world: his father. Julian couldn't count the vast images of Angus that came to him. Ang usKeefe: father, artist, provider—friend.

Julian crushed the letter in his hand. Turmoil twisted his innards like taffy. He wanted to kill her, kill Grimm, kill the world. Julian felt raped and empty. He'd stupidly given her the weapon to kill him.

Julian gathered the letters and folded them together. He picked his bag up out of the corner and laid it on the bed. As he went to the dresser to retrieve his belongings, Julian heard the front door open. He didn't care who was here, he was leaving. The Devil himself couldn't prevent him from leaving this house of sin.

Julian threw his clothes and toiletries onto the bed, then shoved them inside the bag. The pile of letters sat patiently, waiting to be packed away. Julian didn't know if this was everything, nor did he care. He would leave naked if need be; Julian just wanted to flee before anything else could happen.

Suddenly, he heard a voice from behind. "What's the matter? What are you doing?"

He turned to see Elena standing there. She was clad in a black wool cape. Julian thought it was appropriate; all witches should wear capes.

"I'm leaving. I'm going home." Julian didn't want her to see him crying and diverted his eyes.

"Tell me what's wrong?" Her concerned tone was genuine.

Perhaps she didn't know anything about this, maybe Grimm was at the core of the mystery. His heart refused to listen to such nonsense. Julian knew his heart couldn't lie.

"I trusted you!" His words lashed like a whip. "You are nothing but a whore."

Elena gasped at his atrocities. "I won't stand for this. What's gotten into you?"

At that point, Julian lost what little self-control remained. He seized her arm, reeled her down to the bed, and shoved Elena's face into the pile of folded letters.

"You, you tell me." He pressed her face hard into the mattress.

She started to gasp and struggled to scream. "I don't know what you're talking about!"

"Liar, you lying harlot!" Julian's accent flared with his anger, making it almost difficult to understand his words. "Look at them! Every letter I wrote is here: un-mailed! I trusted you!"

"Please," Elena exclaimed. "You're hurting me!"

"I should kill you!" Julian relaxed his grip on her. "I just want to leave. I'm leaving you, and your husband, to rot. You deserve each other."

Elena struggled to her feet. She coughed, rubbing her throat dramatically. She watched as Julian resumed packing his things.

"Please, don't leave!" Elena pulled at him. "I love you! Don't leave me here!"

Julian and Elena heard the workshop door slam, and Grimm's footsteps heading for the bedroom. He gasped in surprise upon entering. Elena was pleading to his hired hand, confessing her love. Julian was packing, angrily pushing Elena from his side.

"What's going on?"

"I'm leaving." Julian stated. "My father has died, and I just found out. I have to go."

Julian wanted no confrontation. He was not going to tell Grimm of Elena's deception. If he left now, he would punish Elena enough for everyone.

"It's not true!" Elena shouted. "He's leaving because of you!

You old fool, can't you see?"

Julian could see by Grimm's expression; he was completely confused. "My father's dead. I have to go." Julian fastened his bag and hoisted it upon his shoulder. "I need to go home. Now."

Elena went to Grimm. "It's all your fault. He's leaving because of you. You destroy everything you touch. He's in love with me."

Grimm's eyes exploded in surprise, "What?"

Julian could see her attempting to implicate him. "No, that's not true." He pushed past both of them, "I've got to get my tools from the workshop, and I'll be going."

Mention of the workshop stunned Grimm. He didn't want Julian going in there alone. It was his territory. As Grimm started to follow Julian, Elena grabbed his arm.

"He loves me, do you hear? I drugged you, and we made love. In this bed. Under your roof." Elena watched as the words sparked Grimm's jealousy. "I gave myself to him freely. Something I would never give to you. I gave to him."

Grimm looked upon her with disgust. "You are a liar."

Elena had to provoke Grimm. She realized Julian was lost to her. The only benefit remaining was Grimm would hate her enough to cast her out. Then she could return to her family.

"I think I carry his child." Elena's statement stabbed Grimm. She could see the pain in his eyes. "I will give him a child. Another thing I will never give you."

Grimm shook with rage. Jealous tremors rocked his hands and arms. Suddenly, Grimm pushed Elena aside, and he stalked from the room.

Elena followed him like a hyena, waiting to pick the scraps of flesh from the floor. He stalked to the workshop and opened the door. Inside, Julian was gathering his mallets and tools. He was packing them in his bag when Grimm entered.

"Don't leave, Julian," Grimm unexpectedly pleaded.

Julian would not face him and kept working. "I'm sorry. I can't stay. Perhaps, I can come back after my affairs have been settled."

Grimm realized he would not be able to convince the young Irishman to stay. "Then tell me one thing." He took Julian's arm and turned him face to face. "Do you love her? Did you make love to her?"

Julian's soul screamed out in protest. He had committed so many sins, he refused to commit another. Julian looked Grimm in his bottomless eyes, "I slept with Elena. She came to my room and seduced me."

Elena entered the workshop and heard the trailing words of Julian's confession. "Tell him how much you loved it. Tell him how I made you feel the moment your seed went deep in me. Tell him."

Grimm could no longer contain his resentment. It began with Sennett, continued with Julian, and he knew it would not end with them. Elena would always cheat. She would always torture him with others.

His feelings went beyond normal shades of jealousy. As he looked at Julian for what seemed forever, Grimm could see every inadequacy he had ever owned. Julian was handsome, strong, talented—and he could dream. It was more than Grimm could take.

"I understand, Julian." Grimm was unusually calm. "Let me pay you for your troubles, and you can leave. I know how difficult it was for you to come here in the first place." He went to the workbench and retrieved a small sack. "I hope this will be enough."

Grimm opened the drawstrings. As the bag opened, his vindictive spite focused on Julian. He looked at Elena with disguised contempt. She must pay, he thought. She must pay.

"Elena." Grimm paused before revealing the contents of the sack. "If I could persuade him to stay, what would you do?"

Julian thought Grimm misspoke. "I said I can't stay."

"Anything you want. I'll do anything." Elena whispered.

"Very well." Grimm reached in the bag.

"I said I won't stay, and…"

As Julian's words trailed, Grimm opened the bottle to the potion. He shook the bottle at Julian and said the magic words.

Ator malcuth theraputae.

Elena knew those words. She knew what they could do. But it was too late. Julian looked upon Grimm as if a fool or madman stood in front of him. Suddenly, though, Julian's expression contorted painfully.

The grain came swiftly to Julian. I watched, and laughed, as his skin turned wooden.

Every shred of my jealousy was woven like silk into the wood that formed around Julian. Elena's helpless cries made me feel rich. I gave her what she wanted, everything she desired. Julian was now here forever, never leaving her side. It was her desire.

She was completely mine. By her own testimony, I own her. As for Julian, I now waited for his dreams to be mine, too.

CHAPTER 30

It had been two days since Julian became part of my collection. Elena became quiet and distant. Finally, I had crushed her spirit. She sat in the workshop, near his place on the carousel.

I placed him by the bear. His face was frozen in fear. His lips caught in mid-protest. I enjoyed looking at him, too. To me, Julian was a trophy equal to Gustav, but for many different reasons.

I defeated my wife's lover. I captured him, put him on display for her to see daily. She would never forget she was mine: I wouldn't let her, and neither would Julian.

She rarely spoke to me after Julian became mine. But, I hoped, that would all change soon. It did not matter, though. I was getting everything I ever wanted. All of their dreams were now mine.

As the sun set, Grimm entered the workshop. Elena sat near Julian's frozen form; her eyes were red from crying. She had not yet noticed her husband's presence and spoke candidly to Julian. "I look at you. I can't believe my eyes. You stand there, unmoving. I hope that it isn't you, but I know it is. What has he done to you? I knew he was up to something when he would visit the *Phuri Dai,* but I never envisioned him courting this kind of horror.

"I did love you, believe me. I regret that this has happened to you. I only wish I could help you now. I regret that I hid your letters. I thought you would leave, like Sennett, leave me here forever."

Grimm listened. He enjoyed her vulnerability. "Don't mourn for him, dear. Now you have him forever. Consider it my gift to you."

"I didn't see you there." Elena felt naked in front of Grimm.

"Somehow I find that hard to believe. How do I know you aren't manipulating me? After all, everything that comes out of your mouth is a lie or deception."

Elena did not have the strength to defend herself. "Perhaps, you are right."

"Perhaps." He moved close to where she sat. "Stand up, I have something for you."

Elena obediently rose. As she stood, he gently took her hand. He selected a slender finger and placed a ring upon it.

Elena felt the band of gold slip on smoothly. She lifted her hand to inspect the gem. It was beautiful. On her hand, a large, clear stone rested. The diamond was flawless. She estimated its weight to be well over seven carats.

"It's beautiful." Elena gazed into the stone's prismatic facets.

"I hoped for a greater response than that." Grimm lifted her chin with his finger. "Do you not like it?"

"I do." Elena was melancholic. Then, she mustered the courage to speak out, "Let him go. He's done nothing but help you with this damn piece of machinery."

Grimm considered her proposal, then smiled. He enjoyed having power over her at last. To him, it was better than the most expensive wine or extravagant food. It was almost as good as owning Gustav's dreams.

"He slept with my wife, perhaps impregnating her. Is that not an attack worthy of his imprisonment?" Grimm enjoyed taunting Elena.

"You are an evil man."

"And you are an evil woman."

"We deserve each other."

He nodded, "I do not disagree."

Elena turned from him. She gazed upon Julian's face once

again. He was so sad, captured forever with terror on his face. What would the world say? What could they say? She did not feel as bad for Julian's fate as she did for her own. Here was the proof of what Grimm would do to her for the rest of her life. He would steal from her what she loved just because he could.

My turmoil changed so suddenly. It was like the first day of a new spring; even the wind tasted fresh and clean. Elena transformed into a mouse, but I did not trust her. She would not be able to bury her fire long. For now, I enjoyed having control over her.

I broke her like a wild mare. It was meant to happen, though. Haughty princess, arrogant woman. She lost sight of what she truly was all along and that was property. She was the property of her father, and now she was mine. A fair purchase. It was only a matter of time until she would be taken down from that lofty finial of fantasy only to crash down in her reality. I was her reality. I took great satisfaction in that fact.

She sat quietly in front of Julian. Elena whispered and stared, talking of her sorrow. She was a different creature; sad, demure, lonely. It was troubling to an extent, to see such passion tamed. But I relished the taste, nevertheless.

That night, when she quietly slipped into bed, my greatest conquest appeared. At last, God was loving me. This time, I would not fail.

Elena wearily retired for the evening. Grimm watched as she left the workshop and dimmed the lamps in the house. Her vigil at Julian's feet troubled Grimm. Soon, he would insist that she abandon her pitiful watch. Julian was not coming back.

Grimm hoped for a different reaction from Elena. He assumed she would be overjoyed, her greedy soul satisfied with the gift of her lover. Julian was her prize for all time. She reacted quite differently, though.

Grimm still could not understand what she saw in Julian.

True, he was handsome, but he was a poor Irish fool who would never take her away. Grimm went to Julian's figure.

He stared at him. "What is it? I've attempted to give her everything. I've even given her you, but it's not enough."

Grimm was solemn, but happy. Everything he wanted was his. He sat on the edge of the platform. Behind him were all the figures, Julian, the women, Gustav. It was all Grimm's, the dreams belonged to him.

The workshop was quiet. As he looked toward the windows, he noticed brief movement. Then, around him, Grimm felt the haze falling. Gustav was dreaming, or was it Julian? The notion came to him in a worry, what if Julian dreamed? He was a man. His dreams would not be those of a silly child. His dreams would be horrific.

He hadn't prepared for Julian's dreams. Julian's dreams would obviously be different. He was a man, he had loved women, and experienced many of life's lustful pleasures. Gustav's dreams were innocent, those of an unadulterated boy. Julian's could be quite darker, possibly sinister. He was an adult. He known heartbreak and sadness. That would affect anyone's dreams. Grimm smiled and savored the thought, a new dimension to add to the collection.

Strands of fine web started to knit through the air. The portal was opening. As each shimmering thread formed a funnel, the droplets of mysterious liquid filled the room. Then, Grimm remembered the potion. It was on the workbench.

He jumped up off the platform and hurried to the bench. He looked for any movement, any action that could signal he had visitors.

This was, perhaps, Grimm's favorite part: the hunt. Another dream captured for the collection. He located the potion and decided to keep out of sight. Grimm wanted to see what appeared and be able to assess the dangers. It would allow enough time to hatch a plan.

Grimm waited. The fog grew thicker. Slowly, the mist crept

across the carousel, seeming to lick at Julian, Gustav, and the other characters. It moved in sensuous tides, surging against the carousel, then pouring onto the floor. Fingers of creamy droplets moved to fill the cracks and crevices. It also choked any light coming from the lamps and stove, until only eerie highlights remained.

Something was in the room. His heart felt as if it might explode. Movement stirred the vapor, but Grimm still couldn't see what had materialized.

Then he saw it; a brief glimpse of something black. The shape was enormous and moved like the wind itself. Grimm attempted to focus his hearing on the creature. Perhaps, he thought, any sound the beast made would betray its true identity.

There was sound. Grimm was ecstatic, overjoyed. He knew that sound, it was the sound of Zoltan's hooves. As Grimm made his revelation, Zoltan stepped from the fog. He was godlike: a Friesian Stallion completely improved upon by Gustav's imagination.

"Not this time, I've waited too long for you, fine horse. You are my crown jewel." He watched Zoltan go to Gustav. He nudged the boy with his nose, then licked the wood.

Grimm contemplated his attack. He did not want to startle the stallion. If he lost control, Grimm wasn't sure what kind of damage could be done. Also, Grimm did not want Elena to return, and strange noises would surely bring her running. He wasn't going to get away, not this time. Zoltan would be the only horse on his carousel.

He opened the small bottle, took it in his left hand, and cautiously stood. Zoltan was unaware of his presence and continued to concentrate on Gustav. As he watched the horse, Grimm faltered momentarily. The beauty was intoxicating. It was like nothing he had ever seen before.

Zoltan was different than when Grimm had seen him last. He was even different from the original Grimm had created for the king. Gustav's mind had improved upon Zoltan. He was humbled in the presence of the horse's beauty.

The bridle secured around Zoltan's head was set with radiant jewels of every color. They seemed to possess their own miniature suns which glinted brilliantly. Along Zoltan's back, the jewels continued. Twisting black leather secured a gold saddle. The saddle, upon closer inspection, was the gilded claw of a giant bird. The talon wrapped around Zoltan's muscular torso.

The closest he had ever come to a dream stood before Grimm. It was clear his own creation made for royalty paled in comparison with the Zoltan of Gustav's dreams. Zoltan was a reminder of his own failure. It was time to claim Zoltan for himself.

Grimm stepped quietly from the shadows. Zoltan was stoic, and oblivious to his presence. Grimm walked up to the stallion, admiring his curly black mane which shined like ebony. Grimm reached out and touched the calm beast's skin. He was cool to the touch, but wet with the mysterious condensation.

Grimm could see he was not going to protest and was saddened. The horse was not there for war or a parade, he was there for Gustav. The expected fight, a raging steed equal to a god, remained stoic. Zoltan's nostrils flared. Grimm cast the drops of potion onto Zoltan. As the solution splattered, he uttered the magic words.

Ator malcuth theraputae.

Zoltan did not fight the transformation. His black coat became infected with the spreading grain. As it crawled over the horse's body, every detail was recorded in relief. History would see the horse I created. Everyone would realize I was a dreamer. At last, the grain had completed its colonization. Zoltan stood proud, preserved forever in my zoo of dreams.

I was happy. For the first time in my life, I was happy with myself. The world would see that I was a dreamer. I had the visions of Heaven. I had cheated God, and there was nothing left to be done.

CHAPTER 32

Another day passed, and Elena still sat in front of Julian most of the day. Occasionally, she would dust just to have something to do. Other times, she would make a cup of tea and return to her position near Julian's feet. Grimm dismissed her grief. He knew Elena would get over Julian, the only variable was how long. Until then, Grimm was comfortable waiting. Somehow, Elena made grief attractive.

He left her alone that day and went to the village. There was nothing special on Grimm's mind, he felt sympathy for Elena, and gave her some time alone. Soon, though, Grimm expected Elena to become a wife in every respect.

Elena was glad she had time alone. Grimm could never be gone long enough for her taste. She sat, sipping a cup of tea, and watched Julian. Elena didn't really know why she sat and watched him. Perhaps, she couldn't believe what she saw the other day. But Elena had seen things far more bizarre in the trailer of the *Phuri Dai*, things in which Grimm would not dare dabble. It was not surprising to see Julian turned to wood, she just never expected it.

Elena thought back: all of those nights Grimm would visit the family; his secret meetings with the *Phuri Dai*; it all made sense now.

"All for what?" Elena said.

She looked at the carousel. It was beautiful, but it had ruined her life. This contraption of sin, this vulgar piece of sculpture and bolts, she hated it.

"I hate you, bastard." She spat at Julian's figure. "You were going to leave me here. Now, look where you are."

Anger was taking the place of despair. Slowly, the fire of rage chewed at her heart, it was uncontrollable. "You're the one rotting now. Think of it, he gave you to me as a prize. But all I can do is look at you. I can't touch you. I have no chance of getting away now. Sennett, my family, now you? I can't stand the sight of your face."

Angrily, Elena looked around the platform. She located one of Grimm's mallets nearby. Taking it in her hand, Elena sneered angrily.

"I will make you as ugly as you are. I hate you. I hate all of you!" She started to swing the hammer. "I can't stand the sight of you!" The first blow impacted Julian's jaw line. "You left me here!" Another blow crashed across Julian's neck and face. "You left me with him!" Elena slammed the hammer against Julian's jaw again.

Then, she stopped. The face of the statue was cracked across the chin and up the nose. The fracture passed under Julian's eye and extended through an ear. Elena suddenly became frightened. She had not realized the intensity of her rage. It was if she watched a stranger commit the assault on her husband's work. The cracks were more extensive than she realized.

Elena climbed onto the carousel. She carefully inspected the damage. As Elena surveyed the web of wounds, she noticed the wood was wet along the joints. The cracks resembled miniature stream beds, and liquid was seeping from deep within the statue.

Elena touched the substance. It was sticky to the touch. If it was a real carving, this substance could very well be glue. But she knew this figure was supernatural, the work of demons. Elena smelled the drop of coagulant on her fingertip. It smelled sweet.

Then Elena heard a faint sound. The voice was so soft it could have been the whisper of an angel. She paused to focus her hearing. The muffled voice was coming from inside Julian— Julian's statue. He was alive! Somehow, Julian still lived.

"Julian!" Elena cried and clawed at the fractured face.

The hammer blows had cracked the wood down to Julian's

skin. Elena pulled at the chunks. Pieces loosened and fell to the platform. All of the sections were coated with the mysterious substance.

"Hold on!" Elena's fingers were raw from constantly clawing the fractures.

As one large piece fell from the side of Julian's face, Elena saw skin. Now, she was able to grasp large slabs of material. Elena peeled the wood away like boiled eggshells. Gradually, she exposed more and more of Julian's face. He was red, irritated, and covered in the solution.

Then a key piece was wrenched from the statue. Julian could breathe. His nose and left eye could now be seen. Julian's nostrils flared, sucking life-sustaining oxygen into his starved lungs. Dancing wildly, his eye probed the room.

Elena saw that he was starting to panic. "Calm down, I'll get you free soon. If you don't calm down, you're going to hurt yourself."

Grief and fear emulated from Julian's eye. He seemed to understand every word, and his breathing slowed. Elena picked at more of the wood. Steadily, she freed his mouth. The mysterious sticky mixture dripped from Julian's lips. He gasped, gathering oxygen.

"Help me." His voice was hoarse and weak. "I'm dying."

Elena backed down from Julian. She retrieved the mallet, and fiercely attacked different parts of the wood. She beat Julian's arms, and they began to crack. Fountains of oozing fluid erupted from the fracture points. The wood crumbled with each strike.

Julian's skin started to show. He could move and writhed like a worm. Gradually, he was able to free one arm, and began to peel his prison away. Elena hammered at Julian's legs, hoping to speed his liberation. Large cracks spread across his thighs, calves, and hips. Motion was returning to Julian. The more he struggled, the more the wood splintered. Shards of brittle matter showered around his feet. The sarcophagus of wood could hold him no longer. Then, the confining walls collapsed completely.

And he fell to the platform littered with his cage's broken shell.

Elena was able to get Julian to the fireplace. He was soaked, and shivering. The liquid had crusted over, but Elena capably removed most of it with a rag and warm water.

He slept for several hours. Elena constantly checked the window to see if her husband was returning. What would he think—what would he do if he found Julian alive? She realized Grimm would not be coming any time soon. He was probably visiting a local brothel, entertaining some whore spending money on them instead of her.

Julian started to stir. Elena sat by him and stroked his hair. He was so handsome. She touched his eyebrows and followed their arch with her index finger. Then Elena traced the lines by his eyes. They weren't there when Julian first arrived.

Julian gradually opened his eyes, "Where am I? What's going on?"

Elena smiled, there was so much to tell. She laughed, but Julian did not. "Think, do you remember anything of the last couple days?"

Julian's face contorted in difficult thought. "I remember leaving here…then…I was somewhere else…" His expression turned to that of a helpless child, "I know none of it makes sense."

"Maybe it's just as well you don't remember anything."

"I do, though. It's just so foggy, so confusing." Julian's face changed, he remembered something. "I remember you hitting me with something. I couldn't breathe. I was choking."

"That's right. I saved you." Elena hoped to spark obligation in Julian.

Julian, however, recalled the reasons he was leaving. "I'm still leaving. In fact," he struggled to get up, "I think it's time to leave."

"You're not ready to leave. You can't, you aren't strong enough." Elena tried to convince him otherwise.

Julian was strong enough, though. He quickly regained his

composure. "I remember what you've done to me. I'll never forget that."

Julian pulled away from Elena who was grabbing at him. She scrambled to her feet and followed Julian. He went into the workshop. There, Julian paused as he confronted the carousel. He looked at the pile of splintered fragments on the platform.

"Something's not right here." He looked at the monstrosity. "I can't believe I had any part in this. God, please forgive me."

Elena silently stood as Julian located his belongings among the ruins. He still didn't understand what happened, Elena thought. Perhaps, God had decided to spare Julian the pain.

"Take me with you," she pleaded. "I can't stand it here."

Julian paused before exiting the workshop's outer door. "It's your home, you belong here."

And he walked out the door. Elena helplessly watched the door close. Julian passed the now cold forge. He passed the snowbank where the hands lay buried and kept moving down the path. It was time to go home.

Grimm came home a few hours after Julian had left the house. He found Elena sitting by the fire, a cup of cold tea in her hand. Her face was stained with tear trails. Grimm could sense her state of mind, fragile and low. He could not resist confrontation. Perhaps, her fire had returned, or perhaps she had, at last, been broken completely.

"Hello," Grimm said cordially. He removed his coat, and circled Elena. "Don't mourn for him, Elena. He never wanted you."

She laughed as if a clown danced just for her. "What do you know about it? We made love so passionately." She deliberately glanced at Grimm. "Just as Sennett made love to me."

Grimm sensed Elena's confrontational nature surfacing. He had missed it. In fact, he realized how much he enjoyed it. The pleasure came from insulting her, hurting her, attempting to break her. The more she fought, the greater his passion grew. Grimm would beat her, and if he didn't defeat her, he could take pleasure knowing he caused her immense misery.

"That's true." He moved close by her and selected a piece of wood to place on the fire. "Isn't it enough for you to know your lover is here with you forever? I think, as a husband, it is the best gift to give. Truly selfless, wouldn't you say?"

She laughed again. "He was never yours to give."

"I thought you would want him, just as you wanted gold and jewels?" Grimm's tone was antagonistic.

Elena did not immediately respond. In her head, she carefully put her response together. "I did want him, now I don't. So, I set him free."

Grimm didn't understand what she meant. He curiously mulled the words—set him free, set him free.

"Husband, you look confused." Elena rose to confront him. "I set him free, I let him go, opened his prison."

"What?"

Grimm turned on his heel and went to the workshop. It was an impossibility! There was no escape. Did she set Gustav free? Did she know Gustav was real? Surely, she would begin to suspect that the boy did not die in the river. No, his loving uncle imprisoned him with magic and raped the child's imagination.

The room was dark with afternoon shadows as he approached the carousel. Elena had told the truth. Only a pile of wood and crusty residue remained where Julian once stood.

"It's true." Grimm stated with no emotion. He was numb, unable to react the way he wanted. "You did this. You did all this?"

Elena had followed her husband into the workshop, "No, you did this. It was my pleasure to let him go. Look at me," she demanded, "I want to see your face."

"Why did you not free the others?"

"I have no interest in what black magic you are dealing in. You will pay for that in time. I knew Julian would hurt the most of all. He was your victory over Sennett—to take what he had and deny him my love. But I found it again. And I would again and again. I wanted you to know that I did this to you."

He wanted to cry, but she couldn't know that. Elena would take that sword and slice his soul apart. He mustered every ounce of pride and strength to support the facade. Any sign of emotion now would be the end.

He turned and looked at the pile of wood. As he continued to scan the waste, Grimm found some of the pieces still bore Julian's imprint. One section mirrored his ear and neck, another his lips.

He turned back to Elena, "So, you didn't like your present. How unfortunate."

Elena nervously watched him come down from the platform. "I've made some tea. Would you like some before dinner?"

"Yes, that would be nice."

"It's in the kitchen, I'll get it."

He carefully observed Elena's passage from the workshop. Grimm did not trust her. He suspected every movement, every thought Elena had.

Soon, she returned with a tray and two cups. Elena placed the service on the workbench and poured tea into each cup. The steam climbed around her face, creating a beautiful scarf of misty lace.

"Don't just stand there, come join me." Elena picked up a saucer and cup.

Grimm accepted her invitation and took the cup she held. "Thank you."

"Before we drink," Elena said, "I propose a truce. Julian is gone, Sennett is gone, Gustav is gone. There is no one else for us, we are alone. Let's make the best of it." She paused and raised her porcelain cup. "Husband."

A month ago, even hours, Grimm would have believed her. But now, he did not know what to believe. Her words made sense, there was no one left in their life. No new lovers, no new friends, only enemies married and sharing a home. Grimm considered her proposal and lifted his cup.

"Truce," he said.

He watched Elena sip the hot tea. Slowly, Grimm took a chance. As he lifted his own cup, a familiar smell shocked his nose. Grimm couldn't place the odor, but it was sweet. Then, as the first drop touched his lips, Grimm remembered. She had placed the magic potion in his tea. Grimm blamed himself, he never thought Elena would look for the potion.

"How is it?" Elena could see his hesitation and hoped her words would prompt him to drink.

"It's a little hot." Grimm avoided the liquid skillfully. He blew on the steaming brew to validate his claim.

"How about some cool water? Would you like me to get you some?"

"Please," Grimm accepted.

What a fool he had been. She did not break at all, Elena deviously pretended to be in pain and despondence. And now, Elena attempted to poison him. Grimm grew angry as he reviewed her actions.

Elena returned with a small shot glass full of water. "Here."

Grimm scrutinized Elena as she added the water to the tea. Instantly, the steam subsided.

"There, that should be cool enough now." Elena put the glass down.

Grimm reached for the tea, "Thank you."

With his other hand, Grimm inconspicuously pushed the empty glass from Elena's reach. He wanted no potential weapons near her hands. She smiled as Grimm raised the teacup. Elena momentarily turned away to retrieve her own tea. And Grimm took advantage of her.

With his free hand, Grimm seized Elena's arm and shoved it behind her back. He could stand her no longer, she would leave soon, just like Julian. Grimm would not permit that. Elena struggled, she screamed at him, raked his skin with her claws. He was going to make sure she would not leave. She was part of him now, he owned her outright that not even God could disavow.

"You bastard!" She kicked him like a horse. "Let me go! I will kill you!"

"I know." Grimm pinned her against the workbench. "I will not live with that threat over my head. Not the one where you kill me, the one where you cheat on me with other men."

Then, he struggled to open her mouth. Elena fought him every inch of the way. She bit at him; he punched her hard across the forehead. Elena cried and screamed threats, all of which Grimm now knew she would execute if freed.

Much of the tea spilled from the cup, but there was still enough in it to be effective. He managed to open Elena's mouth after thrashing her into submission. She gagged and gargled as Grimm poured the cool tea down her throat. He could smell the potion on her breath.

Elena coughed, "Let me up!"

"No. I will not give you up. I will have you forever. I own you."

Ator malcuth theraputae.

As he muttered the words, Elena choked. She grabbed her throat and attempted to scream. Her shriek choked to a hoarse whisper. But her face still echoed her inner pain.

The grain came from within. It crept through her chest, and up her neck. Elena's face and head darkened in color. Then, patterns of grain started to form. She tried to move, to scream, but found herself quickly losing mobility.

Grimm grabbed her around the waist. Elena's weight was increasing significantly as the potion spread throughout her body. He struggled with her and carried her to the carousel. Grimm hoisted her onto the platform. He dragged her to a place near the center and positioned her.

Elena, however, was still able to move slightly. She strained, she stretched, anything to get away from Grimm. Her arms extended, her hands flexed, but it was too late. The potion had finally completely consumed her. Elena stood frozen, forever fleeing the husband she never wanted.

The solution was so simple. I never considered making Elena part of my collection, but then again, she was another dream I desired to have. I knew if I didn't, I would lose her one way or another. She would either kill me, leave me, or I would kill her. This way I could have it all.

Or so I thought. I would go watch her. Elena's face was more beautiful in wood than in reality. Her complexion was so smooth, her beauty flawless and intoxicating. Now, I could watch them all.

As I sat there, day after day. I wondered what she thought about in her prison. I knew Gustav dreamed, and they would visit. Would her dreams bring Sennett or Julian back to my house? I did not know.

I considered the thought of liberating her but knew it would be a mistake. I did long for my wife's conversation, but I knew I would only tire of her. I could not deny my fear of her, it grew daily. Now, I had the power, but I had a strange feeling it wouldn't last too long.

As days passed, I began to feel unusual. Sensations of fear erupted in me as I slept, then as I worked. I wanted to finish the carousel quickly so I could find another man to finish the calliope. I would visit Elena and tell her my plans. Then, I would tell Gustav. They were my family, and I owned them.

In the afternoon, on a bright sunny spring day, I went to see Elena. I climbed onto the carousel. Now I could touch her at my convenience, but even in a state of suspension, Elena rejected me. I explained to her the fine points of our new relationship, I knew she could hear me.

As I talked to her, a strange sensation seized me. I became afflicted with an unknown ailment and stepped down from the carousel. I wondered if I had contracted some disease. That would be one of the only ways God could take my treasures away.

I leaned against the workbench to steady myself. My joints stiffened, and motion was nearly impossible. Had Elena somehow managed to poison me? Was this her revenge?

Breathing became difficult, my thoughts wandered. I tried to make sense of everything that was happening, but it was impossible to ignore the pain in my hardening body. The illuminated vapor began to fill the room, and webs of light wove throughout the room. It was then that I knew it was her revenge.

One of my belongings was dreaming. I then realized it had to be Elena, Gustav was innocent, and revenge was a stranger. All of my symptoms suddenly made sense. I looked down at my skin; it was darkening. Painful buds thrust from each of my arms. At first, I thought my veins were erupting. My legs were losing all momentum and felt as if they were melting into one giant stump.

I had to get to her. She was the only one who could stop this transformation. It was her revenge, she always talked of her dreams of me as an ugly, disgusting, warped tree. She was having the dream again.

I rushed with all my ability to the carousel, but it was like walking in river mud. I climbed on the platform. I reached for Elena, but it was too late.

I screamed her name, as my arms pulled in my sockets. They stretched, vinelike. My fingers had vanished, and darkening tree branches spreading forward. They entwined about Elena, spread across her entire body. I had to wake her. My feet burst from my shoes, but they were no longer human feet. Huge roots contorted my legs as they fastened to the carousel platform. I couldn't stop her, I couldn't stop Elena's revenge. Every organ in my body solidified. I could feel my blood cooling, thickening.

My transformation was complete.

I stood alone, yet with all my dreams. At last, together.

Forever.

AFTERWORD

Long ago, there was a young man who wasn't afraid to dream, and he wrote a book.

Twenty-five years seems like a long time when we think about it being ahead of us in the future, but we realize it's just a quick flash in history after it has passed. Time offers strange perspectives. When I realized my first novel was coming up on its 25th anniversary, I began to reminisce about how it all started and what my life was like way back then. What would prompt a young college student to write a dark fairy tale about a man who could not dream? In many ways, the characters were all fractals of my reality back in the early '90s.

Dream Thieves is a history marker for me—of a time when I was just realizing how much I loved to write. Stories would consume me as they always did and still do. I remember starting this book. It took about 2 years to complete the first draft. The world was a very different place then. The things I can remember happening at that time was that Princess Diana just died, Leann Rimes won a Grammy at age 14, *Titanic* was in the theaters, and everyone had AOL. One specific sound that makes me smile to this day is the screech of a dial-up modem.

I was working as a bouncer at the *Spaghetti Bender* in Ypsilanti, Michigan where I attended college at Eastern Michigan University. I wrote *Dream Thieves* in a notebook with a ballpoint pen. I still write most of my stories like that. I would write whenever I could sneak it in. I would write in class when the teacher wasn't paying attention. I am sure they thought I was taking copious notes. I wrote at my midnight security guard job at a hotel by the highway. I wrote in coney islands—a uniquely

Michigan concept for a restaurant much like a diner. At the hotel, I was able to study in the early morning hours, but more often I would sneak into one of the offices used by staff during the day and write.

After the first draft was done in my notebook, I wrote the second draft on a PC using WordPerfect. This was before Word or Office or anything like that existed. WordPerfect was the jewel of word processing programs. I would save the book on a 5 ¼ floppy disk and take it with me in my bookbag. I remember when I was an intern at WXYZ-TV Channel 7 in Detroit, I would also sneak in writing the same way. I was the public relations intern, and when I had some down time, I would slip that floppy into the drive and peck away. I looked very busy.

I was able to use some financial aid refund money to buy my first PC. It was an off brand called Gold Star, and it was a piece of shit that I bought at Fretter Appliance in Ann Arbor. I was a newlywed, and we were so poor we lived a lot off financial aid. Gold Star went bankrupt, reorganized, and emerged as LG —the manufacturer that is still around today. It may be gone by the 50th anniversary of *Dream Thieves*, who knows. Fretter Appliance also went bankrupt. I remember their tagline in all their commercials: "I'll give you 5 pounds of coffee if I can't beat your best deal."

Back then, I didn't understand how publishing worked. Or agents. I was getting short stories published in a lot of places, and an agent wasn't needed for litmags, zines, and journals. The hunger for short horror was ferocious, and I found out about these little publications via AIM and AOL. There were fantastic publishers and editors putting out some remarkable horror and dark fantasy short stories. To me it was a golden age. I discovered Clive Barker and, of course, Owl Goingback. *Weaveworld* and *Crota* respectfully upset my entire ecosystem in the best ways possible. I was also enthralled by Poe, and consumed anything I could find written by or about him. And this new guy I started reading by the name of Neil Gaiman—he was going places.

My creative writing professors enjoyed the short stories I wrote in class. In fact, one of them and one of my fellow students (who happened to be the editor of the college literary journal *Cellar Roots*) encouraged me to submit one of my stories for consideration. It was accepted. The story was called *The Damned* and it really caused some consternation among readers because it involved a luxury car dealership that sold cars for your soul. Tucked inside my copy on my bookshelf, I found a scathing critique from a fellow student admonishing me for breaking the rules of the assignment and for being a shitty writer in his eyes. Thankfully, the editor, the committee that selected it, and the readers thought otherwise.

I would frequently print out stories (on a dot-matrix printer) and let my friends read them; however it was great to have an actual saddle-stapled magazine to give out. They were free around campus, and I would grab about 5 or ten every time I could. But my greatest fan was my mother-in-law, Rose Carol. More about how she saved *Dream Thieves* from being lost forever is coming up.

Whenever I went to Borders Bookstore (bankrupt) and looked in the horror section, it was saturated with books with skulls and embossed blood drips on the cover. I don't know why every horror novel in the '80s and early '90s had to have a skull on it—I suppose it was the stereotype at the time. I would read the blurbs, and thumb through them. I found the stories boring and derivative—literally a retelling of whatever horror movie trope was popular in the last ten years. Every now and then I found something worthy, but I usually read the zines. Mainstream publishing just seemed to not care that their books were junk. Then everyone seemed to stop publishing horror novels altogether.

One thing to remember about trying to sell short stories and novels during this time period was that everything had to be mailed via the US Postal Service. No one accepted email submissions. Only printed, put-in-a-big-manilla-envelope, postage-metered submissions were accepted. And you had to include a self-addressed stamped envelope for a response, AKA the SASE. Ebooks in any form was in its infancy and there were more than enough people willing to strangle it to death in its crib. It reminded me of the old argument that TV would kill the movies, or that CDs would doom the recording industry. We know now that the Chicken Littles were just terrified of becoming irrelevant. A lot of them did, thankfully.

I decided I would try and submit *Dream Thieves* to some agents, and publishers that accepted unsolicited submissions. That was a thing back then, you could actually send manuscripts to horror and fantasy editors directly. Unfortunately, the gatekeeping has gotten quite ridiculous since then. Manuscripts had to be photocopied. As I recall, agents at that time did not accept dot-matrix prints of manuscripts. At my job at the hotel, there was a revolutionary new piece of technology called the "laser jet" printer. Over the course of a couple nights, I printed sections of *Dream Thieves* and assembled a full manuscript. I printed ten copies of my manuscript to send out. Back then, a writer would have to wait months and months to get a response, and multiple submissions were discouraged. There were a lot of rules, and it was indeed slower than a snail.

Over the course of nearly two years, every agent rejected me. The one or two publishers I submitted to also rejected me, but they gave the excuse that the market wasn't good for horror anymore. The feedback I got from the agents was positive and they loved the story, but they thought they couldn't sell it in the current market. At that point, I developed my personal philosophy about being a successful author: writing makes me a successful author, not the external validation of being published. I kept writing and moved on to the next project. I kept selling short stories and made enough to qualify as a full member of the Horror Writers Association.

I don't recall how I found the call for manuscripts from a new publisher, but they were going to be different than the others.

They were going to be electronic only. This new publisher was called Hard Shell Word Factory, and they were going to publish books on 3 ½ inch disks in .rtf format for you to read on your computer. Also, they accepted email submissions. I sent *Dream Thieves* to them from my AOL account, and it was acquired in less than a month.

The book was published, and I found a new world that was just emerging for authors. There was an entire community dedicated to the success of eBooks. This was before phones got smart, and kindle and nook readers hadn't been invented yet. Amazon (not bankrupt) had only been around for a few years, and still only sold books. This new community discovered or started little magazines, websites, and blogs that were willing to review eBooks. I enjoyed a lot of good reviews, which some are included in this anniversary edition. *Dream Thieves* was the first eBook to be nominated as Best First Novel by the International Horror Guild after we submitted it for consideration.

Hard Shell Word Factory decided to expand into paperback publishing because new Print-on-demand technology made it possible for little publishers to compete with the big ones. I was gaining good reviews and *Dream Thieves* was taken seriously. This is when I attracted the attention of one of my favorite horror novelists, Owl Goingback.

EBooks kept growing despite the doomsayers I encountered along the way. However, running a publishing company is hard work and Hard Shell eventually went out of business, and *Dream Thieves* went out of print. You never forget your firstborn, though. *Dream Thieves* was still in my heart. As the years passed, I lost or gave away all my paperback copies. I had one 3 ½ inch floppy on my bookshelf and that was it, and it later went missing, too.

The years passed. I kept writing. I eventually acquired agents and were dropped by them after they couldn't sell my work. They loved my work, but it was a little too odd and deviated from popular horror and fantasy that was on the shelves. I sold more short stories, and also novels as an indie author.

Twenty plus years later, when I started writing the dark fantasy adventure series *The Bloodstream Saga* for Fractured Mirror Publishing, I remembered that the 25th anniversary of *Dream Thieves* would be rather soon. I sent the team an email explaining what *Dream Thieves* was and if they would be interested in a 25th anniversary edition. They said send it, and they would see if it was something that would fit with them.

This is when I encountered a huge problem. I could not find a copy of *Dream Thieves*. It was out of print, and it was not available on Amazon anymore. I had given away all the copies I had. I didn't know how to contact the publisher anymore. And I was too intimidated and embarrassed to email Owl and ask, "Hey do you remember me? The little peon guy from 25 years ago?" Yeah, that wasn't going to fly.

Over the last 20 years, my life underwent dramatic changes. I came out of the closet at 43, I became a doctor (of education— not the kind that helps people), learned I had synesthesia, and it was a symptom of being on the autism spectrum, and diagnosed with Limb-Girdle Muscular Dystrophy. I moved a lot in just a few years as I was out on my own again since I first went to college. The job market in Michigan was horrible, so I decided to pack everything I had into a U-Haul and moved to Philadelphia with my future husband. That was where he lived, and we had a long-distance relationship for a few years before that. My life was still in boxes that I hadn't unpacked in years. Unfortunately, I didn't find any paperback copies of *Dream Thieves* in my things. I did find, however, that 3 ½ inch floppy disk version.

But how was I going to recover that file? Who used 3 ½ inch disks anymore? I was able to locate an external 3 ½ inch drive on Amazon that plugged into my USB port. I was in business! However, I discovered as I tried to retrieve the file that .rtf formatting was a relic. The file would only download as a text file. *Dream Thieves* was an unformatted blob of text. I set about formatting and revising from page 1 before I could send it to the Fractured Mirror team. Eventually, I did get the manuscript sorted, and it was enthusiastically accepted as a new project.

However, I didn't have a paperback copy. The wonderful foreword written by Owl Goingback was lost because it only existed in the paperback version. I was heartsick. I wanted the world to see those words. I resigned myself to just going forward without it. Then, something both sad and amazing happened. My biggest fan, my former mother-in-law Rose Carol, had become frail and needed to move into a care facility. As my ex-wife was packing up her mother's things, she came across copies of all my reviews and newspaper clippings. She had saved everything I had ever done. My own mother didn't do that.

Best of all, there was a copy of the paperback version of *Dream Thieves* in the storage box. I cried. The original artwork was in the box, too; but somehow it didn't seem to work for the story anymore. Emily, Alex, and Allison at Fractured Mirror created a gorgeous book—it's in your hands right now. My greatest thanks goes to Rose Carol, though. Without her, I would have lost my very first book, a very important part of my soul, and I will always be grateful to her. Because long ago, there was a young man who wasn't afraid to dream, he wrote a book, and someone loved him enough to save it.

ABOUT THE AUTHOR

STEVEN LEE CLIMER is a born creative and works in the written, visual, and aural arts. He has been writing fantasy, horror, and science fiction for kids of all ages, for over 30 years. He is the author of 15 novels, including the award-winning *Dream Thieves*, and *Demonesque*, which was optioned for a feature film.

His short stories have appeared in print and online publications in North America and the UK. Steven is also an accomplished acrylic and oil painter, and when not writing and painting, Steven composes chill EDM music under the name SugarBuzz. His music can be experienced on Spotify, Apple Music, iHeartRadio, and Amazon Music. He believes there are different voices and moods for each creative medium—like family harmony. He lives with the love of his life in Philadelphia, and they are the proud dads of two dogs and two cats.